Amish Snow

Roger Rheinheimer

Sabellapress   USA

www.sabellapress.com

Library of Congress Control Number: 2009936311

ISBN: 978-0-9825469-1-8

Amish Snow

CHAPTER ONE

Switzerland, 1526 A.D.

16th century religious Europe is in chaos. Martin Luther is trying to reform the corrupt Catholic Church from within while others openly defy the religious government's iron fist. The rebellious grassroots movement draws more and more supporters and they become increasingly bolder, questioning the church-state on many issues. Their determination to re-baptize themselves (the Catholics scoffingly call them "Anabaptists") is a flagrant affront to the church practice of infant baptism. This ultimate offense brings swift and terrible retribution. Thousands of men are dragged from their homes and burned or drowned. So many, that for a short period in history, surviving Anabaptist men take multiple wives, the widows of their best friends and brothers: one more reason they are so hated.

All week, the cold had expanded, plunging deeper, creeping into every crevice, under every rock. The snow crunched. The wagon axles squealed.

Jakkob shifted his weight on the icy wagon bench, soothing the impatient team of horses he had brought to a halt on his favorite spot high on the bluff. He could see Zürich in the distance and felt his throat tighten. The low slung ice clouds engulfed the small city, swirling and embracing the coal smoke as if inhaling, and then drifted on, sullied. When the winds were just right, Jakkob would get a whiff of the acrid stench of dust, dried horse droppings and decaying carcasses, left to rot on the street where they fell. Raw human waste ran slowly down the open ditch in the middle of most streets, lazily winding its filthy way to the cesspool at the edge of town.

Sometimes he could see the Devil's horns in the smoke spiraling up from that wicked place.

1

In the early years of their marriage, Jakkob and Orpah were casual Catholics, like all their friends, socially religious. Life was full of other distractions, God could wait. Go stand by the wall, God. They had kids to raise, crops to plant, a garden to grow, a house to build. But with time and the responsibility of a family, they grew stronger in their faith and their bond to each other.

Life was calm and fulfilling.

Then a small group of farmers split with the Catholic Church over the issue of infant baptism. It should have been a small thing, and Jakkob took his family with them.

The townsfolk didn't care if the strange farmers and carpenters in the valleys south of Zürich sounded and looked different. The country folks kept to themselves, they would say. But the state church's official position, its decree, was to baptize infants.

This affront of adult baptism by the Anabaptists was a blatant act of insubordination that could not be tolerated.

This time they had crossed the line.

It had been almost a month since Sarah first knocked on the front door.

"Hello, Sarah. I'm so sorry to hear about your husband. Will you come in?" Orpah embraced the young widow warmly.

"Yes, please, thank you," Sarah answered, curtseying to the older woman and stepping inside, stomping the snow off of her high-top, laced-up leather boots, tiny boots.

"Here, come over by the fire, you must be freezing." Orpah took the coarse wool blanket from around the young woman's shoulders. She shook the snow off, shooed several squawking chickens out of the way and hung the shawl on a wooden peg on the main vertical house pole. Several more hens peered down from their perch on a crossbeam, trying to comprehend this human activity, cocking heads first one way then the other.

The two women, one old enough to be the other's mother, made small talk: *how was the crop last year, that sure is a nice table.* And then Sarah finally asked, "Is Jakkob here?"

Orpah studied Sarah, older hazel eyes scanning young dark brown eyes, the young girl quickly dropping her gaze to the floor. Orpah realized for the first time why Sarah had come over. It hadn't occurred to her that this young woman, this girl, would be interested in an old man like Jakkob. He was nearly thirty-five.

"Why do you ask?"

Sarah blushed and continued studying the freshly swept rough hewn wood plank floor.

"I have nowhere to go. And I can't feed myself." She looked up plaintively and continued, "I don't want to impose, but God told me in a dream that I was supposed to marry Jakkob. I am strong. I can help with the chores. I know how to milk a cow —"

The older woman silenced Sarah with a wave of her rough, cracked hand and looked away. After a moment, she turned back and said, "Of course, child, if it is God's will, I'm sure Jakkob will be willing. God has been good to us, there is plenty to eat."

The first years of Orpah's marriage to Jakkob had been an innocent, happy, blissful time. Two vines intertwined. Neither of them ever imagined she would be the "first wife".

But so much had changed.

"Jakkob, it's time," Sarah called from the next room. She had been up for an hour, working hard to gain Orpah's acceptance, building the fire, adding fat cut from the loin to the ever-present huge kettle of bubbling porridge. Porridge with no beginning, porridge with no end, always there. It slowly morphed from vegetable-based to meat-based as the seasons changed, but it was always there, over the fire.

Jakkob offered a quick prayer, turned onto his hands and knees, and stiffly climbed up out of his floor-level straw-mat bed. He walked, limped, to the doorway, the limp a result of an unfortunate encounter with his mule. The mule had spooked, who knows from what, and wrapped Jakkob's left leg and the reins around a small oak tree, breaking the leg and the tree. Orpah was convinced a witch had tried and failed to enter the mule, and added a special mixture of herbs to the porridge for weeks to ward off any evil spirits, until Jakkob's leg improved and he ordered her to stop. The Catholic Church had begun their witch hunts, and he wanted no part of the trouble that could come from being accused of witchcraft.

Jakkob's long flowing white beard and matching hair (they used to be blond, unusual in this Swiss community) could be seen from far off. As was the custom of his religious community, he shaved his upper lip and most of the chin below his mouth, leaving a heavy white band of beard hair under his chin and up the sides of his face. His variegated blue eyes pierced a face permanently reddened from too much sun and icy wind. Jakkob was over two meters tall, and the floor creaked under his eighteen stones of sinew and muscle.

God had blessed Jakkob with two sons, the oldest just now fifteen. Although both boys were going to be as big as their father, he reserved the hardest work for himself. There were two girls, too, but... well, he supposed the women could use some help. Some said girls were God's way of punishing lustful thoughts. Boys were the real prize.

"What are you going to do about the Summons?" Orpah asked from just outside Jakkob's room.

The ambitious, ruthless Deacon from the Zürich Church had delivered the Summons yesterday. Jakkob and the boys had been gone at the time, and the wives and daughters had been terrified, crying hysterically, at the savage arrogance of the Godly Catholic. He had stormed up in a thunderous flourish, dressed in

4

his finest cloth, riding a huge black horse, and had hammered the square cut nail through the dreaded announcement into a finely shaped porch post without even dismounting.

"Orpah, you know that if it is God's will that I join my Brothers in Heaven, then I am ready to go. I do not plan to attend the Meeting tomorrow. I answer to a Higher Power, and He has instructed me not to go." Orpah shook her head, opened her mouth to reply, but Jakkob's stern look made it clear there would be no discussion.

This is how it always started, she wanted to say, this trouble with the church. In spite of her faith, Orpah was petrified at the thought of how she would survive if Jakkob was taken too. But she also accepted her fate as God's will, and knew the only choice she had was to trust that God had a greater plan.

"Let's eat then," she said softly. "There is work to be done." She turned away from the door and stepped back over to the fireplace, and stirred the porridge.

The small, one-story cottage had filled with the early morning medley of sounds and smells, the smoke from the popping fireplace, fresh baked crispels, and Orpah's special recipe of boor loin sizzling in the skillet.

And the unmistakable odor of pending doom.

The new snow was less than fifteen centimeters deep, and Jakkob slowly trudged to the barn, hunched over, leaning into the bitter cold. There were fresh footprints in the snow, hollowed out craters in the sparkling morass of brilliant cream. Jakkob glanced around, saw no one, and stepped inside the massive wooden front double doors.

Jakkob loved the barn, with all the familiar smells: the hay piled loose in the overhead mows, the smell of leather on horse, and the unmistakable smell of manure, recent piles steaming up from the frigid dirt floor.

Jakkob glanced around the usually tidy barn, quietly absorbing the remaining remnants of last Sunday's service, fifteen shouting, screaming, rollicking Anabaptists, bellowing their praise to the Almighty. Finally, exhausted and panting, they had leaned or fallen on anything they could find: three-legged rough hewn stools, overturned wooden buckets, piles of blankets. Two members had been dunked, shrieking, in the large wooden half-barrel that now leaned upside down against the rough wooden planks of the end stall. Jakkob strode over, lifted it effortlessly, and returned it to its normal place behind the round-rung ladder going up to the haymow. Everyone preferred to hold these baptisms outside, in a river or lake, but these were dangerous times. Jakkob spent a few minutes returning everything to its normal place, making it look just like it always did.

"Who amongst thee knowest this?" the Catholic Bishop spoke in the formal language he reserved for official Church business. He paused and peered down at the parchment in his hand and continued, "Jakkob Ammon?" He looked around the room at the six men, pious men, men he had carefully picked for this holy task.

The men had arrived through the massive door at the bottom of the outside stairs to the church, walking down the short hallway and into the room, ducking through the low door, taking their seats around the big table. The sticky tar torches leaned up against the wall of the hallway, black soldiers in a row, and the men had to turn sideways to move past them. The Bishop was always there, lantern lit, parchment in hand when the men arrived, some still reluctant, some eager.

"I do." It was the town baker.

They all knew Jakkob.

"What do ye know of him?"

The baker paused, looking around the room, relishing the moment.

"Ammon is a huge man, a farmer, father of four." An earlier Anabaptist had gone berserk when they grabbed him, and one of the Churchmen had been severely injured. These heretics were usually strong, hard workers, so the churchmen had changed their methodology; several men glanced towards the back of the room at the clubs leaning against the wall. The baker paused, licked his lips and continued, raising his voice, "He has been re-baptized, immersed in the river," the man on his left began to nod, "and he has taken a *second* wife." The men were all nodding, now, murmuring to each other, grim teeth clenched.

"And the second wife is just a child! It is an affront to God Himself!" The baker had begun to sweat and the town blacksmith slammed both huge hands down on the table in front of him, spilling his goblet of water. The men were agitated, talking loudly: *Let's go get him... Heretic... She's just a child... Two wives!*

The Bishop smiled to himself and then raised his bejeweled right hand, slowly bringing order back to the room, his room. Church doctrine required two confirmations before action could be taken. "Who else amongst thee knowest this Ammon?"

The men all started talking again, each more eager than the next to add his knowledge of this heretic: *He's a maniac... Witchcraft... Incest... Let's get him!*

The Bishop raised both hands, once again silencing these men, his neighbors and friends, and then slowly said, "By the power granted unto me by the Lord our God and His Most Holiness, Pope Clement VII Himself, I hereby beseech each of thee to accompany my loyal servant, the Priest, on this Most Holy Mission, to retain the integrity of the Scripture, to purge our land of this heretic, this polygamist, this Devil-worshipping Raven of Unholy Practices."

With a roar, the men rose, each grabbing a hand-hewn club and tarred-up torch, and rushed up the stairs and onto the street, the Priest out front, nostrils flared.

CHAPTER TWO

Jakkob was perfectly comfortable with his new pair of wings. He found that he could not only flap his way up to great heights, dizzying heights, almost to Heaven, but with a little practice hover in one spot, like a giant hummingbird. He had always expected his wings would be bright white, and was a little puzzled that they were the dirty golden brown of wheat ready to harvest. Jakkob slowly, calmly, soared over Zürich, up one street, banking sharply, and down the next one.

It was still early morning dark, but Jakkob could see every detail of even the smallest objects, even through the ever-present coal smoke. There were the paving stones that made up the front steps to the Church, a hundred copies of a hundred Summons nailed to the board; over there were a couple of sleeping dogs, curled up together to stay warm, their moist breath hanging in the still, frigid morning air, like smoke curling up from a discarded cigar. The blackish mixture of gases from the smoldering, coal-burning fireplaces drifted lazily up from the rock chimneys, forming a low black-cloud ceiling just above Jakkob, the underside illuminated by the yellow-flamed gas powered lights on the street corners. The soot from the dirty air began to collect on the tiny brown feathers on the leading edges of his wings, slowly turning them a filthy dark gray, like the front of uncleaned ceiling fan blades in an opium den.

Jakkob had the calm of someone that knew he was untouchable, invincible. He continued his lazy tour of the town, circling the spiral on the Catholic Church, the highest man-made point for miles around. He curiously examined the gold shingles and the wooden cross at the very top, spreading its knotty arms to all. Even though it was still completely dark, he could see his farm in the distance — evidently night vision came with the wings, he marveled — and slowly spiraled upwards through the sooty air to the clear air above to get a better look.

Something wasn't right. The lanterns in the house should be on by now, and the boys should have already gone to the barn to begin the chores. Both structures were pitch black.

Banking hard to the right, Jakkob flew towards the farm, fanning his wings faster and faster, calm slowly replaced by unease. The still completely dark farm grew larger, and as he approached, he could see the huge splash of crimson streaking the fresh snow just outside the front porch, like someone had tossed a bucket of red paint off the bottom step. Gathering more speed, Jakkob dove towards the front door, wings tucked at half-spread, cold wind streaking past his ears, eyes watering and tears streaming back across unshaven cheeks and flying off of frozen ears. At the last minute, the patriarch tucked his wings tight to his body, knowing he could pass right through the door to find out what was so dreadfully wrong.

The massive wooden door shattered, sending huge splinters in all directions, skidding across the rough wooden floor into the next room. Jakkob was jolted awake, and in the fog of the first few seconds was bewildered, stupid, not understanding why he didn't easily pass through the door with wings folded. The shock of the exploding door was immediately followed by men shouting: *Where is he! Let's get him! Careful, he's strong as an ox!* Rough hands grabbed him and dragged him from his bed, the hand-hewn "Baptism" clubs imbedded with Anabaptist hair cracking his sleepy head, nearly knocking him back into his dream. Through the shouts of the men and screams of his family, now all hysterically awake, Jakkob sluggishly realized that he had been dreaming, and that the dream had turned into the nightmare he knew was coming. He was surrounded by maniacal devils, their brightly burning torches casting evil, swaying shadows on the walls, billows of black smoke rushing upwards and flattening against the already smoked-stained underside of the thatched roof.

The Servants of God, ordinary citizens by day, dragged him across the floor towards the destroyed front door. His night clothes caught on one of the splinters that had wedged into the pile of firewood by the fireplace, tearing the long sleeping dress Orpah had made for him. The shouting men dragged him outside, roughly bouncing him down the front steps he had so carefully crafted from a large spruce tree he and the boys had cut, into the still-dark, early morning frost, clothed only in the now bloodied and torn nightdress. He offered no resistance, yet the men continued to beat and kick him, binding his arms tightly behind him with thick, rough, hemp rope, blood-stained rope. Once securely bound, they heaved him up, covered with snow and blood, and threw him into the back of the black, horse-drawn hearse.

Jakkob's family hung onto porch posts and railings, wives on their knees, screaming, hysterical.

The squad was led by Priest Argular, a small man physically, barely a meter and a half tall, but a giant in political and financial influence. He particularly liked using the hearse, which he had discovered long ago had a great quieting effect on those few Anabaptists that lost their faith, and in the face of this final "baptism," put up a last-minute, completely futile resistance.

Jakkob, bound and gagged and thrown on the floor in the back, painfully felt every jolt of every frozen rut. Three burly men rode in the back with the stunned, motionless Jakkob, and three men on horseback raced alongside. Priest Argular was out front on his magnificent black Friesian stallion, the one he had taken from a Dutch visitor, "For God's work," he had explained to the hapless foreigner.

The men always wore their finest Sunday clothes for these raids, and except for the mortal component of their mission and the frenetic pace, could all be headed for early morning mass. The farm grew rapidly smaller as they raced away, and finally they slowed their pace. Even though they had performed this same, tough-but-necessary task many times before, the adrenalin still coursed through their bodies, and they talked in excited, slightly lower tones. The horses had all caught the fever at the farm, screaming and prancing and pawing, but had started to calm, except for the Priest's stallion, fresh and excited. The Priest, an expert horseman, seemed totally oblivious to the prancing steed, his jaw set in righteous determination.

The procession turned slightly northeast, heading for a well-known passage through the foothills on the southwest end of Zürichsee Lake. Zürichsee was a long and narrow lake that stretched all the way into Zürich, fifteen kilometers to the northeast. Approaching the pass with Priest Argular in the lead, the church/city leadership fell into single file to make their way through the narrow opening. The southern approach to the corridor was a fairly mild ascent, up about two hundred meters from the valley, and then gradually dropped at the same rate on the other side.

Cold and painful stabbing crept through Jakkob, as he slowly regained some of his senses from the earlier beating. One of the men had purposefully broken his left leg, evidently knowing his prey well enough to focus on the area of the old injury the farmer had lived with these past five years. The broken bone had not penetrated the skin, and Jakkob had a fleeting thought that perhaps God intended a miracle and even that leg would heal. The blood from his savaged head had pooled in the hearse, and had matted on the wood and burlap the churchmen had put in the back of the fancy wagon to protect the fine linens there for normal use. He tried to move his throbbing head and found the coarse mat under his head moved with it, stuck to his scalp with dried blood. He tried to free his matted hair, but couldn't with hands bound behind him, and gave up and lay back down. One of the guards saw his efforts and with his boot roughly kicked the burlap away from Jakkob's head, shooting bolts of pain and light behind his eyes.

Jakkob rolled back on his side, it was impossible to get comfortable, and began softly repeating his favorite prayer, The Lord's Prayer. "*Vater unser, der Du bist im Himmel. Geheiliget werde Dein Name. Dein Reich komme. Dein Wille...*"

The same guard kicked again, kicked the gentle, hard working family man in the head and snarled, *"Halt den Schnabel!"* The bound man continued his prayer silently, offering no resistance. The grim procession jolted down the long, gradual slope that led onto the frozen lake. The hearse and its four-hooved escorts slid out on the ice, the torment of the frozen ruts suddenly changing to smooth, even, easy traveling. The horses slipped and slid, struggling on slick footing. The men grew quiet and stern with the task that was quickly approaching. Even though God's word was quite clear on infant baptism, the Priest always grew somber as the final moment approached, the moment he was to carry out this necessary purging of heretics. He was God's instrument, and these ceremonies were an important part of furthering God's plan on earth. And his own.

The Priest always went back to the same place, a secluded cove that other, less convicted church members kept clear of snow. The procession finally came to a stop, and each member took his accustomed spot. The same three men that had yanked Jakkob from his warm bed an hour ago threw him down on the smooth, snow-cleared ice, still bound tightly with the rough hemp rope they always used: worn, stained, holy rope.

One of the men grabbed a huge burlap sack, one made especially for this ceremony, one that had been constructed from many smaller sacks. The local tailor never asked what the church needed with these huge sacks. He knew.

Early on, the executioners had simply put the heretics inside the huge sacks and tied it shut with rope. But they had found it was much more effective to also wrap rope around the outside of the sack, so the renegades were bound tightly inside and out. If there was no possibility of struggle, it would bring the ceremony to a much more dignified conclusion. There had been an ill-fated incident last winter where a rebel had slipped completely beneath the ice and they had to wait until the spring thaw to retrieve the body. So the group had learned also to tie a rope to the feet of their subject. Sometimes the unbelievers were able to stand, sometimes not, it mattered little. On a couple of occasions, they had been dead when they arrived, and that troubled the Priest; he wasn't able to give them a final, last chance to repent.

This one was strong, and big, but had great difficulty standing, wobbly on his remaining good leg. God's messengers busied themselves cutting the three foot wide hole in the thick ice, chopping at the same spot that contained the jagged ice from previous baptisms. The Priest readied himself for the conclusion of preserving the world from nonbelievers and heretics, and preserving his spot in the social and economic order of things.

Three burly assistants soon finished tightening the rope around Jakkob, and then there was no sound at all except that of their labored breathing in the early, still-dark morning. The other members of the group had lit their wood-tar torches, and if anyone had been watching, it would have made an eerie sight: the Priest in his fine ceremonial dress standing three meters to the west of a fresh hole in the lake, a hole barely large enough to fit a man through. In the middle of the line of six men, there was a strange, huge shape (could it be a person?) standing erect in what appeared to be a burlap sack from neck to toe, his bloodied head sticking out the top. One of the men threw a rope around his neck, securing the bag, and the folds of the remaining sack fell draped around his chest and shoulders, rope binding him like a sloppy mummy. Next to this figure, a tight semicircle of men, dressed in fine clothes, three on the north side and three on the south side, stood at casual attention. The flickering torches made devilish, dancing shadows on the cleared ice all the way to where the snow was piled up near the bank.

The Priest faced the poor, misdirected farmer, and asked, "Ye knowest why thou art here, Herr Ammon?" No response. "It is not too late. All thou must do is repent, denounce these heretical —"

At this, Jakkob began again repeating his prayer, loudly, "*Vater unser, der Du bist im Himmel. Geheiliget werde Dein Name. Dein Reich komme. Dein Wille —*"

The Priest was instantly angry. He wasn't going to listen to this supreme hypocrisy on this heretic's last minutes on earth. Although extremely rare, others had been defiant, and the Priest nodded to the man immediately to Jakkob's right, who swung his Holy Club into the the big man's head, at the base of his neck, smashing white hair, skin and bone, and Jakkob fell with a sickening thud, spider cracks shooting in every direction in the ice as his weight crashed down.

The Priest quickly finished his recitation, and with no more ceremony, the three men roughly pulled the remaining burlap up over the non-believer's head, tied it shut with a short rope, and Jakkob was shoved, head first, into the icy-slushed waters for his final baptism.

The Priest, now sweating profusely in the early morning cold, turned his back on the ceremony and said simply, "It is done."

Jakkob was among the first of the Amish, as they would later become known. He was unrelated to Jacob Ammon.

CHAPTER THREE

Pennsylvania, 1964 A.D.

"Well? Anyone?" Mr. Phend peered out through his thick black-rimmed glasses at his eighth grade algebra class, waiting for the answer to question 19, the square root of 47. Not one of the twelve students looked up, instead busily studied the carved-up sloping wood tops of their desks. Finally Ezra raised his hand, just slightly. "Yes, Ezra?"

"6.856." They were supposed to work the questions long hand and round the answer to the nearest thousandth.

"Yes, very good, thank you." Mr. Phend glared disapprovingly around the room. "Why is it that Ezra is the only one in my class doing his homework?"

Mr. Phend had scolded his class many times before, and without waiting for a response turned to write the answer on the blackboard. A big wad of crumpled paper and saliva arced through the room and splattered Ezra square on the back of his neck. The classroom erupted in laughter, but immediately went quiet when Mr. Phend angrily spun around. He saw Ezra wiping his neck with the big red handkerchief he always had hanging out of his rear pants' pocket.

"Who did that?" the teacher angrily demanded. Silence. "If I find out which —" The gray classroom bell hanging on the painted cinder block wall above the big round classroom clock loudly clanged. It was the end of class, and in spite of his attempt to keep everyone there until he "got to the bottom of this," the rowdy adolescents spilled out of the room and down to their old gray metal lockers that lined both sides of the wide hall.

"Hey, Ahmo, wait up." It was Jonathon. Ezra paused without turning around. Jonathon walked up to Ezra, leaned over and sniffed his shirt loudly. "Ah, Ahmo, you smell so good." Several passing girls who stopped to watch started giggling.

This was Ezra's last year at the small country school and he hated every minute of it. He had longed to be part of the gang, talking to friends about girls, cars, and the latest movie they had seen. But instead, the other students smirked at his too-short pants held up with wide leather suspenders, dirty white socks and dull, scuffed work boots and straw hat, smelling of kerosene smoke, horse manure and body odor.

Jonathon was the school bully, and not a day passed that he didn't yank one of Ezra's suspenders or knock his hat off, his torment of choice earlier that same day. School had just started for the year, and Ezra wore the flat-brimmed straw hat that was the summer custom among the Amish. Mr. Schneider, the coach, saw the hat flying through the air, saw Jonathon smirking and the crimson slowly rising in Ezra's cheeks, and without much emotion said, "Knock it off, boys." Jonathon mouthed his customary "sorry" and the minute no one was looking, made a fake lunge at Ezra, his mean laugh echoing down the hall.

Ezra didn't have friends at school. The closest to a friend was William, the Negro. Ezra was the brunt of a lot of jokes and snide remarks, but he had blond hair and blue eyes and those northern European fair-skinned good looks. If he had worn his hair and dressed like everyone else, he would have been just another student in this rural German community. But William, with his brown-black skin and kinky hair would often show up with scrapes and cuts that didn't quite fit with his explanation of how he got them. One time, Mr. Parker, the science teacher, sent William to the bathroom five times during one science class, to "wash the dirt off of your hands." William's hands were not dirty, but he clomped down the hall in his ever-present third-generation wingtips and washed his hands again and again, never complaining.

Once, in the seventh grade, Ezra had asked his father if he could sleep-over at William's house, the little faded brown asbestos siding house on the outskirts of town, the poor side of town, by a small creek that meandered through the tall oak and hickory trees lining the dirt streets. 1964 Lancaster County social

16

order was very structured, institutionalized even, with white folks, even Amish white folks, higher up the social order than people of color, and the Amish father sneered at his naïve son's request. It was a morning question, the best time to ask difficult questions, Ezra had learned.

"We don't sleep-over with niggers. And I don't want you to be hanging around with that colored boy, you understand?" As usual, Ezra started to argue, but his father's curled up fist silenced the debate, no debate at all, really. Ezra decided not to press the sleep-over question, but went out of his way to befriend the young Negro at school, eating lunch under an old oak tree at the edge of the playground, catching up with him in the hall, helping him with his homework at recess.

Ezra didn't understand exactly why he had to attend public school. The preachers all said education was to be avoided, "It led to pride," and yet his father made him go. Something about "*die Engländer* (The English)" laws required public school through the eighth grade. English was what the Amish called everyone else.

Ezra wore the Amish "uniform," a mixture of plain, coarse clothing with eye-hooks and suspenders, no zippers or buttons. And there was Jonathon, always waiting for Ezra, looking for a chance to bedevil the strange-looking boy who never fought back.

Ezra's twin cousins were another story. They were a year behind Ezra, and each day on the way to school they slipped into an old abandoned barn on Jeb Miller's place. The broad-brimmed summer-straw hats came off and the rough pants, suspenders and shirts were exchanged for blue jeans and white t-shirts, shiny black narrow belts and burgundy penny loafers they had secretly bought at Woolworth's. Each penny loafer had a shiny new copper penny inserted in the slot for that purpose, Abe Lincoln looking up expressionless at the two boys. Their t-shirts were rolled up at the sleeves, holding their cigarette packs, showing off muscles honed by the hard work they had done every day since they could walk. They shared a hand-held transistor radio blaring a tinny rendition of the Beatles' "Love Me Do." Their bowl-cut hair was a problem — left alone it looked like Moe's of *The Three Stooges* — but they slicked it back as best they could, and it wasn't that different from the current style, the ubiquitous duck's ass, or DA. Everyone knew they were Amish, of course, it was a small community, but they came to school with an attitude as big as the gymnasium, and they were left alone.

Jonathon had made the mistake one day of picking on the blond twin, the taller one. "Hey Ahmo," had barely left his lips when the shorter twin hit him hard, hit him on the side of his head with hardened knuckles, knocking him onto the gravel under the swing set. Jonathon grabbed at and missed the swing chain, spinning the metal seat and both chains wildly in the air.

Both twins stood over the crying bully, the tall one saying, "Get up sissy, come on. Not so tough after all are you?" The bully lay there with his arm up as if to ward them off until the two had had enough and walked away. Mr. Schneider saw the whole thing out the tall window in his classroom, and did nothing. He secretly applauded these two young men "acting like boys", and couldn't understand why Ezra didn't defend himself. "Strange people," he muttered to himself. "Just leave them alone."

Ezra saw the whole thing, too, and wondered how the twins pulled off this double life, why no one went to the Amish Bishop or the twins' father. Fighting at school, and then every Sunday morning, there were the twins, front and center, leading the hymnal singing, helping with the metal folding chairs at whoever's house the Sunday morning service was held, smiling, hugging friends and neighbors. Their father struggled just trying to buy food and clothes since his wife had died, and as long as they weren't trouble at home he was oblivious, disinterested.

Ezra was the oldest of five surviving children born to Nathan and Rebecca Neuenschwander. The second oldest, a boy, had been stillborn and the fourth child, Sarah, had died when she was only five years old, died of a variety of complications from birth defects. "It is God's will," the Amish patriarch had

18

brusquely told his weeping wife. Daniel, ten this past February, was very bright, but had a habit of lying, lying when the truth would have done as well.

Seeing the constant combativeness between his older brother and his father, Daniel kept his thoughts to himself, his mouth closed. He would often attempt to disrupt his father's abusive pattern with humor, Amish humor: "Daniel, why are the milk buckets not washed?" his father would bark, and Daniel would answer, "The cats wanted to lick them clean," or "I turned them upside down," broadly smiling while he answered. Usually this worked, depending on the time of day, and Nathan would turn his attention back to Ezra, who never deflected, always stood straight and took whatever his father dished out head-on. The brothers were not close.

Naomi, nine, was slow, slow to learn. Yet she was mellow, even-tempered, with a knack for invisibility. Her mother had to repeat everything three or four times, and her father just ignored her. "She chust ain't right in the head," Naomi's cousins would whisper, just within earshot. The youngest boy, Joseph, five, took it on himself to look after his older sister, steering her away from problems and danger on a daily basis. He could often be seen, with his gray pants, cloth suspenders and blue, long-sleeved shirt, streaking across the house to help his sister retrieve a doll or put a pan back or remind her not to stand on the open oven door, gently and patiently helping and explaining how to do it properly. The youngest, Hannah, ten months old, was colicky, face screwed into constant protest, screaming her discomfort. Rebecca had tried everything, ginger and other herbs, but nothing seemed to help. She had finally begun holding her hand over the child's mouth until the baby passed out, the only relief against the constant shrieking. She had persuaded herself it was better than what she and the child would get from her husband if the howling didn't stop.

Ezra's father, Nathan, was a stern German from a long line of stern Germans. He had the same straw-yellow hair as his ancestors and had passed it down to his oldest son. Beaten by his

19

father, beaten so hard that he would carry a limp to his grave, he vowed to break the pattern, to treat his family with respect. Early in the marriage, he largely succeeded. He was a good, acceptable, father and husband, if cold and distant. But slowly, over time, he lost the battle, as the house filled with more and more children. His resolve to stop drinking and adhere to the Amish way of nonviolence began to crumble. The man was pious and remorseful through his bleary-eyed morning hangovers, but as the day wore on, his piety surrendered to the cheap whiskey he smuggled home from the occasional trips to town. Over the years, too much drinking had taken its toll, and he lost the fight, lost the will to do better, and had turned mean.

Ezra had approached one of the Bishops with his father's drinking. That lone attempt resulted in a lecture to Ezra on his need to "respect one's elders."

Ezra didn't fit in even among the Amish. The other kids at church seemed to be happy, peaceful, contented, and even joyful. He had tried to embrace the faith. When the protracted Sunday morning services came to the long prayers, Ezra would squeeze his eyes shut tight and pray with all his might, but all he saw was his boozed-up father, mouthing the very words the preacher was saying, meaningless words. Ezra tried talking to God, but God didn't seem to be listening or didn't care, he decided. He could see God leaning up against the wall, arms folded, expressionless, watching him. He finally quit trying.

Ezra didn't mind the hard work that was so much a part of growing up on a farm with no electricity, phone, or even curtains or mirrors in the house. In fact, working hard had been a satisfying distraction, and he had grown strong enough to easily snatch Jonathon up and throw him out the schoolhouse window. But — that was "not our way" his father had so often yelled at him, an inch from his nose. "You get in a fight at school and you gonna wish you never come home," he would bark, slurring his words. "We don't fight."

Ezra's mother could have been pretty, but it had been too many years since a smile had crossed her face, and she looked tired and sad and resigned. She had been an attractive young bride, but the years spent carrying huge loads of laundry to the basement, washing them by hand, hauling them to the back yard to clothespin them on the line to dry, almost always nursing a baby, and then being available for her husband's rough nightly demands, had left her chronically exhausted. She was kind at heart, and if she had had the energy to think about it, probably was a True Believer. She was simply too tired to think about it. She hated the way her husband treated the children, especially the eldest who was always quietly defiant, but the *Bible* made it very clear that the husband was the head of the household and the wife was to obey him. "Treat your wives as I treat the church," was what Jesus had instructed, and the Amish Bishops, all men, had uniformly interpreted that to mean wives didn't talk back. Ever.

Several months earlier, just before the family's customary early dinner, Ezra's mother was standing at the old, propane, chipped-porcelain stove, feet planted wide to brace against the onslaught of needy children, stirring a large pot of stew, the usual staple for the large, poor family. Young Hannah, to be their last, was crying, as usual, in a cloth sling hung around the mother's neck, a dress-yanking child on both sides, clamoring for what children clamor for. She nervously glanced over her right shoulder when Nathan stumbled through the back door demanding to know why dinner wasn't ready.

"*Wo ist meine Abendessen?*"

"It's almost ready," she answered wearily, warily.

"*Sprechen Sie Deutsch!*"

Rebecca looked over her shoulder again, opened her mouth to reply when the young boy on her right screamed and pointed, pointed at the flames licking up the long bonnet tie ribbon she had let fall in the flame of the front burner. Jumping back, she slapped the flame out against her dress and turned in fear towards her drunken husband. His raised left hand slapped her hard on the side of her face, no time to duck, and she fell hard across her young daughter still clinging to her dress, barely

21

able to break the fall, barely avoiding crushing the now shrieking baby in the wildly swaying sling. She lay on the floor for a moment, crying, and then her husband's rough, strong hands helped her to her feet. She saw a flicker of regret in his bloodshot blue eyes, the Nathan of old, but it went out like the real flame she had just extinguished.

The meal that night was like so many evening meals any more, hushed, no, "How was your day?" no, "What are you doing tomorrow?"

When he came in from chores, Ezra could sense things were worse than usual, and noticed the burnt ribbon his mother still wore, the black smudge on her apron, the red welt on her face, her refusal to look up. After his father had "retired," slumped in the torn cloth chair in the living room, he asked her what had happened.

She stood up slowly and began clearing the table. Her eldest son walked over in front of her, took the dirty plates from her and set them in the sink. "What happened, Mother?" He spoke in English, accented English, so different from the English neighbors.

"Ezra, first you have to promise you won't be to do anything," she said earnestly, taking his hands into hers. Ezra had grown increasingly defiant of his father, some of it normal adolescence, some of it a resolve to end the abuse, resolve he had taken to speaking out loud to his mother.

Ezra hesitated, and then promised, "Okay." A pause, then, "What happened?"

She continued to busy herself with dishes, then in a shaky voice, said, "Oh, nothing, really, my *schnur* caught ablaze with the stove and I had to put it out. Father was a little impatient."

Ezra said nothing for a minute, looking at his mother's pocked face, remnants of an early bout with untreated measles. "He hit you, Mother. I shall honor my word tonight, but if it should be to happen again, he will for sure regret it." Ezra worked hard to speak like the English, but when excited, or angry, slipped back into the singsong dialect of Amish English, Pennsylvania-Dutch English.

He dropped his mother's hands and she went back to her cleanup chores. Ezra watched her for a minute, then turned and walked towards his slumbering, snoring father, the wooden floor creaking under his almost mature weight. His mother stopped and watched, holding her breath. But the young Amish man simply stood over his father with his hands clenched in tight, white-knuckled fists, then slowly opened them back up and left the room.

CHAPTER FOUR

Jonathon was raised on a small, poor patch of hardscrabble at the edge of the Amish community. His was the last house before the double overhead power lines quit, just stopped, ending at the creosote pole, like long, skinny fingers pointing towards the Amish.

The dilapidated dwelling seemed perpetually in danger of falling down. The paint on the siding was long since gone, the bare wood turning dark gray, like a land-based shipwreck. The rocky ground hadn't seen grass since his mother left when he was five. The run-down homestead was a stark contrast to the neat, fresh, well kempt grounds and white, always white, houses, of his simple Amish neighbors a mile down the gravel road.

Jonathon hated the Amish. Even if he had stopped long enough to wonder why, the answer would have been elusive. His was the kind of visceral hatred the lion has for the weak gazelle: the need to destroy, to consume. And he particularly hated Ezra, "that queer, that bookworm dweeb," he would say to himself. "How can you be Amish and a bookworm?" he would mutter. And he would hate him even more. He took particular delight in tormenting Ezra. At first, the torment had been spitballs, a little shoving, and then expanded to the family, burning a few corn shocks. Soon it escalated to killing their chickens and slicing up leather harnesses. Ezra and his family never shoved back. "What a bunch of pussies," Jonathon would laugh.

"Hey, Jon, how's it going?" Jonathon's father tentatively creaked the grimy, bare wood door open to his son's room. He wanted to be his friend. Last week, Tuesday, his father had discovered the plastic packets with the dried, off-green plant leaves in each of them neatly stacked in Jon's top dresser drawer next to an equally neat stack of one-dollar bills.

24

Jonathon slowly turned from slicking back both sides of his black hair. He used Brylcream like everyone. He slowly, deliberately, put the brush on top of the dresser, and stared at his father. "What part of 'Don't ever come into my room again in your life' do you not understand?"

Jonathon was not large, but at fifteen he was bigger than his father. More importantly, he was a bully, and with the instinct of a serial tormenter, knew when to press, when to back off. It was time to press.

"Look, Jon —" his father started his usual, tentative pleading, then stopped. It had all been said before, to no avail.

Jonathon's face was expressionless, placid. He was relaxed. "See that?" he nodded towards the shotgun hanging on the wall. "I keep #4 shot in it all the time. #4 is especially good for bigger animals." He continued to stare at his father, who was now looking at the floor, at his worn shoes. "Get out of my room. Don't come back in here."

His father opened his mouth to say something, closed it, turned and left without saying a word. He was shaken, and went out the front door and headed to the wood shed, the one he had fantasized about whipping his son in, knowing it was too late now. He picked up the double-bladed ax, looked at the house, and slowly, then furiously, began splitting firewood. Finally, exhausted, dripping with sweat, he crept back into the house, his house, and keeping a wary eye on his son's closed door, pulled the key to his rusty, old pickup out of the kitchen drawer, crept back outside and slid behind the wheel. He pumped the gas pedal with his right foot, stomping on the floor starter with his left, sending small clouds of dust into the air around his feet, and the flat-head-six engine finally coughed to life, stuttering. He angrily ground the floor shifter into reverse, the clutch was nearly gone, backed onto the gravel road, slammed the shifter into first, spewed tire-launched gravel against the old mailbox, and disappeared over the hill.

He never returned.

25

CHAPTER FIVE

Someone had let the air out of Ezra's bicycle tires again. He walked it the three miles to his house, hand-pumped the tires full of air, and leaned the faded red bike against the barn. He walked the short distance to the house, carrying his school books, and entered the back porch. He started to catch the rear porch screen door behind his back, and then let it slam instead. His mother looked up from the sink.

"Wie er an der Schule heute ging, Eshra?" she asked in Pennsylvania Dutch, a peculiar mixture of Low German, unwritten German, and English, a clipped, guttural language. She wore a pale-yellow, full-length dress, dark hose showing on barely exposed ankles. Her dress had the traditional modesty panel sewn over her chest, hardly disguising her ample figure. The work-day Amish bonnet hid her prematurely gray hair, and the long tie ribbons hung almost to her waist.

"School went fine Momma," he answered in English. "Where's Father?"

Ezra's mother glanced at her son and then answered, also in English, "He went to town with Mr. Schilling." Mr. Schilling made his money ferrying the Amish around in his old Chevy van.

"What kind of mood is he in today?" Silence. "Are you alright?"

Ezra's mother was busy cutting up vegetables on a handmade cutting board. She finally laid the wood-handled knife down on the faded brown Formica countertop and turned to her oldest son. "Yes, Ezra, I am fine. It has been calm today. Why don't you go upstairs and change for to do your chores so maybe we can have a peaceful evening?" She wiped her hands on her dirty apron. "Mrs. Herzog brought some more books by. I put them in the attic. But do your chores first."

Ezra smiled at the mention of Mrs. Herzog. She was a retired schoolteacher and had lived in her modest white home at the edge of the Amish community for thirty years. To an alert observer, the most telling difference between the Amish and the English homesteads was the lack of electrical lines running from the road to the houses, and except for the wires, her place could have been Amish. In fact, her house was the last house before the Anabaptist community, and the public wood-cross power poles stopped at her driveway. Just stopped, ended. The city folks that occasionally came out to gawk at the Amish would comment about the power lines ending. And the horse droppings in the road, the "road apples." Some of the fancy car drivers tried to dodge the small, round clumps of horse waste strewn along the road. Some didn't notice, carrying the country remnants back to their garages, wondering the next morning what that awful smell was coming from the fancy wheels of their fancy cars.

Mrs. Herzog had taught many Amish kids in her career, and had run her own small education revolution, her mission to educate the world. She was appalled and fascinated with the Amish determination to live in ignorance, institutionalized ignorance, dependant on "Word-From-Above" for every detail of their lives.

Ezra was her latest target, but unlike so many before him, he was interested, even eager to learn. Ezra's mother was nervous, and early on had asked the gray-haired revolutionary to please not come by the house. But Ezra had pleaded with his mother for more books, and so Mrs. Herzog still came, quietly, furtively, watching for Father, making sure he didn't suddenly arrive at the door. Sometimes Ezra would stop at her house, risky business too, and then hurry back home, down the brown-stained road from their close neighbor, barely a quarter mile away, carrying the *verboten* books in a sack.

Earlier that day, Mrs. Herzog had come to visit. There was no doorbell, of course, not even a doorknocker, so she rapped on the sun-bleached front door with her knuckles. She heard footsteps growing louder, felt the front porch tremble slightly as someone walked towards the front door.

"*Guten Morgen.*" The schoolmarm taught eighth grade German and always greeted whoever came to the door that way.

27

A flicker of a smile briefly lit up Rebecca's face, and she replied, "*Guten Morgen, Frau Herzog.*"

"I know I can't come in, I understand, but here are some more books for Ezra. And some batteries. Ezra stopped by yesterday — l don't worry, no one saw — and said he had worked all the Algebra problems, and did I have the next edition, so I put it in the bag too. I put a copy of *Catcher in the Rye* in also. Be careful with that book, your husband would not like it at all."

The retired schoolteacher had already slipped Ezra a copy of *Riders of the Purple Sage* several months ago, admonishing him to not tell anyone, even his mother, that he had it. She secretly hoped the tormented young man, brain-washed and conditioned to be passive from an early age, would see in Zane Grey's Lassiter another response to his abusive father.

The two women, neighbor women from different universes, chatted for a few minutes longer, Mrs. Herzog doing most of the talking, and then she left, saying, "see you next week" over her shoulder.

His mother knew Ezra wasn't happy at school, but in spite of his unhappiness, or perhaps because of it, he buried himself in his homework. He had asked for her help with his homework once, but soon realized she neither knew nor had the time and energy to help. Ezra not only mastered the work assigned at school, but also began asking his mother if there was any way he could get more books. At first she said no, both of them knowing full well the price to be paid if Father found out, but she eventually started smuggling reading material up to the attic along with the *verboten* flashlight and batteries. "You can't very well use a lantern," his mother had said, handing him the weekly supply of batteries. They both knew they had to be careful; the drunken patriarch had made it perfectly clear he couldn't wait for the eighth grade to be over so he "could get a decent day's work" out of his eldest son. In the meantime, Ezra snuck to the attic after his siblings were asleep, devouring every book, working every Algebra exercise and always, always asking for more.

The family had just finished breakfast. It was a Saturday, and the mood at the table had been almost jovial. Almost. Father was in a semi-jocular mood, a rarely seen state that left the rest of the family on edge. Daniel was helping clear the table when his father said, "That's not proper work for a boy, Daniel, let the girls do it. Joseph can help, he doesn't know if he's going to be a boy or a girl yet." Daniel, always the placater, pulled his hands away from the faded green plastic plate he was about to pick up and glanced at his older brother, who was headed out the door. Without a word, Ezra turned around and deliberately walked back to the table, picked up the plate, and took it to the sink. His father was instantly angry. He grabbed the plate back out of the sink, dripping soapy water on the linoleum, and slammed it down hard on the table where it had been, knocking a glass of water over, spilling it on the floor. He turned slowly towards Ezra, blocking his eldest son's path to pick the plate back up.

"This is the problem I have with you, Ezra. You defy me all of the time and cannot be counted upon to do what you are told." The same spider veins that always turned red later in the day had begun their creep up his neck, disappearing behind the bushy gray beard under his chin, and reappearing on his florid, shaven cheeks.

Ezra's face flushed crimson, white-knuckled fists clenched by his side. Without a word, he turned and walked back to the door to go out, again. His father threw a water soaked, wadded up napkin at his retreating son, splattering Ezra on the back of his hatless head. The rest of the family froze, rigid bodies afraid to breath, waiting. Ezra stood looking straight ahead, hand on the doorknob. Though his head was down, the family watched the muscles of his jaw clench and re-clench before he hissed, barely audible, "You told Daniel to put the dish back. Not me." Then slowly he went outside and slammed the door behind him.

CHAPTER SIX

It was a beautiful weekend in the middle of October, crisp evening breeze rustling the turning maple leaves. It was Ezra's last year in school. The teenage Amish had just finished hauling the last of the corn shocks to the covered storage area behind the corn bins, and was sweaty and filthy. The largest of the farm wagons was filled to overflowing. He unharnessed the two huge draft horses and was hand-grazing them before putting them up for the night. He had finished rubbing the horses down with the burlap bags kept for that purpose and their black coats shined, their rippling muscles glistening in the failing light. In between mouthfuls of the still-green autumn grass, the horses blasted huge streams of moist fog into the cool evening, like benign dragons, clearing their nostrils. Occasionally they would find ears of field corn that had been dropped off of the rickety, gas-run conveyor belt Father had borrowed to fill the bins, and excitedly crunched away. Not too much corn, Ezra thought, don't want them to founder.

Ezra never knew what would set Father off, and tonight it would be the corn. Ezra had seen another welt on his mother's tired face, on her cheek, and almost hoped for a confrontation with his father. Ezra could tell by the familiar flush in his father's cheeks and unsteady gait that he had already begun his evening ritual with his version of grain. The abuse so far had been non-physical, at least with Ezra, muscular and defiant, almost a man. "You're no good and will never amount to anything," and "you're going to Hell, Ezra." But tonight something was different. It was Ezra. He usually avoided looking his father directly in the eye; that just added fuel to the burn. But the young man, tonight, had decided finally to confront his drunken father.

"I've told you a thousand times to pick up that corn, you *schwachsinnig!*" Father shouted, slurred.

Ezra said nothing, but held his gaze steady, directed at his father's increasingly flushed face.

30

"Was betrachten Sie?" Father demanded.

Ezra remained silent, mind racing with visions of his mother's battered face and gunslingers crouching, warily eyeing their enemy. He continued to lock his eyes with his father's, unwavering. The patriarch grew more agitated, left eye twitching uncontrollably, temple muscles flexing, his explosive burst of profanity a jarring contrast to the calm, cool, beautiful evening. Ezra did not flinch, strangely calm and resolved, not nauseous like in the past.

The two draft horses were beginning to fidget, pawing the ground, snorting, wide-eyed, increasingly agitated, sensing the electricity in the air. Ezra, left handed, instinctively shifted both lead ropes to his right hand, not sure what to expect but readying himself.

With a final stream of oaths, the wild-eyed farmer in his black, broad-brimmed felt hat lunged at his "wicked" son, furious and completely out of control, swinging wildly at the boy's head.

Ezra easily sidestepped the sloppy haymaker, and clutching the now jerking and taut lead ropes, hit the drunken farmer hard with his tightly clenched left fist, hit him in the middle of his stomach. His father went down like an overstuffed sack of ground wheat, hitting the back of his head on the sharp edge of the stout metal frame of the conveyor belt, flopping to the earth with a thud and laid there twitching and jerking and bleeding.

The enormity of what he had done hit him, and Ezra stood there shaking. *Turn the other cheek — it is not our way— honor thy mother and thy father — if you get in trouble at school there is bigger trouble when you get home — you're a worthless piece of shit and you're going to Hell—* all pounding in his head. For a minute Ezra stood and shook, not even conscious that he was talking to the big animals, slowly soothing them back under control. "Better put them up," he said to himself. He glanced at the now motionless heap of rough clothes that was his father, black hat laying five feet away, one arm awkwardly bent under his stomach, and tearfully turned towards the barn, the still jittery draft horses in tow.

Ezra quickly walked the horses around the corner of the barn and hurried to the huge, sliding barn doors, already closed against the cool air. He slid the twenty-foot doors open, and quickly put the horses up, tossing a pad of hay to each, forgetting their oats and molasses. He hurried to the house and found his mother drooped in her tattered armchair, near the blazing wood stove, nursing Hannah. Ezra's breath was coming in short, shallow bursts, like a laboring locomotive. His pupils were fully dilated and his peach-fuzz covered cheeks glowed bright pink. She glanced up, sleepily, then alarmed, and asked, "Where's Father?" After no reply from her oldest son she asked, "What happened?"

"I hit him Mama," he said as matter of factly as he could muster. "He tried for to hit me first, so I hit him hard. He's on the ground now."

"Ezra, how could ye? Is he going to be okay?" She yanked her nipple from the suckling baby, covered her breast and placed the now wailing child in her cradle. "He has provided for us and now you hit him!"

Ezra started to protest, to explain, but she cut him off. Then, strangely calm, she said, "I knew this was going to happen someday. You need to go. I have packed some items you will need on your journey. I asked Mrs. Herzog for some help to buy you some English clothes and to call your second cousin, Phil, in Philadelphia, to see if you could to come and live with him. He said OK. He is no longer Amish. He has a television and a car and everything, but I think he is OK. Go into town and take the bus to Philadelphia. I have written the phone number on a note and put it in your bag."

She looked at her son, still ten feet away. "You need to leave now, he will kill you."

Ezra stood still, looking at his mother. She handed him the black canvas bag containing everything in the world that would be his, and he realized she had a depth he had missed. He knew now what had happened to the missing money his father had angrily accused her of taking. He attempted to give his recoiling mother a hug but she pushed him away with, "Nay, you are wicked," gave up and slowly walked through the front door, black bag over his right shoulder.

He walked rapidly, past the barn where he had grown up, exhilarated and terrified. He glanced at his now stirring and groaning father, still lying on the ground, and walked even faster. The gravel crunched under his worn boots as he walked quickly down the long narrow lane past the pond on the left, towards the county road, and for a fleeting moment wished he could undo all that had just happened. Somehow make things right. Impossible, he knew, and didn't allow himself to look back, not even a glance.

"I'll go to my cousin's place," he told himself bravely. He didn't really believe all the drug abuse stories the twins had repeated so many times.

Everything would be fine in Philadelphia.

CHAPTER SEVEN

Ezra briskly walked the three miles to town. He kept glancing over his shoulder, listening for the tell-tale rapid clip-clop of racehorse shoes on asphalt, expecting to see his furious father racing to catch him in the open buggy with the fast black filly, a pacer he bought off the trotter race track. The young horse had not been fast enough for the track but was plenty fast for an Amish family.

Ezra had walked to town before, but never with the intensity of tonight's walk. By the time he arrived at the outskirts of the small sleeping town, he had taken his gray jacket off and his shirt was darkened with streaks of sweat. He was breathing hard, puffing frosty breath into the cold dark air.

The bus station was at the end of the line for this run, and the driver had to turn around to head back to the city. The station was simply a sign hanging by Ted's filling station. Ezra knew from older Amish friends that worked in Philadelphia that there was a 10:30 run and he needed to hurry to catch it. The adrenaline from the fight had worn off, and by the time he rounded the last bend in the county road and saw the single bulb dimly shining on the bus schedule nailed to the wood power pole, he was weary. There was one other person, a man, slouching with his feet stretched onto the bare dirt in front of the bench, ankles crossed, his neck resting on the back of the faded wood and dull iron bench. He was wearing a brown fedora pulled down over his eyebrows, waiting, and was smoking a cigarette. It was Mr. Speicher, the greenhouse owner.

Ezra gratefully sat down on the empty end of the bench, and put the canvas bag next to him. He rested for a minute, and then unzipped the bag and reached inside. There were clothes, not the traditional Amish drab clothing, but blue jeans and flannel shirts and a soft black leather jacket. There was a hard case of some type on top of the clothes, and he pulled it out. A narrow black leather belt, shiny black, encircled the case, holding

34

the lid closed. He undid the shiny silver buckle, and opened the box. On the right hand side on the top sheet of a thick bundle of white, lined paper, his mother had drawn several hearts and had written in big, awkward capital letters "GOD BE WITH YOU." Ezra knew his mother had struggled to write that; she had no education at all, and he had taught her the few words she could read and write. She had also included two #2 pencils, already sharpened, and a small, plastic pencil sharpener. Ezra felt a lump rise in his throat, and returned the case to the bag. He continued to feel around inside the canvas bag, and found a small, soft leather pouch. He pulled it out, and with a furtive look at Mr. Speicher, pulled most of the money out and put it in his right front pocket. He returned the pouch to the canvas bag; he would count it all out later.

"Say, aren't you Nathan Neuenschwander's boy?"

Ezra had noticed that Mr. Speicher had been watching him out of the corner of one almost closed eye. "Yes sir."

Mr. Speicher sat up straight on his end of the bench, pushed the hat up on his forehead with his right forefinger, and took a long drag on his half-smoked cigarette. He tilted his head way back and blew the smoke straight up, like a fire-eater at the county fair. He turned to Ezra and asked, "What are you doing down here so late?"

Ezra thought for a minute, and then replied, "I have cousins in Philly that need some help with a room addition and I'm going to help them for a couple of weeks." Mr. Speicher said nothing, and Ezra continued. "You know how it is trying to get away; I didn't get everything done in time for the earlier bus."

Mr. Speicher still said nothing, and turned his gaze away from the boy, looking off into the darkness. He took the last drag from his now-smoked cigarette and flicked it into the street. Both of them watched it hit the pavement, sending a light show of sparks in all directions.

"Are you going somewhere too, Mr. Speicher?" He didn't want to appear impudent, but didn't want any more questions.

"I'm waiting to pick up my daughter, Cheryl." He knocked another cigarette out of its hard cardboard box, tapped the filter several times on his knee, hard, packing the tobacco, and lit up his face with the flame from the wood match. He inhaled deeply, threw his head back again, exhaling up towards the street light. "The little whore got herself knocked up in Philly." He took another pull on his smoke. "You probably had a piece of her too, dintcha? Everyone else in town did. I've always heard you people are horny all the time." Ezra said nothing, looking straight ahead, expressionless. Mr. Speicher stared at the embarrassed Ezra and then his face softened a bit. "You'd better be careful over there, son," he added.

Cheryl Speicher had been two grades ahead of Ezra. He knew who she was but when she went to the new regional high school two years ago he hadn't seen her since. She had been a wild one, and Ezra had fantasized about her like every other boy in school. He wasn't surprised she was pregnant.

Ezra was relieved to see the yellow headlights of the approaching bus. The driver put on the right blinker, and slowed the dull aluminum bus to a brake-squealing stop, engulfing the bench, the man and the boy in diesel fumes. The door whooshed open, and after a couple of seconds, an elderly Amish couple made their way carefully down the steps. The old man nodded his black hat at Ezra, but said nothing, and they set off on foot, disappearing down the darkened street. A few seconds later Cheryl came haltingly down the steps, carrying a small green suitcase. She had been crying, and when she saw her father, still sitting on the bench, smoking his cigarette, burst into new tears. He slowly stood up, flipped this cigarette into the street near the other one, and gruffly said, "Get in the car," not offering to help her or take her suitcase.

There were no more passengers, and Ezra slowly walked up the three steps into the long, dark bus. He was about to walk past the driver when the man put his leg out blocking his way. "Twenty five cents, Ahmo, you don't get a free ride on my bus." Some of the drivers let the Amish ride free. Ezra reached into his pocket and handed the driver the first bill he pulled out, a five. The driver snatched the bill, stuck it in his shirt pocket and snarled, "No change. Go sit your ass down." Ezra stared at the man, who started to get up. Ezra turned and continued down the aisle. He had ridden this bus once before, when he was twelve, for a one-day field trip to Philadelphia with his class. He remembered the odd smell of the bus, the mixture of stale cigarette smoke, food dropped on the floor, and this time, the pungent smell of old vomit and disinfectant.

There was a young couple in the third seat back on the left side of the bus, sleeping, and Ezra made his way past them towards the back of the bus, grabbing the back of the seat in row five as the bus roared away from the station. Ezra had to grab a seatback with every step; it seemed like the bus driver was deliberately trying to throw him off balance.

Ezra tossed his bag onto the far side of the next-to-last row on the left side of the bus. He grabbed onto the back of the seat in front of him and finally sat down as the bus lurched around a corner, leaving town. He leaned over his bag and slid the top half of the window down a couple of inches, trying to get some fresh air.

"Close that goddam window, you idiot," the driver yelled back. "You trying to freeze my ass off?" Ezra slid the window up, still leaving a crack, sitting as tall as he could to catch an occasional fresh gust, inhaling deeply. He turned back to the bag, and stuck his right hand inside, still exploring the contents. He felt another small case, and pulled out a small soft leather Bible. He held it for just an instant. "I won't be needing that," he whispered, and tossed it across the aisle onto the seat. It bounced off onto the dirty floor. Ezra started to get up to at least put it on the seat, but then sat back down.

"OK, Ezra, here you are." He began talking to himself, a habit he had picked up during the endless hours behind a team of horses. "You're fifteen, been to Philly once, for an entire DAY, you may have cousins that will put you up, but you certainly can't call them at this hour. And you sure can't be for going back home." It would be midnight before they pulled into the city bus station. "So what's your plan? Start with tonight." The driver had been glancing back in his large overhead mirror at this kid talking to himself, so he continued silently. "You have a little money, no job, nothing to eat. What's your plan?"

Ezra continued to look out the filmy window. The occasional lights of a lit-up storefront grew rapidly larger and then disappeared in a flash as the bus roared towards the city. He was determined to not become emotional. He would need all his wits, and emotion would just get in the way.

"The hat has to go." He removed his broad-brimmed black felt hat and put it on the seat behind him. "And the jacket." He shrugged out of the gray, trademark jacket with no buttons and put it in the bag. After a minute, he reached back inside and tossed it on the seat behind him, knocking the hat to the floor. "The suspenders." They landed beside the jacket. Ezra reached inside the canvas bag again, shoving clothes, case and pouch aside, fishing for the belt. He found it, and then laughed; his pants didn't have belt loops anyway. He pulled the black leather jacket from the bag and put it on. "Perfect fit." While searching for the belt, he ran across a baseball cap, a green one with a yellow tractor logo on the front. He brushed his long blond hair back with his fingers and put the hat on. It fit, too. Bless his mother.

Ezra looked out the bus window again, and saw the soft glow of the approaching city lights reflecting off of the bottom of the overcast clouds and had a moment of homesickness; it looked just like the soft glow the kerosene lanterns made on the ceiling of his bedroom. He could only imagine the fortitude it took for his mother to squirrel away the clothes and money, and the price she must now be paying with his father. His eyes began to swim. "Knock it off," he scolded himself.

The streetlights were more frequent now, and in their rhythmic flash across his lap, he could see the obvious contrast between his coarse, gray woolen pants and the leather jacket. He had forgotten about the pants, but it was too late to change now.

The young couple had awakened, and they were looking out the windows and over their shoulders, pointing and whispering, excited and animated. He would change later.

"Five minutes," the surly bus driver shouted.

The city grew increasingly dense with tall buildings, and the young Amish boy stared in awe. The long bus made a final, wide arcing turn into the bus depot, then unceremoniously lurched to the final stop for the night, angle parked at the end of a row of seven other darkened buses.

"Get your bags and get off," the driver barked. The young couple, no longer interested in the teenager in the back of the bus, strode the few steps to the front, holding hands and looking nervous. Ezra slowly rose to his feet, picked up his black bag, and started up the aisle. He stopped, backed up to where he had been sitting and picked up the Bible and tossed it into his bag. He ignored the profanity from the bus driver walked to the front and stepped down into the night. He barely cleared the last step before the driver slammed the door shut behind him and stomped into the terminal.

The bus depot was a dank cesspool of greasy mud and aging urine. "Hey Buddy, got 'ny cigs?"

There were two bums sleeping behind the graffiti-pocked concrete pillar that held the long metal overhang covering the buses. They had stirred awake at the arrival of the midnight bus. Mr. Phend — he had been chaperone for the field trip — had warned the class against talking to the bums. "They're dangerous. Most of them are crazy, deranged, using drugs. They'd as soon cut you as look at you."

"I don't smoke."

Ezra knew you didn't speak to bums, just ignore them, but it was too late. Sensing a new mark — that's why they hung out here — the younger bum struggled to his feet, tattered multi-colored blanket wrapped around him as though he was an Indian chief. He walked up to Ezra and grabbed his shoulder. With a speed that surprised even him, Ezra spun away and simultaneously shoved him, hard, and the shocked bum stumbled and went down. The other bum rose to his feet and moved menacingly towards the young man now clutching his black canvas bag close to his body.

The PPD patrol car slowed to a crawl. The graveyard shift officers usually came by to check for exactly this type of problem, and the two bums scurried around the corner of the depot, out of sight.

"You come in on the twelve o'clock?" the officer driving the patrol car asked out his now open window, wipers beating against the light rain.

"Yes."

"What are you doing coming in so late?"

"I've come in to stay with my cousin for a couple of weeks. He needs some help for to remodel and I have a lot of experience." He decided to stick with the same story.

The patrol officer was probably in his early twenties, a rookie. "Where does your *cousin* live?"

"I don't know. I have his phone number and he said to call when I came upon the town."

"What is your cousin's name?"

"Phil Myers."

"So is he expecting you after midnight?"

"Yes sir. No sir. He knew I was coming but I haven't been able to get hold of him to tell him exactly when."

By now the officer's partner was leaning forward, looking past the driver at the young man standing ten feet away. The rookie turned to the more experienced officer and asked, "What do you think?"

"Just tell him to get the hell off the street."

"I'm not sure what you're doing out here in the wee hours of the morning, but call your *cousin* and get off the street. We're going to be back around in ten minutes and I don't want to see you again tonight. Got it?"

Ezra said he did, thankful they hadn't asked for any identification. He had none. He turned and walked to the pay phone hanging on the wall, the one that still had a cord and receiver. He dropped a dime in the slot and slowly twisted the circular dial, pretending to call a number. He noticed his left hand, the one holding the receiver, the one he had shoved the bum with, smelled terrible. There was no dial tone, but he started talking anyway. He watched the diffused reflection of the disappearing patrol car's red tail lights in the filthy front window of the bus depot, chatting away to no one. After he was sure the officers were gone, he hung the receiver up and retrieved his dime.

Out of sight, several blocks away, the veteran officer looked at his partner and told him, "We're going to see that fella again; those phones don't work. I don't know why those people don't just stay on the farm." The young rookie nodded his agreement.

Ezra looked around to make sure the bums were gone. It appeared they had given up for the night. "Okay, Ezra, now what?" he asked himself.

He thought he remembered a couple of motels several blocks up on the ride in, and could see their flashing green, blue and white lights reflecting against the low overcast. He threw the canvas bag over his right shoulder and headed up the shimmering sidewalk. The night chill mixed with the light mist caused the young man to shiver as he walked. It wasn't more than ten blocks back to the first motel, but by the time he got there, he had warmed, and was no longer shivering.

He was wrong about there being several motels to choose from: there was just one. The other lights came from an all-night filling station with a small café on one end. Across the wide US highway, down a little gravel side street, there was a tavern. The two dim outside lights cast frail rays on several low slung motorcycles with high handle bars, bars high enough that you would have your hands above your head when you rode. There was no traffic this time of morning. Ezra could hear the occasional crash of the cue ball smashing into the pack of billiard balls, hoarse laughter and the cover band butchering George Jones's "She thinks I still care," off key and ear-splittingly loud.

The lone motel, the Paradise Motel, had a ten foot tall flashing neon palm tree dropping a coconut. An unlit, hand-painted sign hung on two rusty chains over the low front porch roof leading to the front door. It read, "Hourly Rates from $2.50," and under it another sign said, "Always Open."

Ezra walked, if not boldly, not hesitatingly, towards the front door, ducking slightly under the low hanging sign. A hand scrawled note said, "ring buzzer to enter," and after several prolonged presses on the small black button, the door buzzed loudly, popping open about an inch. Ezra paused for a second and then entered the front office, coughing slightly at the acrid mixture of stale smoke and a stronger, smoky odor he couldn't identify. The smell was so strong it got on his tongue, and he kept swallowing.

The old man behind the chipped bulletproof glass with chicken wire embedded in it appeared to be sleeping. He couldn't be, of course, he had just pressed the button releasing the magnetic catch on the front door. He slumped in a faded green office chair with red and blue shiny vinyl tape holding it together at the torn seams. He had tight, white, curly hair and his white-stubbled chin rested on his chest. His nose was curved and crooked, like a thick twig that couldn't make up its mind which way to grow. Ezra could barely see his eyes, almost hidden under the black leather driving cap. They appeared closed.

"I need a room." Ezra spoke into the small round metal mouthpiece in the middle of the glass.

The man didn't move.

"Excuse me. I need a room tonight. The sign said vacancy. Do you have any rooms?"

"How fast are you?" The man's mouth barely moved.

"What?

"How much time you need?"

A weary Ezra wasn't sure what the man was talking about. "I need a room. I'm tired and need to get some sleep."

The grizzled old man tilted his head back and peered at the young man standing on the other side of the dirty glass. He saw he was alone, recognized the clipped, accented speech of "one of them."

"Oh, right. Twenty bucks."

Tired as he was, Ezra knew he was being overcharged. He had seen the big sign that said "CHECK OUT TIME 9:30 – NO EXCEPTIONS"; the maximum charge should be no more than $17.50. "How about $15?"

The man didn't move. Finally, with a flicker of a smile — he liked this kid — he drawled, "Okay. Shove the money under the glass."

Ezra reached inside his front pants pocket and pulled out the wad of bills, carefully keeping it below the grimy countertop, out of the man's sight. He slid the three fives under the glass and the man quickly grabbed them, like a white-headed frog snatching a fly, and stuck them in his pocket. He slid the key to Ezra. The key was attached to a faded yellow plastic room marker with a small chain, and he could barely make out the 14, almost completely rubbed off.

"Go back out the front door, turn left, last room on the left." He had given these instructions a million times. "Don't slam the door."

Ezra walked the short distance in the cold, early morning darkness and slowly turned the key in the wobbly door knob lock. The door creaked open, and stepping inside Ezra was engulfed in that same smell he couldn't identify in the front office. Ezra pushed the top button of the light switch in, flipping on the bare bulb overhead light, hanging by two frayed wires. He glanced around the filthy room, and thought of his tidy clean bedroom, and his home. Mother would have cried herself to sleep by now, he told himself, and Father would have — "Stop it Ezra," he said out loud.

The avocado colored sink hung on the wall right outside the bathroom, a convenient place to wash up, but it hadn't been cleaned in months. The mirror looked like a large spider had slammed into the upper right hand corner, sending cracked webbing in all directions. The front window had a similar, larger array of cracks where a stray bullet had evidently entered the room the hard way. Someone had put a small rusty bolt through the hole, washer and nut tightened against bubble gum that squished out from under the washer, sealing the hole. Old, dirty, blue shag carpeting had begun to pull away from the walls, its edges curling up and in.

The room was heated by a military-gray heater that protruded through the front wall, the exhaust hanging out onto the covered sidewalk, its tired inside protruding over the bed. It was off, and the musty smelling room was cold. Ezra opened the metal cover hiding the temperature controls and moved the handle to "Heat." The tired machine groaned and banged to life, loud enough to wake the dead, and Ezra immediately turned it back off.

Ezra thought briefly about taking a shower, but someone else had used the towels. Exhaustion finally overcame the young soon-to-be-ex-Amish, and he lay on top of the unmade bed, his unwashed blond mop of a head resting as lightly as he possibly could on the wrinkled pillow, already covered with a few strands of long, black hair. He dropped off to sleep, sleeping the fitful doze and dreaming of a young man chasing loose horses, fighting his drunken father, and a big city crushing his chest.

CHAPTER EIGHT

Ezra woke slowly, stupidly, his left eye plastered shut with dried tear-salt, his head pounding in time to the impatient open palm slapping on the door, two feet away.

"You in dare, get up, it 9:15!" The maid was standing outside the door, smacking it like she was trying to kill a mulish mosquito.

"Yeth, alright," Ezra managed, thick-tongued.

"Hurry up! They gonna charge you 'nuther night!"

Ezra swung his now completely wrinkled gray pants legs, filthy, not fresh like his mother always made sure, over the edge of the bed. He stood unsteadily, and stumbled to the door. One boot had become untied in the middle of the restless night, and he almost went down, almost tripped on the leather shoelace.

Ezra fumbled with the lock — he didn't remember locking it — and slowly opened the old, paint-chipped door, blinking against the bright sun. The maid, a large Negro woman, almost knocked him down shoving past, into the room. She pulled her large cleaning cart behind her, bristling with brooms and mops. She glanced at the closed bathroom door and said "git yo' self outta heah. Yo' needs to be gone. What you been doin', boy? You smells awful."

Slowly circulating oxygenated blood made its impact in Ezra's brain, and the fuzziness began to clear. Saying nothing, he picked up his bag and jacket, looked around for his hat, remembered, and slowly walked outside. He was bareheaded, his yellow bowl-cut hair completely disheveled and greasy. The maid was still scolding him from inside the room, and he turned and closed the door behind him, her muffled voice raising several indignant, louder octaves at the affront. Someone's radio sang, "I wanna hold your hand, I wanna hold your hand." Ezra smiled slightly to himself, remembering how much his twin cousins loved that song.

Ezra was famished. Breakfast on the farm was usually scrambled eggs, fried potatoes and biscuits. The thought made his mouth water. Swallowing, he said, "Time to eat, Ezra. Where you going to find food? Maybe ask your *friend* in the front office?" He chuckled at the thought, and headed towards the highway, busy with morning traffic, cars zipping past every few seconds, driving too fast. He remembered a filling station in a long building with a restaurant on the other end. He thought he remembered a sign about breakfast.

Ezra walked around the corner where the motel street intersected the highway, and saw the filling station and restaurant about a quarter mile away on his right. There was little room between the fast moving cars on the highway and the ditch that ran beside it, a small, still river littered with cans and paper trash.

Ezra decided to walk on the far side of the ditch, away from the traffic, next to the sagging, rusting, chain-link fence someone erected many years ago. He started across the ditch, and one of his boots, the left one, sank until the putrid goo in the ditch met itself over the top of the leather shoelaces. For the second time in less than fifteen minutes, Ezra almost went down, catching himself on the unsteady street sign. He pulled his boot out of the sucking mud and headed towards the restaurant on the well worn path, next to the fence.

Tired and dirty, he still had a spring to his step. Free from the tyrant father, free from farm duties, the world was waiting. Hell, he had an 8th grade education, he was smart, strong, knew construction well enough to get a job, this was going to be great, he told himself.

The restaurant was really a diner. The five stools at the counter were topped with badly worn burgundy Naugahyde, patched and re-patched with the same colored vinyl tape as the motel's front office chair. The two truck drivers sitting on the far left stools, near the cash register, promised everlasting contentment to the waitress if only she would run off with them. She giggled and asked them to tell her more.

46

The three booths by the front window, with a commanding view of the two long semi rigs parked in tandem out front, barely off the road, were empty. Ezra glanced around and then sat on the far right stool, at the counter, nearest the door. The young man at the griddle, an aspiring cook, just slightly older than Ezra, glanced over his right shoulder and then returned to the hot griddle, artfully flipping the drivers' breakfasts.

"What can I get for you, cutie?" The waitress had decided not to marry either of the truck drivers, and sauntered down to Ezra. She was on her stage, and leaned over, elbows on the counter. Despite his best efforts, he really tried not to look, his eyes fell into the cleavage, deep and wide enough for the Grand Canyon. She caught a whiff of the unwashed teenager, straightened, and asked again, not as friendly, "Have you decided what you would like to eat?"

Ezra retrieved his eyes and stammered, "Could... could I have four eggs and some home fries please?"

Now she was irritated. "The menu says no substitutions. You can get #4: three eggs any style, hash browns and tomatoes. You can order another egg as a side. Is that what you would like?"

Blushing slightly, Ezra said, "Yes, please."

"And how would you like your eggs?" she asked.

"Uh, scrambled, please."

The two truck drivers finished eating, paid at the register, and left, paying no heed to the young man at the end of the counter. Philadelphia had always been a boiling pot of styles, and the young Amish with his black leather jacket and gray wool pants might have looked like any other fifteen year old at the beginning of the 60's.

Ezra asked the waitress if she would mind if he moved to one of the booths, now clean, and she rolled her eyes and asked why.

"I'd like to read that newspaper," he said, nodding towards the one the drivers had left, "and there's a little more room to spread it out."

"Sure, go ahead and move." He was pretty cute, she thought, but he needed a haircut. And a bath. She imagined giving him a bath and caught her breath.

Ezra picked up the rumpled newspaper and turned to the "Help Wanted" section. The area of the classifieds looking for construction workers was half a page long.

CARPENTER HELPER: Must have own tools and car, $1.75/hr.

"Good pay. Too bad about the car and tools," he thought.

CARPENTER HELPER: Limited experience, apply in person, $1.15/hr.

Ezra tore out the page, and marked a dozen ads using the pencil from his bag.

"Here's your breakfast, Hon, enjoy."

Ezra wolfed his breakfast, never looking up, finished and pushed the plate back. He was about to pick the paper back up when the waitress leaned against the table, pressing the top of her legs close to his right hand, and said, "My. When's the last time you ate?" Without waiting for an answer — it really wasn't a question — she asked, "Would you like a cup of coffee?"

Ezra hadn't been allowed to drink coffee at home and said, "Sure, thanks." She returned with the coffee and continued, "I haven't seen you around. Where you from?"

Ezra looked up from the paper and fell into the Grand Canyon again. He looked at the rest of her and saw a young, probably twenty year old woman, not fat, but full figured — isn't that what they say? She had tight, curly, light brown hair pulled up into a messy knob on top of her head, a pretty, mischievous smile that made her freckles dance. Her hands, long slender hands, were slightly reddened by the constant mopping of other people's messes with hot water, and one of her long, pale white nails had fallen off. She seemed happy.

"Arizona."

"You don't sound like you're from Arizona."

"We moved around a lot. My dad was in the Army."

"When did you get to Philly?"

"Last night."

"Where you staying?"

Ezra paused at this question. He didn't know this woman's name and she was asking all these questions.

"Why?"

"Oh, just wondering. Wondering if you needed a place to stay."

Ezra continued looking at the help wanted ads, looked so long she started to leave.

"I'm trying to find my cousin. He knew I was coming, but I didn't tell him exactly when. I need to call him." The pay phone hanging just inside the front door worked; one of the drivers had made a call on the way out.

The waitress walked away, smiling at him over her bare shoulder. "If you don't find him — your cousin is a him, right? —come back here. I get off at 6:00, you can stay with me 'til you find him." She smiled sweetly and he felt the familiar flush creep up his neck. He had intended to ask if she knew where this one construction job was, they had the address in the paper, but she unnerved him and he decided to leave instead.

The waitress went in the back, and Ezra hurriedly stood up and went to the cash register, ready to pay. The young cook had finished scraping the top of his grill, cleaning it for the lunch crowd, and took the three steps over behind the register, ringing up $2.75.

"She likes you," he said matter-of-factly. "Wanda likes you. She likes everyone."

Ezra counted out the change and asked if he could have some more dimes, he needed to make some calls. He shoved the change into his right front pants pocket, the same pants he had put on fresh — was that yesterday morning? You need to lose these pants, Ezra, he told himself. He walked back to the booth, laid down a quarter (he knew you were supposed to tip but had no idea how much), added a dollar, hesitated, then picked up the quarter. He picked up his black canvas bag, shrugged it over his right shoulder, and walked outside. The deafening cyclonic whirl

49

of a passing semi surrounded him with roadside filth, making him blink, blowing his hair.

Further down the highway Ezra could see a grocery store, maybe a drug store, he couldn't be sure, and it looked like there were phone booths out front. He felt a need to get away from the diner, to walk down the highway to make his calls.

This time he walked along the edge of the highway, hunching over against each passing semi, and after a short wait, hurriedly crossed the highway and walked up to the payphones. The first phone was dead, but the second one had a dial tone. He dropped a dime in the slot at the top, and heard the melodic tone signaling he could dial. He knew how to use the phones; he had used the pay phone at Ted's in his home town. He dialed the number on the slip of paper his mother had put in his bag. After a dozen rings — at least it wasn't disconnected — he hung up and retrieved the dime that fell into the metal "change" compartment on the bottom right of the phone.

Ezra made a dozen calls, inquiring about work, and they all said the same thing: no applications over the phone, show up and we'll hire you.

There was plenty of work.

For the first time that morning, Ezra wasn't sure what to do. He wasn't going back to the motel, unless he absolutely had to, it was too expensive — and filthy — but he needed a place to stay. Wanda? He had to admit that was an exciting possibility, but all these English women were... if not whores, at least loose, probably diseased, he had always been told. She didn't look diseased.

"You're thinking like an Ahmo," he said to himself. "Be logical, you can figure this out," he thought. "You have a little money, so you don't have to have a job right away. You do have to have a place to stay and you can't find your cousin. Maybe your cousin moved? Then what? And get rid of these pants. Come back here at 5:00 and go with Wanda? Maybe."

Coming in on the bus last night, he remembered catching glimpses of new houses in various stages of construction:

foundations newly placed, their form boards still hugging the now solid freshly poured concrete, new houses springing up, raw plywood roof decking, defying the rain, waiting to be sheltered with shingles. He would walk out there, he decided, it couldn't be more than ten blocks, to see what kind of work they had.

Ezra walked less than five minutes, along the edge of the highway, when a pickup truck with tools in the back pulled over into the parking lot of the hardware store ahead on his right. Two men got out, glanced at the approaching boy, and waited for him. They were in their twenties, tanned and fit looking. When Ezra came abreast, the driver walked over, hand extended.

"Hey, I'm John, need a ride?" John had a very slight Southern accent.

Ezra hesitated, then took the proffered hand and shook it, briefly, withdrawing it quickly. "I'm Ezra."

John appeared to stifle a smile, Ezra couldn't tell for sure, and continued. "Not to interfere with your morning stroll, but me and my buddy"— he nodded towards the other man —"run a framing crew and we're looking for more help. Business is crazy. Do you have any experience? You look like you could work."

Ezra hesitated and John continued, "Hey, no big deal, see ya later." He turned to leave.

"Actually, I am looking for work."

"Actually?" He mocked the young Amish and then grinned disarmingly.

Ezra reddened slightly. "I have some carpentry experience and am looking for a job. What are you looking for?" He was a bit defensive.

"Carpenter helpers. You wouldn't believe the druggies we get showing up, wanting work to buy their next hit." He looked at Ezra. "You a druggie?"

"No."

"We pay good, $1.15 an hour. Pay every Friday. Cash money. Got any tools?"

Ezra said he didn't, at least not with him, and John said that was OK, how about it, you wanna work?

"Yes, I need a job. When do I start?"

"Right now. Hop in." He glanced down at Ezra's gray pants. "Where'dja get the pants?"

Ezra ignored the comment and climbed in, holding his black bag, sitting in the middle of the front bench seat of the three-year-old 1961 Ford. His left knee bumped against the air conditioner John had installed under the dash, in front of the Hurst floor shifter. He had heard about these new air conditioners but had never seen one. Wires ran everywhere. John slid in beside him on the passenger side, had to close the door twice to get it to shut. Someone had run into the door.

"Be careful you don't kick a wire." John noticed Ezra looking down.

"You like music?" He saw Ezra looking at the push button radio in the middle of the dashboard.

"Yeah. Sure."

They merged with traffic, John's buddy power-shifting and squealing the tires slightly between first and second, a rubber-asphalt chirp, tools in the truck bed flying. John twisted the left knob of the radio, bumping Ezra's knee with his own. The radio slowly came on, and then the rollicking melody of The Dave Clark Five's "Glad All Over" filled the truck cab, bouncing off the windshield, the two carpenters rocking to the music. Ezra moved slightly to the music. How lucky could you get, he grinned to himself.

CHAPTER NINE

"Where you stayin'?" John asked loudly, over the music. The three young men were headed to the development of new houses and the promise of Ezra's first job in Philly, radio blaring "Surfin' U.S.A.".

"Not sure yet. I have a friend that waits tables at that diner down the road, and I may stay with her for a couple more nights." He made it sound like he had already moved in.

"Wanda?" John asked incredulously.

"Yeah, Wanda. We're friends."

John and his friend stared straight ahead, not daring to look at one another. Then John glanced at his friend and they burst into raucous laughter.

"What's so funny about that?" Ezra was defensive, again.

John and his friend were still laughing. "We call her CB, *community bicycle*. Everyone's had a ride, that's all." John chuckled. He stretched his right leg forward, shifting to his left side, and pulled a small plastic packet out of his pocket and handed it to Ezra. "Here, take this, you're gonna need it."

Ezra glanced at the aqua blue package, shrugged and put it in his pocket. He was still defensive. "I can take care of myself."

"Oooookaay, you take care of yourself, then."

After that first day's work, Ezra asked if he could leave at 5:00 sharp. In spite of John's willingness to either put Ezra up for the night, or at least drive him back to the diner, Ezra insisted on walking back to see if Wanda really meant he could stay with her. But John wasn't going to tell him what to do; he thought that was Ezra's decision to make. "Yeah, sure, take off. Will we see you tomorrow, Ezra?"

"Yeah, I'll be here."

"Ten bucks says you won't. Deal?" Ezra tried to stifle an embarrassed grin and shook his head yes.

Wanda's face lit up when he walked in, dirty gray pants now also covered in sawdust in spite of his best efforts to brush them off, riding low on his hips, no belt or suspenders. She ran over and hugged him, igniting the crimson on his neck. "I'm so glad you came back. I'm just getting off."

They left together, out the back door, Ezra ignoring the look from the un-amused cook, watching them leave. They climbed into her dented and scratched 1956 Chevy blue and white two-door. She fumbled with the ignition key, then got it right, twisted it, and with a throaty roar, the 327 CI V-8 engine snarled to life. Ezra loved the car and the resonant rumble of the dual-exhaust glass packs, but politely declined her offer to let him drive. He had driven Mrs. Herzog's tractor a few times, but never an automobile. But Wanda didn't need to know that, he told himself.

For a minute, she just sat and looked at the young man in her passenger seat, the big engine gently rocking the car, making the handle on his canvas bag vibrate. Finally she smiled, patted his left knee with her hand, and noticed him looking at the broken fingernail.

"I broke that first thing at work this morning trying to get some pans out of the cabinet. I hate it when that happens. I'm gonna fix it as soon as I get home." She seemed to be out of breath. She pulled the column shifter out of park and into reverse and backed out of her gravel parking place.

She seemed in a hurry, he thought, spewing gravel behind the positraction rear wheels as the car squealed onto the highway, Wanda barely looking for traffic. She lived in an apartment less than ten minutes away, and he began to have doubts about his decision to stay with her, even for the night. These English women are trouble. Maybe I should just get cleaned up, have something to eat and then leave, he mused to himself, moving his lips but making no sound.

She turned the Chevy into a parking spot in front of an older but tidy apartment complex, turned off the engine and as the V-8 pinged and snapped cooler, sat there for another minute looking at a now nervous Ezra. He looked back, blinked, and then looked straight ahead, out the windshield. She grabbed his canvas bag, as though she could sense he was thinking of bolting, and headed up the concrete walk to her first story front door, merrily waving at the bemused neighbors and swinging the bag.

He was timid, she wasn't, and they no sooner stepped inside the front door than she tossed his black canvas bag on the green shag carpeting and started stripping him of his clothes. She took off his jacket, then the shirt, but by the time she got to the gray pants, the dust from the day's work made her cough slightly. She backed up and said, "The bathroom is over there. Why don't you get cleaned up?"

Ezra filled the rust stained claw foot tub with hot water, lowered himself in with a grateful sigh, and began to lather up, when Wanda slipped into the room clad in nothing but her desire, her ample body a Milky Way of freckles. She slid in with the overwhelmed young man, splashing sudsy soap-water on the faded yellow linoleum floor, and fulfilled her fantasy of washing him, over and over.

The lambskin Trojan was still in his pants pocket.

"Look at them red, white and blue eyes. If it wasn't for Visine, you'd bleed to death. What the hell you been up to? Did you go over to Wanda's?" John droned on and on about Ezra's "patriotic eyes." The exhausted, freshly-scrubbed Ezra had shown up the next morning, on time as promised. He put his black canvas bag under an old oak tree, visible from any of the houses they were working on.

"You gonna work in those fancy duds?" John nodded at Ezra's new, stiff, dark blue jeans, shiny belt and his rust-red checkered flannel shirt, price tag hanging off the left sleeve. "Shit, you look like you fell out of a catalog. I'm gonna have ladies lined up one side of the street and down t'other waitin' for your cherry ass to get off work. How the hell you gonna bend over and pick anything up? Don't you have no regular work clothes?"

Ezra muttered something about none of your business and spent the next eight long hours of eternity determined to put in a good showing, running on fumes and adrenaline; this was his first full day on the job.

Ezra returned to Wanda's apartment that night and the next ten nights, waking up one morning with white-hot burning where his penis used to be. It got worse by mid-afternoon, and finally he could no longer stand it and reluctantly asked John about it. It had taken all his courage to ask John, but who else could he talk to, he asked himself. John didn't laugh, not this time, and said, "Didn't you use no rubbers? Hell, you can't ball the likes of someone like Wanda without no rubbers. I gave you one that first day, didn't you use no rubbers? Welcome to the clap. You need to get over to the hospital right away."

Ezra slipped his leather tool belt off and walked, limped, to the nearby hospital. The young male physician sternly lectured him about morals and loose behavior —"look what happens." He told Ezra to go back outside and dust off the sawdust first, "What, were you born in a barn?" He shot him full of penicillin, and in a couple of days the burning went away.

CHAPTER TEN

"Hello?"

"Yeah, hello." Pause. "Who the hell is this?"

"This is Ezra Neuenschwander. I'm trying to reach Phil Myers."

Silence.

"Is Phil there?"

The voice on the other end of the line was thick, like talking through a wool sock. "This is Phil. Who the hell did you say you were?"

"This is Ezra Neuenschwander. I'm your cousin. I don't think we've seen each other for five years, but my neighbor, Mrs. Herzog, was for to call you and see if it was to be okay for me to stay with you for a while." Nervous, the old speech pattern returned.

Nothing.

"Look, I'm sorry, I thought — "

"I remember!" Phil sounded proud of the fact he remembered. "You're the little runt that went skinny dipping and we stole your clothes. Right?"

Ezra felt his neck start to warm, but decided this wasn't the time to deal with a five year old affront. "Yeah, that was pretty funny," he lied. He paused, then said, "So you married? What you been up to?" He concentrated on talking like his cousin, mirroring his speech.

"Married?" Phil laughed, a hoarse laugh, like it wasn't natural. "Why would I want to get married? There's more poontang in this town than you could possibly take care of in a lifetime."

Ezra wasn't sure what he meant, so said nothing. The line was silent long enough that Ezra started to hang up.

Then, "Look, I'm sorry Ezra, I had a rough night last night. I'm not usually a prick. Yeah, Mrs. Herzog called a month or so ago and asked if I had room until you figured out what you were going to do. I guess things got worse with your ol' man, huh? Anyway, I got a back porch that's insulated and has a bed. You can stay there for a while. How long you think you'll be here?"

Ezra was relieved. Phil wasn't his first choice, but he needed a place to stay and at least he knew him. "I don't know. I got a job and it looks like it's going to be a good one, so money is no big deal. In fact, I have some money my mother —" He caught himself, wishing he hadn't said anything about the money.

"Hey, money's cool, man, that's good. You got something to write with? I'll give you directions over here. When can you make it? You want me to pick you up?" Phil had instantly turned friendly.

"Just a minute, let me get a pencil and paper." Ezra let the pay phone receiver hang straight down on the metal, spiral cord and fished in his bag for a pencil and paper. "OK, I have it, what's the address?"

"You know what, I apologize for my manners, I insist on picking you up. You don't know the city. Tell me where you are and I'll come right over." Too friendly.

In spite of Ezra's protest that he could take a cab, his cousin was now determined to pick him up.

"I'm out front at the pay phone of a little diner on the northeast side of town, on U.S. Highway 1, just east of the river."

"Is that the one just down from the Paradise Motel?

"Yeah, that's the one. The food's not that great, but the people seem friendly."

"So you know Wanda?"

Ezra hesitated. "Yes, I do think that is her name, I'm not for sure."

Phil laughed. "Cuz, let me help you with your city living. There is no way a fresh young man, fresh meat from the country, is gonna stop at that diner without Wanda taggin' him, so cut the crap, OK?" He was still laughing. Then he stopped. "Look, I can't pick you up there, I had some trouble there once, old story, just walk down to the hardware store and I'll be by in less than thirty

58

minutes, ok? I'm in a beige VW van. It has some flowers painted on it."

Ezra walked back inside, sat back down in his favorite booth next to his black bag, and asked Wanda if he could have another cup of coffee. She pretended not to hear him, so he got up, grabbed the coffee pot that had been fresh hours earlier, and poured his own cup. He returned the coffee pot and tried to make eye contact, but she was busy looking elsewhere.

It had been a couple of weeks since he had moved in, and she had become increasingly detached, distant. She looked a little tired this morning, and Ezra wondered how he could have missed the lines around her eyes and the sag to her walk. He finished the coffee, put a quarter on the table, and walked over to put himself squarely in front of the woman. She wasn't happy about it, and glanced at a couple of truck drivers that had been watching, increasingly interested in the deal between their favorite waitress and this young man.

"I just talked to my cousin. He's going to pick me up after work today," he said. "I'm going to stay with him tonight, but I'll come by tomorrow if you like."

She looked at him and said, "Don't bother. I like men that come and go, and it's *waaay* past time for you to go."

Ezra could feel his neck redden — everyone was watching — and before she could turn away, he grabbed her by the arm. She winced and yelled, "Ow!" She suddenly looked just like his mother. Ezra dropped her arm like he had been burned, and before he could move was grabbed from behind by the two truckers, big men, and dragged past the booths and tossed out the front door. He had not fallen down, barely catching himself, and had just turned around to face the diner when Wanda appeared through the front door, the door guarded on each side by the two men, as if sentries at a castle. She threw his black bag at him, throwing it overhead, awkwardly, like a kindergarten baseball player. It fell in front of Ezra with a thud on the muddy, greasy gravel. He picked it up, and when he looked again at his former lover, she simply smiled and waved her broken-fingernail right hand from her waist, a little wave, barely wiggling her fingers, and said simply, "Bye-bye."

Ezra stared back, took a step forward, and then with a start saw his father's reflection in the big picture frame window in front of the restaurant, the black-clad shimmering figure bearing down on him from behind. He whirled, dropping the bag, right hand up to ward off a blow. There was no one, only the two huge tractor trailer rigs, diesel engines idling, blocking the busy highway. He turned again, looking at the snickering men and smirking Wanda, picked up the bag and walked down the side of the highway, heart gradually slowing to a normal rate.

"That went well, Ezra." He searched for some humor, failed, and continued to calm himself. "These English women—" The thought trailed off, but his mind filled with the girls he had been raised with, polite, deferential girls that understood this was a man's world. Girls that weren't "all painted up," as Father had spat so many times. "So why don't you go back home, then?" Finally he shouted, "Stop it!" He paused, reached in his bag, felt the Bible, shoved it to the bottom and jerked the zipper shut.

Thirty minutes had come and gone. It had been almost an hour since Ezra hung up the phone with his cousin. He had all but decided to leave, not sure where he would go, when a sputtering VW van, painted in wild, psychedelic colors, wobbled across the edge of the highway where storm water ran, and motor knocking, pulled up to the bank of payphones. The four cylinder, air cooled engine wheezed and whined off, and a man in his late twenties climbed out of the van, followed by a cloud of smoke. The smoke drifted past Ezra, and his nose recoiled at the same acrid smell he had first encountered in the motel lobby.

"You Ezra?" The man offered his hand. "You've grown. I'm Phil. Been a while, huh?" Ezra shook the soft, limp hand of his cousin, trying not to stare. Phil had on a shiny black, long-sleeve shirt and faded, white-splotchy blue jeans that looked like someone had spilled bleach all over them. A four-inch band of wild-colored tassels was sewn on the bottom of each pant leg. He had long, dirty brown, tightly curled hair, kept more or less out of his face with a single, thin leather band tied around his head. His beard and mustache were thin and scraggly. "Where are your things?"

Ezra explained that his things were in the dirty bag, deciding not to describe his final moment with Wanda.

"Travel light, that's what I always say," Phil said. "You takin' that to a new level, Cuz. Toss it in the back and climb in. Watch out for Roxie."

Ezra had no idea who Roxie was, absurdly expecting a cocker spaniel. But when he opened the reluctant, squealing rear door, he almost tossed his bag on top of a black haired girl partially curled up under a multi-colored blanket, long bare arms and longer legs uncovered.

"Oops, sorry, I didn't —"

She looked up, dreamily, sleepily, and said, "That's all right Brother, no problem." She had the longest, blackest, prettiest hair Ezra had ever seen. He started to close the door, aware he was staring.

"Are you Ezra? You're cute. Wanna climb in back here?"

"Roxie, shut the hell up," Phil said. "Can you leave at least one male in Philly that you haven't balled?"

Ezra closed Roxie's door and climbed into the front passenger seat, coughing slightly. Phil leaned over and whispered, "I gotta get rid of this nymph."

Roxie called out, "I heard that," and then, "Drop me off at Penn," and then was silent again.

"Where at?" Phil asked her.

"I don't care. Houston Hall."

Phil leaned over to Ezra again, "She's working her way through the frat boys."

"Shut up, Phil," came flying up from the back.

The wobbly van drove south on 34th Street, turned west on Spruce, and pulled in front of the huge student hall. Hundreds of Phils and Roxies were milling about, skin color mainly sifted-flour white, dotted here and there with rubbed-oil ebony, hair everywhere, wearing clothes that would had been discarded by conservative parents a decade ago. Handmade signs waved like square sails in the breeze, *END THE WAR!!* and *PEACE* in the brightest colors Ezra had ever seen. Grim-faced police with their straining police dogs, intently watched, looking for trouble.

Roxie poured out of the van, scanning the crowd, eager. Phil and Ezra pulled away, and last saw the young woman jump up on a wooden box beside a young man handing out some type of flyers, helping him shout at passersby to join some march somewhere.

Phil lit a hand rolled cigarette. He knocked it out of a Marlboro box, but it wasn't a Marlboro, Ezra could see. Phil had been smiling since they pulled off campus, and was in a good mood. "I love that place," he muttered, pulling up to a traffic light.

The smoke filled the small van, and Ezra rolled down his window, trying for some fresh air. He tried to place the smoke smell. It wasn't cigarette smoke; plenty of his friends and neighbors smoked. No, it was like — it was like the time he helped Mrs. Herzog clean up along a drainage ditch on the back of her property. They had cut all the weeds and brush, and raked it up in small piles, looking like round beaver mounds along the banks. He had burned them one at a time so they wouldn't burn out of control, and in among the normal, ordinary smells of grass and woody brush, a different, strange smell mingled, like a ghost, like a thief in the night. That's what it was, he remembered. He had heard stories of a strange weed that could be found along the banks of some of the creeks and drainage ditches, a strange weed that, when smoked, made you feel good, great.

"You want one?" Phil offered the red and white cigarette box.

"No thanks, I don't smoke."

"You look like you could use a smoke, Cuz. Jeez, lighten up, man. C'mon, take one, you'll like what it does."

Ezra waved him away, again, and Phil, with a shrug, ground the psychedelic colored bus's transmission into first and rattled away from the now green light. He still seemed happy, or at least mellow, but when he saw a black and white patrol car parked by the side of the road, ahead, facing the same direction, he lowered the smoking cigarette and grew quiet.

"Fuzz," he said quietly.

"What?"

"Fuzz, heat, the man —" he glanced at his puzzled cousin, and added "police, man! They catch you with weed and you get your head busted. No jail, just busted heads. See this knot?" He pointed to the top of his forehead, on the right side. "They always take the MJ, though, the assholes. Roll your window up, man! Don't look at them! Don't look at them!"

Ezra wasn't sure what his cousin was talking about, but rolled his window back up before pulling alongside the police car. They crept past, barely moving in crowded traffic, and as the van inched forward, Ezra heard his cousin mutter, "Shit, shit, shit," under his breath. Ezra glanced in the outside mirror on the passenger side, drawing a "Don't look!" from Phil, so he leaned back and looked straight ahead. Finally, Phil drew a breath, exhaled, raised the crooked, still-smoking cigarette to his dry lips, hissingly inhaled, held the smoke in his lungs, and then with smoky breath said, "They turned off. Philly cops are the worst, man."

Phil gradually relaxed again, his body resembling less a frozen corpse and more a warm blooded human, and turned on the AM radio. In a world of rock 'n' roll, Phil preferred Tony Bennett, Peggy Lee, Steve & Edie. Sinatra's "Fly Me To The Moon" filled the van, the crooner's silky voice soothing and caressing. Distant thunderstorms added their looming crackle to the music, and the speaker cut out with each bump in the road, bare speaker wire finding bare metal.

They drove along in silence, Phil happy and content. Ezra was lightheaded. He looked out the window, watching the streetlamps and trees dance past, houses in the background, like the set of a play. His mind drifted to the quiet serenity of the countryside, Mother churning butter, Father in a sober moment, then drunk and whipping the horses.

"Stop it," he commanded himself.

CHAPTER ELEVEN

Philadelphia – 1970

"Have you seen my bag?" The tension between the two had been building for a long time. But lately, it seemed to Ezra that his cousin was intent on pissing him off. Running him off. "Phil?"

Phil looked up from the kitchen table. He was putting white powder in small plastic bags. He shrugged, held both hands palms up, and went back to his work.

"Come on, I know I'm living here on the cheap. But $25 a month doesn't give you the right —"

Phil stood up angrily, sending the chair flying across the room. It slammed against the aging cabinets, adding another ding. "Screw that bag! What *is* it with you and that bag! Do you sleep with it too? Do you suck your thumb, stroking it 'til you go to sleep? What is your problem, Ahmo?"

Ezra shouted, "What the hell is it to you? You sit there stuffing your little plastic bags with coke, busting my ass about my bag? You've got a different whore jumping through here every night, higher 'n a kite, payin' 'em with snow, and you're bustin' my ass about a bag?"

The cousins stood nose to nose, fists clenched. For a long moment, the only sound was their labored breathing, adrenaline pumping, veins bulging. Then gradually, their breathing slowed, fists became hands once again, and Phil picked up the over-turned chair with one hand and shoved it back in place, sat down. He took a double sided razor blade and returned to moving the white powder into small mounds. "I threw it away. It stank."

"You threw my bag away?"

Phil looked up. "Yeah. So what? Get a new one."

"My mother gave me that one."

The two cousins had almost come to blows before, but each time Ezra had backed down. Phil knew it would be a bad idea to take on his muscular cousin, and thought he may have gone too far this time. Phil had once asked Ezra to help him move a hide-a-bed, and before he could help Ezra had picked it up in the middle and asked him where he wanted it. Ezra could probably crush him with three fingers. Pushing drugs didn't build the kind of muscle that construction work did.

"What about the Bible?"

"I don't know, was it in there? Did you ever read it?" Phil looked up, placating. "Hey, look, I'm sorry. I didn't realize it meant so much. It was all beat to hell, ripped, falling apart. I'll buy you a new one."

Ezra continued to glare at his cousin. Phil was the kind of guy he would avoid if they weren't related — and the rent so cheap. And strange as it seemed, Phil seemed to like having Ezra there.

"You still thinking about going to Toronto?" Phil attempted to change the subject and placate his bigger cousin.

On one of their rare real talks, Ezra had mentioned that he was thinking of moving. The Vietnam draft was in full force, and his under-the-radar life had become increasingly difficult — no bank account, no driver license, cash for everything. He had been reading about Toronto, and Canada, and the city intrigued him. What he didn't tell his cousin was that he didn't want to get caught in the illegal, violent world Phil swam in, a real possibility. He had seen the same dark, plain car parked across the street from Phil's apartment too many times lately. Phil had quit offering Ezra either a piece of the business or some of the product; Ezra always refused. Ezra had started to move out dozens of times, go someplace else, but for some reason never did.

"I'm thinking about it."

"What about your job here?"

"It was great at first, but now — John's been visiting your store."

Phil glanced up, and then returned to his packaging. Ezra had been complaining about the increasing drug use on his crew. Friday paychecks were now coming late, sometimes on the following Mondays, sometimes Tuesdays. One had bounced and they still hadn't made it right. Ezra had saved most of his earnings over the years, so he had plenty of money, but still — it was his money. And the men were complaining, asking Ezra what was up.

"Jonathon's in town. And the twins," Phil said.

Ezra had been looking out the window but turned sharply around. Ezra had heard Jonathon had gone to prison. He had tried to keep in touch with the twins, but they were hard to keep up with. "Where did you hear that?"

"We're doing a little business. Those Amish kids are insatiable. You know that." He didn't look up.

Ezra said nothing, reached for his bag, remembered it wasn't there, grabbed his old, frayed hat with the yellow tractor logo, and left, slamming the wooden screen door behind him.

The black sedan with the small round hubcaps was parked across the street. Ezra stared at it as it slowly pulled out of its parking spot and crept away, turned right, and disappeared.

CHAPTER TWELVE

Detective Swansen and his partner, Detective Black, were parked outside of Phil Myers' house, engine idling, watching. The rear floor of the city-issued dark sedan was littered with crumpled hamburger wrappers, empty soft drink cans, and a couple of girlie magazines. Detective Swansen was behind the wheel. He slapped his partner on the shoulder, "Here comes Blondie."

They were interested in Phil, but the carpenter with the long yellow ponytail that had just stepped out of the front door had been living there for a long time, and they were watching him, too.

"He saw us. Let's go."

The detective lowered the automatic gear shift lever from *park* down into *drive*. The transmission clunked, and they slowly pulled away from the curb, big V-8 growling out of the twin tailpipes. They drove down the tree-lined street and turned right.

"I don't think Blondie's in on it," Detective Swansen said.

"Why not?"

"He's former Amish. A jerk-over."

"What are you talking about? Amish? He doesn't look Amish."

"*Former* Amish. Jerk-over. *A J-O.* When one of them innocent little farm boys gets yanked out of that life, they say they've been *jerked over* into our world."

Detective Black rode in silence. Finally, he said, "You think every kid you see that isn't dealing is a former Amish. What is this fascination with those people?"

"I dated a young JO one time. She was different, wild, but I didn't know exactly why, then she told me. Now I can tell. They talk funny. They're jerky when they move. They even smell funny." More silence, then Detective Swansen said, "Let's take 'im downtown. They always cry when you arrest 'em. Five bucks says he'll cry like a baby."

Five dollars was the standard bet between the two veteran vice detectives. Detective Swansen was wrong only once, and his partner was tired of paying.

"You got no reason to haul him in. Forget it."

"Chicken shit."

Detective Swansen was a veteran of the Philadelphia police force. He had been on the job just over eighteen years, and was counting down the nineteen months left to go. He was tired, ready to retire. He was a good cop, he knew. He had more than paid his dues, and had earned the right to coast. At fifty-one, he was young enough to enjoy the almost adequate pension he would receive, and occasionally thought about what he would do to earn enough extra money. Some type of private security, maybe some cases for the lawyers in town, although the prospect of more law enforcement made him ache. Maybe something entirely new, like opening a coffee shop or selling cars. Not that he had a clue how to do either.

His wife worked at the city utility department, and had often told him to take a couple of years off, relax, go fishing, there was no hurry to do anything. She didn't mind staying on, she often told him; in fact she enjoyed it. In another eight years she could retire, and between the two retirement incomes they could live comfortably, if not in luxury.

The detective had been secretly squirreling away some of the money that every detective, especially a vice detective, was offered. His public servant salary almost forced him to take it, he remarked once to his partner, but it didn't amount to all that much; he hadn't been greedy. Besides, how would he explain the money to his wife?

The detective had let his health deteriorate. He looked older than he was, partly because his chronically reddish face had gotten fleshy, and partly because he had gone bald. His gray, bushy eyebrows looked like they were in danger of falling off his face, shading his brown, almost listless, eyes. He had long since quit going to the gym, and the main exercise now was the daily ritual of lifting a heavy mug of beer at Rusty's Tavern, the local

PPD hangout. He often joked that he needed to alternate drinking between his two hands so he didn't get muscle bound on his right side, always guaranteed to bring a round of laughter and another beer.

He had always been a smoker, a light smoker, three or four cigarettes a day. Lately, Detective Black had been complaining that the smoking had moved back inside the car again, in spite of their longstanding agreement to keep it outside. "Maybe I should start eating more beans, so I can add to the aroma," his partner would complain.

"Go ahead, blow us both up," Detective Swansen would shoot back. But he would take the smoking back outside, and the two veteran law enforcement officers would settle back into the kind of comfortable working rhythm that comes from having seen it all, together. And having the utmost confidence that the other one had his back.

Swannie, as he was known around the station, was a poor, indifferent dresser, and simply didn't care that his spit-shine black shoes didn't match his equally worn brown suit. He dismissed his wife's criticisms with, "I'm comfortable," and she had long ago quit saying anything. Swannie was not quite 5' 8", slightly overweight, and tended to slouch whether he was driving or riding, making him look even smaller. He was a civil servant with a gun; not flashy, perfectly comfortable keeping within department guidelines, and his name seldom came up in conversation. He was just there, adequately doing his job, and liked it that way.

Philadelphia, like any other large city, had its share of crime, and the recent increase in drug activity brought a corresponding increase in other violent crimes. The two detectives had seen a surge in the amount of gang activity, ranging from the vicious Latino gangs from Central America to the more *civilized* gangs like the Ravens, with their black leathers and thunderous herd of motorcycles. The Ravens were home-grown criminals, with a certain sense of what constituted *acceptable* criminal activity, unlike the imported varieties whose brutality knew no bounds.

The Ravens were attracted by the boom in residential housing, and weren't opposed to taking temporary jobs as construction workers, partly as cover for the more lucrative drug business they operated, and partly because of the large numbers of customers found in the ranks of workers.

The foreign gangs *expected* their members to kill, the home grown gangs killed only out of necessity.

CHAPTER THIRTEEN

Ezra reached into his sweat stained leather nail apron and grabbed half a dozen nails with his right hand, like a slow motion internal combustion engine, simultaneously pounding the last nail with the huge framing hammer swinging from his left hand. A solid blow set the pointed end of the three inch nail half an inch into the two-by-four bottom plate of the wall, and then the big hammer went up over his head, down between his feet, driving the nail deep into the plate. The serrated face of the 22 ounce hammer left a miniature waffle print in the board, the nail head buried in the center of the depression.

Ezra could layout, cut and nail a twenty foot framed wall in fifteen minutes, by himself. At nineteen, he was six feet of bronze, chiseled muscle. His long, thick, slightly wavy blond pony tail swished side to side with each swing of the hammer, like a pale yellow fox tail stuck in the fork of a swaying tree. Ezra glanced towards the girl standing next to his pickup truck. It was the girl from last weekend, what was her name? *Cindy?* He couldn't remember for sure.

The girls liked Ezra. He was a lot of fun, always telling stories, great in the sack, generous, sort of, with his money. He liked them all, and sometimes, in a moment of weakness, told a girl where he worked. He never made any promises, but they would still show up and then he would have to tell them, politely, firmly, to not come around anymore.

"Why do you tell 'em where you're workin' if you don't want 'em to come over here?" John asked.

"Dunno," Ezra mumbled. "Maybe I just like the attention."

Ezra occasionally thought of Wanda, his first, a self-conscious grin taking over his face. He had been naïve back then, but what a blast that had been. Since Wanda, there had been a lot of girls: some were quiet, some were loud, some could cook, some were demanding. He particularly liked Mandy — quiet, passionate Mandy — but she left when he couldn't tell her what his feelings were. She would take his head in her delicate hands and plead with him to open up. He couldn't, so she left. He was usually the one to leave, not get left, and that bothered him for a couple of days.

"Who's that?" John was making an effort to run a good business, but the illicit chemicals were mangling his mind.

"Uh... Cindy?"

John laughed. "Are you sure?"

Ezra smiled back and said, "Yeah, I'm pretty sure." They both laughed.

Cindy saw the two men looking at her, laughing. "Are you laughing at me?" she screamed. The two men simply shrugged and John turned away.

"No, we're not — Cindy," Ezra yelled back.

"My name's Paula!" Furious, she whirled and kicked another dent into the passenger side door of Ezra's battered white pickup and stomped off.

"You got off easy this time." John had seen this scene plenty of times before. He wasn't sure why Ezra attracted so many girls. "What is it with you and women?"

"I don't know," Ezra shrugged, "they just keep coming around."

John lit a cigarette with the still burning stub of his last one, inhaled deeply, then flipped the spent one into the street with his right middle finger. Both men stood there for a minute, surrounded by the sound of pounding hammers and whining circular saws.

"I hired another carpenter. He sounds like he's a Colored boy, says he knows you. Name's William. Says you went to school together. I haven't met him yet. He called on the ad." They were behind schedule, and John was desperately looking for more help.

Ezra said nothing.

"Do you remember him?"

"Yeah. I do. I didn't know he was a carpenter."

Ezra thought back to eighth grade and the little time he and his Negro — they preferred to be called Black now — friend had actually spent together. They never had a *sleep-over* at each other's house. Ezra didn't even ask to bring The Negro home. Father would have been angry at the question. And William's father didn't like the Amish. "Those people are weird," he told his son. So the boys shared a few lunch hours, said "hi" in the hall. Ezra hadn't thought about him for years.

"He's been working that project on the south side, the one I passed on. If he's no good or steals, run his ass off."

"I'm sure he'll work out. He was a good kid when I knew him."

William pulled up in his 1965 T-Bird at 6:45 the next morning. Ezra watched him effortlessly climb out of the five-year-old spotlessly waxed shiny black car, grab his leather nail apron and hammer from the trunk, and walk briskly towards the construction site trailer. He was tall and muscular, dressed in faded blue jeans and a black t-shirt. He had let his hair grow, they called it an Afro, Ezra knew, and had a black terrycloth sweat band tied around his head, like a too-tight corset, his long curly black hair puffing out above and below. He seemed self-confident, almost cocky.

He approached Ezra and said, "Hi, I'm William. Where can I find Ezra?"

"I'm Ezra."

William studied his old schoolmate for a bit, head cocked slightly to the left, right eyebrow arched. He smiled slightly and offered a huge hand. "You look different."

Ezra smiled back and said, "Yeah, so do you."

The two young men spent several minutes discussing William's experience; it ranged from framing subfloors to running a small trim crew to finishing out the interiors of the new houses. He would be a good hand, Ezra thought.

John came down the steps from the construction trailer, vigorously chewing the gum that alternated with the smokes, watching the Black man intently, listening. His mouth was open, popping with each chew. Ezra finished his questioning and told William to join the crew on the third house on the left. They were framing second story walls. William turned to leave.

"I catch you stealing, I'm gonna bust your ass," John called after him. "And you work for me — your name's gonna be Billy, or Boy, your choice."

William stopped, turned back, walked up to the owner. He looked down at the shorter, slightly overweight man and said nothing for a minute. Then, in a perfectly even tone, he replied, "The name is William. And if I catch you stealing any of *MY* stuff I'm gonna bust *YOUR* ass."

John's mouth dropped open and his gum fell to the ground. He turned a slightly paler color, sputtered something unintelligible. He spun on his left heel in the mud and stomped up the three concrete steps to the dirty white metal entry door to the trailer and slammed it shut. It didn't catch the first time and he slammed it again and again until it latched.

Ezra stood for a minute, watching his black high school classmate climb the aluminum ladder leaning against the partially framed house to the second story. The William he knew would have said nothing. But that was a long time ago, and evidently William had decided to push back. William isn't going to last long, he told himself. John is a coward, but if William mouths off like that to one of the bikers working there— in fact, he continued to himself, growing slightly irritated, if this uppity — he stopped, looked up at William working a strong, steady pace alongside the other workers and left the thought unfinished.

Ezra had intended to work on the same crew as William, but decided instead to help the crew on the other side of the street, framing the first floor walls of a newly poured foundation. There were ten more foundations scheduled to be poured the following week, and the framers were lagging behind. The three bikers were trying to keep up with two Amish men framing the house next door, and it was no contest. He would lend the bikers a hand.

One of the bikers had snapped red chalk lines the night before where the walls were to be framed on the newly installed plywood subfloor. They used red chalk instead of the traditional blue, because the red lasted longer in the all-too-frequent rain. Some of the lines had become pools of dirty bloody water in the overnight drizzle, and valuable time was lost sweeping the water off of the already warping plywood, waiting for the wood to dry a bit, re-snapping the chalk lines. The Amish had snapped their lines the night before, too, and then had sprayed clear lacquer over the red lines, so this morning the outline of wall locations were perfectly visible. Half of their walls already stood.

The bikers grunted their acknowledgement as Ezra picked up the circular saw. "I'll lay out the walls," Ezra said, "and cut the cripples. You—" he nodded to the closest biker— "grab the studs, make sure they're crowned, and you two nail 'em up." Ezra had explained, over and over, that if you didn't put all the crowns — the bow in every two-by-four board — up, the finished wall would be wavy, one stud bowed one way and the next bowed the opposite way, and the cabinets hung on the inside would look like a fishtailing miniature train wreck.

He glanced at the Amish crew next door, even-paced, not a wasted motion. "Come on," he told his crew, "let's kick some ass."

Ezra preferred old fashioned hand-nailing (he thought it produced a tighter fit) but these three men would have none of it and nailed everything with high powered compressed-air framing guns. The air guns were as powerful as their gunpowder cousins, and all too often a worker would get in a hurry, just catching the edge of a board with the strongly shot nail, and cry out as a hand, an arm, or a leg became the unintended target. The guns were all equipped with safeties, but that slowed them down, they all said, so the safeties had all been disabled.

Accidents were common.

A couple of crew-leaders had removed the safety guards on their circular saws, too, until one of the best lead men forgot and put the still spinning saw-blade down on the plywood deck and the saw immediately jumped across the top of his foot. One of the young workers passed out from the sight of all the blood, hitting his head on a stack of headers, and Ezra made everyone put the guards back on.

Ezra had been working for about an hour, and the four-man crew had finally hit stride. They were gaining on the two-man crew working next door.

"*Sprechen Sie Deutsch?*" The Amish worker on the next house, less than ten feet away, was talking to Ezra.

Ezra was listening to Stephen Stills singing "Love the One You're With" on his transistor radio. He glanced up, began to answer, caught himself and then said, "What?"

"*Sprechen Sie Deutsch?*" the man repeated.

"I don't know what you're saying. Speak English."

"Oh. I'm sorry. I thought you —"

"You thought I what?"

"I thought — I thought you spoke — maybe —"

"You thought I spoke your language?" Ezra was amused. "Whatever gave you that idea?" Ezra wondered what had given him away. He had purposefully burned all the Amish out of himself a long time ago. He thought.

The young Amish carpenter muttered sorry and went back to work. Ezra watched him for several minutes then turned and picked up his hammer.

CHAPTER FOURTEEN

"I don't think so." John shook his head, dumbfounded that the overweight biker would even ask for a job.

John was sitting outside on the small concrete porch of the construction trailer having a smoke, Camel unfiltereds. The biker had roared up through the muddy gravel parking lot on his deafeningly loud motorcycle. He was shirtless, sagging belly bouncing on the gas tank between his leathered legs, leaving a grease mark on the glossy black paint. He cranked the throttle on the huge bike several times before shutting it down, the sharp retort rocketing up and down the street. He grinned at the appreciative workers waving from the top of the houses, then dismounted, as if from a steed. He was covered in a kaleidoscope of multi-colored tattoos: two-headed dragons, a dagger buried in the middle of his breastbone, tattooed blood running down his oversized, hairy belly. The tattoos writhed with every exaggerated motion, straining to escape their skin-deep prison.

John stood and walked back inside. He sat behind his cluttered desk, coffee stained paperwork, ashtray overflowing with half-smoked cigarettes, packs of gum nearby. The biker followed him in, the trailer floor groaning. Even over the smell of stale cigarettes, he could smell the biker. The cacophony of odors created from greasy hair, cigarette smoke and drug induced toxic sweat almost knocked John out of his chair.

"Why the hell not?" the biker asked, voice like a rasp on hard wood.

John felt his blood pressure rising, and caught himself. He really didn't want to start Tuesday morning antagonizing a biker, in spite of the .45 in his desk drawer. There were a lot of them.

"The only openings I have are for roof deckers," he patiently explained, "two stories up, 6/12 pitch. I'm looking for monkeys, not —" *an elephant* — he thought to himself.

"Not what?" the tattooed man demanded.

"Look. I'm sure you'd do good with the basics, framing, laying out walls, floor decking, but I'm full up with those crews. Why don't you try the project down the road? I heard they were looking."

The development down the road, miles away, was a cluster of two and three story houses. The dark-haired twin was on top of one of the two-stories. He grabbed the end of the plywood sheet the Raven shoved his way. He muscled the bottom edge in place, then let it slap down hard on the second story roof trusses, shaking the entire building. He kept glancing at the straw-hatted worker on the house next door, effortlessly outworking him by a wide margin, two sheets to every one of his. He rapidly stapled the last sheet down, the staccato "bang-bang-bang" of the air gun ringing in his ears, half of the staples missing the rafter beneath it.

The activity on this busy street was intense. The air compressors struggled to re-fill their tanks as the workers rushed to use the compressed air in their various air guns faster than the compressors could refill. The loud "boom-boom" of the framing guns, shooting three inch nails into two-by-four's and two-by-six's, competed with the sharper report of the rapid-fire staple guns furiously fastening roof decking and window trim. The shriek of circular saws was deafening.

The men up on the houses shouted dimensions to the workers standing on improvised islands of scrap wood in the mud. The men on the ground cut the pieces and heaved them back up to the rooftop workers, tossing the light ones and sliding the longer, heavier ones up over the roof edge. The shouting would rise to a fever pitch as a worker lost his balance swatting at the swarming mass of mosquitoes and almost rolled off a rooftop, then subsided to laughter and normal shouting as he grabbed on to one of the air hoses at the last minute.

Above the din of the laboring compressors, air-guns and saws, the portable transistor radios blared their competition, rock-n-roll on one house, blues on the next, Mexican on another. The satirical protest music of the '60's had given way to the bland songs of the '70's, "I'd Like To Teach The World To Sing" and "I'll Be There" and "You're So Vain." The syncopated beat of the Mexican music was timeless. The blues were all the same, telling the stories of man, or woman, troubles.

This particular day, a Tuesday, had defied the forecasters. They had called for rain, again. But every so often a bit of blue appeared between the lower layer of misty clouds rapidly moving one direction and the much higher mass of dirty-gray broken overcast slowly drifting the other way. The workers had been able to rest up yesterday from the excesses of the weekend, and were as fresh as construction workers ever got. The project manager looked pleased at the progress.

The standard issue construction-worker uniform, except for the Amish, was frayed-bottom cutoff jeans and no shirt, on sunny days. The cutoffs were so short the men appeared naked behind their leather nail aprons. Sunburned, scarred, sawdust covered legs bottomed out to dirty-white ankle socks and work boots.

The degree of spring sunburn depended on ancestry: northern Europeans started the summer bright pink then turned dark red and finally dark mahogany, the Mexicans and Negroes turned slightly darker, or, for the darkest-skinned, unchanged. The white-skinned workers had their bottles of baby oil. Once the skin stopped blistering and peeling, the oil produced a deep dark tan and now, by the end of summer, they were all pretty much the same skin color, their hair and eye color the most obvious ethnic dividers.

The Amish had learned long ago to protect themselves from the burning sun, and wore their broad-brimmed straw hats, and tied red or white handkerchiefs around their necks. They worked in long sleeves, regardless of the temperature, and seldom burned.

The whores came around, especially on Friday, payday. They liked construction workers. Most of the carpenters were hard-bodied, flat-bellied, had money and didn't mind spending it. The Amish in particular were fascinated with these ladies-of-the-night, and would stand in small groups huddled together, heads covered with sweat-stained, sawdust-covered straw hats, on top of the unfinished houses, glancing and whispering, never talking to them.

The twin was on top of a three story house, balanced on the three-and-a-half-inch top plate of an outside framed wall, setting rafters, twenty-seven feet from the ground. He paused and took a deep breath, started coughing. He thought he could smell the fresh that always came after prolonged rain, a fresh blended with the musty smell of the mud and the wood that had gotten too wet for too long. He could *almost* smell it, but all the other stuff he had put in his nose along with the constant cigarette smoke had all but destroyed his sense of smell. He could smell the sawdust, though, the ever present sawdust. Different kinds of sawdust, the fine kind from the plywood blades, sawdust mixed with the glue that held the plywood together, the coarse sawdust from the dimensional lumber, acrid sawdust from the treated lumber. The sawdust from the bottom plate treated lumber smelled bad, arsenic forced into the wood to keep it from rotting.

The twin had gone off the roof one time, skiing down the plywood on the loose sawdust, tripping on a power cord three feet from the edge, grabbing and missing the aluminum ladder, and had landed on his back in the mud. The workers had laughed their heartiest at that stunt, even before anyone knew whether he was dead or not. Everyone except the workers in the straw hats.

The twin looked down the long street at the twenty houses taking shape, and the workers swarming all over them. There were two straw-hatted crews on this long block, and as usual, their houses were rising out of the ground faster than the others. They shouted dimensions back and forth in a curious mix of 17th century German and current English, with the occasional "two-by-four" and "plywood" punctuating otherwise indecipherable language. They were distinctive looking, with their ever-present straight-brimmed straw hats, beards with no moustaches, their sideburns shaved to leave a gap between beard and head hair. They shaved under their lower lips and the fronts of their chins, and had page-boy haircuts. The shirts and pants were their uniforms, usually gray, sometimes blue, with equally drab suspenders to hold up the pants. They chose not to use the leather nail aprons, no one knew why, and instead used the complimentary cheap cloth nail aprons with the name of the lumber company on the front. Their thick flat carpenter pencils were always stuck up under their hats, sharpened end up, leaving pencil marks on their temples, and they had their retractable tape measures clipped to one side of their suspenders. They stuck their huge twenty-two ounce framing hammers inside the cloth-string nail aprons that tied behind their backs, and how they got anything done at all with that get-up was a marvel, but they always, always outworked the English.

It was rumored that they didn't mind a nip of homemade wine in the evening, but no one knew that for sure and they never talked to anyone about anything but work, preferring to keep to themselves.

All the work was piece-work; they got paid for completed work, not by the hour, and the straw-hats made more than anyone, and their work had the least re-dos. This particular developer had never stiffed anyone, so the word went, so you would probably be okay to get paid at the end of each job instead of every Friday, but then, where would the weekend money come from, the city workers asked? Some of the straw-hats even waited until the end of the month to get paid. They just took their money back out to the country and gave it to their families, so it didn't really matter to them. The twin remembered those days in the country, although the memory was fading, and an almost wistful look crossed his face, and then departed.

"Hey, Brother, ye have to make hay whilst the sun shines, don't ye?" he shouted at one of the straw-hats on the next house.

The twin knew perfectly well they didn't talk like that, but it never failed to bring guffaws from the other workers. The young Amish man just smiled and waved, and went back to work.

Sometimes at night, late at night, the twin would lie on his cheap, dirty bed at the local cheap, dirty motel, and miss the days when he was part of the controlled, secure Amish life. But through the tired haze of too much booze and too many chemicals, the feeling would pass. He never really *was* part of all that, he would drowsily remind himself. Somehow, it just hadn't taken with him, or his twin brother, all that religion and clean living, although they had managed to fool everyone into thinking it had. Or so they thought. It was a bizarre life, strict and God-fearing on the one hand, with one intriguing exception. When Amish teenagers turned sixteen, they were allowed, encouraged, to participate in *Rumspring*. This church-sanctioned rite of passage allowed the teenagers the freedom to drive cars, live away from the farm and see what the English world looked like.

He remembered the parties well, and remembered the justification the Amish Elders had given for them: "Let them sow their wild oats," they would say, "and they will return and be with us forever." That worked most of the time; over ninety percent of the kids returned to their families and were baptized into the church. But some of the youngsters discovered that the pleasures of the flesh were too strong and never went back. The twin never went back, except to supply the partying, and it paid well. He had an occasional twinge of guilt, just a twinge, but the wild times and wild sex always drowned it out.

He never really thought about getting caught dealing drugs. It was a game, an exciting, thrilling game, and the money was just part of it. The potential for danger was part of the thrill, with no real thought that the danger could be real. And he would drift off to sleep.

Construction sites had always been problem areas for law enforcement, and when the economy boomed, as it had the last couple of years, the problems multiplied: theft, assault, drugs, the occasional shooting. The number of concealed handgun permits shot up, and project managers who never had a reason before started wearing weapons on their hips.

The detectives hated going on construction calls. They often picked up nails in one of their tires and the mud was difficult to wash off of their car. And they seldom solved anything. Construction workers were a tight-lipped group. Most of them were stealing or using, the cops were convinced, and the rest were too intimidated to say anything. So they made no arrests, filed meaningless reports, and groused about the latest flat tire or the mud.

The latest boom had also seen a big influx of young, twenty-something workers from the surrounding rural areas, the "quiet people," very odd, very religious people. The detectives knew little about these odd-dressers, except that the young men that came to town to work construction were mostly very polite, very hard working, and never any trouble. They were usually driven, for a fee, to the site by one of the large vans that their less religious neighbors would hire out to bring them to town. The vans would usually show up again at quitting time to take the happy workers back out to their farms, where, rumor had it, they put in another couple of hours of equally hard work feeding horses and mucking stalls. On rare occasions, some of the young men would stay in local motels, the cheap ones, so they could get as much work done per week as possible, and even fewer of them would end up staying more and more weekends.

Lately, the twins had begun to show up in the local bars, drinking and swearing. Their effort to conform bordered on competition. Their overzealous drinking, swearing, and generally obnoxious behavior would create a nuisance, and sometimes the unwanted attention of a biker or two they unwittingly insulted. The local PPD had been called in a couple of times to the Kountry Klub to break up the drinking and shouting before it got out of hand. So far, no charges had been filed, the brothers grinning that no one had been seriously hurt. The two crime-weary detectives both knew it was probably just a matter of time until they would be called in to investigate a dead body.

CHAPTER FIFTEEN

Ezra slowly walked the familiar ten minute route to Rick's, a small counterculture café hidden behind a little market run by a Chinese family that spoke no English. Like everyone else, Ezra went through the motions of shopping for fresh produce in the colorful, overflowing baskets on the sidewalk, nodding and smiling at the incomprehensible chattering of the store's owner. Purposefully hidden from abusive law enforcement, the café relied entirely on word of mouth, and the exclusive aspect made it a popular hangout.

It was dusk, and after a few moments, Ezra ducked between the hanging rows of multi-colored beads covering the entrance to a small, narrow alleyway, the beads clacking together, swinging and swaying behind him like reeds at the bottom of a river. The uneven brick walkway made walking difficult, and he stumbled towards the far end. The brick-walled buildings rose three stories high on each side, intersecting the darkening sky.

The short passageway led to a plain metal door, a gray door with a white porcelain doorknob. The door was always locked, and Ezra knocked the secret code, two raps, a pause, another knock, and the door opened. The local cops on the beat knew the cafe was there, of course, and occasionally amused themselves rousting a few potheads, kicking the door open, pistols drawn.

Jerry Rubin had stopped in once, a year ago, and his picture was plastered all over the place.

"Hey, Ezra." Charlotte was older than Ezra, probably in her thirties, and always wore the same dress, a floor length pale green paisley print that complimented her gold, wire-rimmed granny glasses and Ivory soap complexion. She had been going braless long enough that her nipples, quite visible through the thin fabric, appeared to be making a glacial creep downward, succumbing to gravity. Six months or so ago, she had accused Ezra of getting her pregnant, "You knocked me up!" but he pointed out that he was only one of probably thirty candidates. She had laughed heartily, "Only kidding," she chuckled, and they had been good friends ever since. She wasn't pregnant at all, but was clumsily trying to persuade the young carpenter to return to her futon bed. She had three, small, distinct tailbones, and had thrilled at his carefully counting them over and over with his cracked, calloused fingers, pretending to lose count at two and starting over. Ezra, as usual, had lost interest early.

"Hey, Shar, how's it going?"

"Good, good." She smiled sweetly at him.

There were half a dozen other patrons, earnestly huddled over a large, round Formica and chrome table, quietly, fiercely, conspiring over some important issue. Charlotte took the group their fresh, whole-grain muffins. As an occasional treat for her most trusted regulars, she would spice the batter with Mary Jane. Charlotte smoked pot throughout the day and handled it well. A "functioning pothead," Ezra called her.

The incense was intense, thick, a futile attempt to mask the smell of the smoldering cannabis, and Ezra always coughed when he first stepped in from the outside. She offered him a toke, as usual, but he declined, as usual. The café walls jumped and danced with their psychedelic colors, with posters of Hendrix and The Who plastered around, angled this way and that. The flat black ceiling disappeared behind iridescent planets and stars and a quarter moon hanging from invisible fish lines, the planets seeming to hang in mid-air above the fish net draped from dozens of gold colored chains. Three dimensional, bathed in a flood of black light and slowly undulating from the rotating fan on the floor in the corner, the brilliantly phosphorescent objects were a "high" in themselves.

"Hey, Jim, cover for me for a bit, huh?" Jim nodded yes, she blew him a kiss and mouthed "Cool." Jim was her business partner and occasional lover when no one new was around. If Charlotte hadn't invented free love, she was the self-styled pioneer of the Flower Children. Jim would say she hadn't laid all the men in the world, "Why, she had missed at least five on the east coast alone."

"You bet, Shar, a girl needs what a girl needs. Hey, your high beams are on." Charlotte folded her arms across her puckered nipples, stuck her tongue out at him and turned to Ezra.

Charlotte glided the short distance from behind the counter, moving to the music of Hendrix's "Foxy Lady," miming the words, moving her hands and head like an Egyptian queen, and plopped down on the yellow-haired carpenter's lap. She buried his face in her bosom and stroked his long, yellow pony tail. Ezra was in an indifferent mood and quickly tired of her gyrations. He gently guided her to the chair on the other side of the small table.

He sat for a minute while she continued her sitting dance, snapping her fingers and sliding around the oak seat. Ezra sipped on the thick chicory hot drink. The sign by the coffee machine said the owners refused to support the "growing coffee mega-conspiracy perpetuated by corporate America's greed, on the neck of illiterate, poor farmers." So they served chicory and assorted herb teas.

Jim brought Ezra a muffin, a plain muffin, "No *electric* muffins, please." He wolfed it, scraping the remaining crumbs into a small mound and picking them up with his thumb and first two fingers, popping the last bit into his mouth.

"I'm thinking of moving to Toronto," Ezra finally said.

She stopped moving, hands suspended in the air, fingers unsnapped. "Whatever for?"

He thought for a minute. "I dunno, I just think I need a change. I've been reading up on Toronto, and it seems like a really cool place. Philly is nice, but it's just too close to —" he almost slipped. Too close to all that I'm trying to escape is what he wanted to say, but caught himself. She was not a confidant. She lit another joint, inhaled deeply, smiled slyly and offered him another toke. He waved her away, again, and continued. "Things haven't been going too well at work. I can't keep good help, the ones that stay are stoned all day long —" She made an expression of fake shock and surprise — "and we have had way too many accidents. Living with my cousin is trouble. The cops are snooping around, the paychecks are slow or no good, the bikers are —"

She stood abruptly, suddenly angry, unrestrained breasts waving their concurrence. "Go, then, screw you. You're in for a surprise if you think those cold Canadians are going to love you like you been used to. Good luck, Ahmo." She spun and walked off, granny dress swishing and lightly brushing the unswept floor, slamming the kitchen door behind her.

Ezra was stunned. How did she know? Could he never shed his past? Being far from his roots seemed like an even better idea now. The other patrons glanced up, looked distractedly at the hapless former Amish, who simply shrugged.

Ezra ducked between the perpetually undulating beads, shook his head no at the Chinese marketer's offer for produce, and wandered aimlessly down the sidewalk. He slowly ambled towards the main shopping district, walking towards the bottom-lit clouds hovering over the bright lights of the store fronts and streetlamps. He turned up the collar of his black leather jacket. The afternoon chill was descending like a hungry wolf.

Woolworths loomed several blocks ahead, and Ezra smiled ruefully at himself. Woolworths was the favorite store of the Amish; was he drawn back to this store like a bug to an open flame?

Even from this distance, he could see the familiar dress, especially the bonnets, of the Amish women, children in tow, entering and leaving, they would be buying their fabrics, sewing needles and thread, he knew. One van would leave and another would pull up, park in the special parking area to the east of the store and another dozen Amish would pour out and march towards the front door, nodding and waving to the small parade going the other way. Ezra had never been homesick, he often told himself. Not once, never nostalgic. He watched with a detached mild interest at these quaint people wandering the streets of worldly Philadelphia.

But wait — there was something very familiar about the Amish woman that just stepped out of the van onto the parking lot pavement, pausing to exchange words with another woman, an English woman, familiar hand-gesturing. Two children were at her side, about the age of his two youngest siblings. Was that his mother? Was that Joseph and Hannah? He couldn't be sure at this distance. The Amish woman reached into her paper bag and pulled something out, probably a fold of fabric, he thought. The two women stood there for a minute, touching the cloth, nodding and gesturing, the children fidgeting.

A late model medium blue Chevy SS rocketed around the corner. Ezra could just hear the squealing tires. It roared past the drugstore, and slid to a stop in front of the women, at a rakish angle to the curb. A leather-jacketed man jumped out of the passenger side, ran to the small group, striking the familiar looking woman, knocking her to the ground, grabbing her purse and her paper bag. Ezra tried to yell but the sound caught in his throat. He tried to sprint, but his legs may as well have been imbedded in freshly set concrete. The man ran back to the car, jumped back inside, tires smoking as they fishtailed away from the curb, his hand out the window, arm in the air, waving an obscene one-fingered gesture.

The woman slowly got to her feet. She waved off the offer of assistance from the others near here and the store manager, who frantically shoved his way through the front door after witnessing the ordeal.

Ezra stayed until the police arrived, watched the cop car pull over to the curb, the red light from the single bubble-top slowly rotating around, lighting up the woman's face with each pass. He watched the uniformed police officers climb out of the black and white car, put on their stiff-billed captain's hats, holster their night sticks, move the gawkers aside, finally reaching the distraught woman. She appeared to be shaking her head no, but one of the officers returned to the patrol car anyway. He reached inside and pulled the microphone through the open window, speaking into it. Less than ten minutes later, a long, black Cadillac ambulance appeared from behind Ezra, siren wailing, cherry-top red light also slowly spinning. It raced past the watching carpenter, and pulled in behind the patrol car, the two beams of red chasing each other around the block of brick buildings.

The woman slowly returned to the van, assisted by the children and another woman. Ezra could imagine her urge to leave the city and return to the safety and comfort of her home in the country. No shopping this trip.

The ambulance driver was the first to leave, talking briefly with one of the officers, and then slipping back into the emergency vehicle. The light went off, and he drove away, back past Ezra, the car appearing to grow larger, then whooshing past. The officers returned to their car, turned off the red beacon and pulled away in his direction.

Ezra instinctively stepped back, tripping on the uneven cobblestone sidewalk. He went down, scraping his black leather jacket on the jagged brick building corner, bloodying his left hand reaching for a handhold. He scrambled away on hands and knees, crawling into an alleyway, seeking refuge in the darkened space from the officers and his past.

Ezra rolled over, watching the patrol car move past. He was sitting on the filthy brick paving, urinal to the world of bums, feeling the wet, frigid stench soak through his pants, hands cold and sticky, chest compressed and short of breath. He finally stood, wiped his hands on the cold lamppost, and walked unsteadily away, away from downtown, back towards the motel strip, the familiar strip.

"Well, then, Ezra, how's it going?" he asked himself. His face softened, the stress lines began to fade, and the open dry mouth began to moisten. "Good job with the Amish woman. Johnny-on-the-spot, everyone can count on ol' Ezra, ran right down there and kicked the shit out of those two hoodlums, good to have you on the team, boy if you're down for the count all you gotta do is call Ezra —" The young carpenter quickened his pace, still muttering to himself.

91

It was still early, a Friday evening, and Ezra returned to his apartment, showered, changed clothes and oiled the scrape on his jacket. Phil was gone — somewhere, wherever Phil went at night. He decided to go back out — or stay in — or go back out. He picked up one of Phil's ever present glossy girlie magazines and distractedly thumbed through the worn pages. With a sigh, Ezra tossed the magazine back onto the coffee table, and grabbed his leather jacket and hat and headed for the front door, out the door, down the sidewalk.

1971 Philadelphia was a wild place for a young man, especially a tall, muscular, brutally handsome young man, one that seemed indifferent to money, but always had plenty and didn't mind sharing. Even in a time of extremes — extreme dress, extreme sex, extreme political protests — Ezra stood out. He had bought several pairs of too-tight, purposefully too-short black jeans. The bottoms of the jeans' pantlegs were decorated with tiny dangling braids that bounced against his shiny black, pointy-toed cowboy boots. He wore a belt of colorful cloth, tied in a knot, dangling down in the front, a sly nod to Dr. Freud and the fashion of the day.

A new club had opened, he had heard, and he absently wandered towards it. The music and strobe lights grew louder and brighter as he ambled closer. There was a line out the front door of the new place, and several girls recognized Ezra from the other, older clubs around town. One of them ran over, hugging him in her best Marilyn Monroe impersonation, bending her left leg at the knee, foot wiggling in the air. Ezra pried her loose and moved inside with the next group of people, smiling slightly and shaking his head no.

Mick Jagger shrieked "Honky Tonk Women" at deafening decibels. Drunk and stoned patrons were unsteadily dancing every conceivable combination of steps in the middle of the peanut shell covered oak parquet dance floor. The new owner — Canadian, someone said — had hung a huge ball in the middle of the cavernous room, covered with tiny mirrors, and the DJ occasionally flashed multi-colored beams of light on it. The tiny

92

refractions ricocheted around the room like a million lost meteorites frantically searching for home.

There wasn't a black light to be found.

"Hey, Ahmo, whatcha doing down here? I took you more for the C and W scene."

Ezra had mentioned he liked country music one time, and Phil had never let it go, annoying Ezra no end. The DJ had taken a short break, and the low level buzz of people talking and the shuffling of still-dancing feet filled the huge room.

"Phil," Ezra replied coolly. *Ahmo*, he mused to himself. Phil is the one, of course. I wonder how many people he has told. Ezra tipped his hat to a familiar, laughing, waving couple, and wondered if they were laughing at him, wondered if they knew.

Phil leaned over and whispered, "See that tall fox over there, the one in black?" Ezra wanted to leave, but his cousin knew his Achilles heel and Ezra looked in spite of himself. The woman in question was striking, probably as tall as Ezra, wearing a dress, a long, black strapless dress. She had black hair, cropped short. She looked back, smiled, and waved, a small, waist-high wave like Queen Elizabeth might have waved, fingers tightly pressed together, hand rocking from side to side, like she was unscrewing a light bulb.

Marvin Gaye began belting out that he had "Heard It Through the Grapevine," and attempting to talk became utterly futile once again. Phil was trying to shout something into Ezra's ear but Ezra decided to walk off, nonchalantly, making a slow arc, closer and closer to the dark haired lady waiting on the other side. She was watching the young, bushy-haired man make his way closer out of the corner of her dark eye. She was standing with two other girls, and as Ezra casually moved closer, they covered their mouths with their hands and giggled, giggled too hard, almost laughing.

Marvin was finished, and Ezra eased up to the tall woman. He was in his comfort zone, and brushed up against her arm and said, "Hi. I'm Ezra."

Her two friends were now openly laughing, turned and left, still laughing. "Yeah, Phil told me who you are. You're the Amish fellow, right? I'm Pam. I like Amish men."

Ezra was pissed, looked around for Phil, but couldn't find him. "Do I look Amish?"

"Whoa, cowboy, I didn't mean anything — Phil said —" She had a husky voice, a smoky voice, gravelly, purring.

"Phil's a cokehead, he can't even remember his own—"

Pam leaned towards Ezra and smothered the rest of the comment with a wet kiss, Ezra eagerly kissing back, leaning into the kiss. It was a good kiss, but something wasn't quite right. He didn't mind big-boned women. In fact, he grew up with stout women and they were a bit of a turn-on. This woman had a bra on so tight it could have held a piece of furniture secure on a moving van. Her breasts were in no danger of moving. He caught himself staring at her makeup, thick and splotchy up close, and noticed the laughing couples over her broad shoulders.

"So what's your sign, Tiger?" She took his right arm, tightly, and even through his leather jacket, her left breast felt like a small round bale of wheat straw, tightly bound with some type of wire.

Ezra's flight response had kicked in, but it was dueling with another primary drive, an even more powerful drive, and lost. He relaxed slightly and after a pause said, "Aries."

"Oh, no kidding!" She purred the way a lioness might purr, a low, guttural purring. "Mine too, isn't that amazing? Hey, Phil tells me you're quite the carpenter, is that right?"

Ezra admitted he had been working with wood for a long time.

"I know it's late, Tiger, but I have this cabinet door that just won't close right. Do you have time to come over and look at it? I would be most grateful." She batted her heavily made-up eyes, fake eyelashes in danger of flying off.

Ezra looked at the tall woman again, then said, "Sure, why not. Where is your place?"

94

"It's about a five minute walk from here. Would you like a ride?"

"No, that's fine, we can walk."

They headed for the front door, why were all these people snickering and nudging each other, he wondered. Chill, Ezra, you're going paranoid, he scolded himself. He caught a glimpse of his cousin, through the haze and people, ducking out the front door. Was he laughing too?

Something crashed behind the departing couple, followed by shouts of "Fight! Fight!" and the approving roar of inebriated spectators lusting for violence. Ezra and Pam stopped, turned as one, arm in arm, and watched the combatants swinging wildly at one another, unsteady on the peanut-hulled floor, missing, taking turns falling down. Two large men in starched, white, long-sleeved dress shirts ran across the dance floor, slid to a stop, shoved cheering onlookers aside. Each grabbed a fighter and twisting an arm behind him, headed for the front door, passing close enough to Ezra and Pam to brush against them. The entire scene seemed choreographed.

Ezra smiled slightly, and shook his head, ponytail swinging. They turned back towards the front door, and his mind returned to the oddly attractive woman on his arm and the casual encounter coming up. Cabinet door, that's a new one, he smiled to himself. The crowd had lost their interest in Ezra and his date, maybe he imagined it all anyway, he wondered, and they made their way through the still-excited throng, pushed the heavy wood front door open and stepped into the cold night.

The club owner had hired off-duty cops to park outside, and they were shoving the now chastened and handcuffed pair of former fighters into the back of their squad car. The officers were handling them roughly, banging their captives' heads on the top of the open, black and white door frame. Phil was there, too, shouting, "Do you have any idea who you're dealing with?" He pointed a finger at his own chest. "My boys were just having a little fun, what's the matter with you? Let them go! Do you have any idea who I am?"

95

"One more word from you, you stupid coke-head, and you'll be in the back with your *boys*, capice?"

"After all I've paid —"

The closest officer shoved Phil hard, both palms against his chest, knocking him against the trunk of the patrol car, looming over him.

"Shut up, goddamit, I'm gonna shove this nightstick —" The other officer walked over and put a restraining hand on his partner's raised arm.

Their voices dropped to the point Ezra could no longer hear what was being said, but they appeared to be agreeing. Soon Phil got up and stepped away from the car, shook both officers' hands, and with a wave and a grin to Ezra, swaggered away.

Ezra and Pam had stopped long enough, just outside the huge door that the cold was beginning to penetrate their jackets and their skin. They began down the long walk, intending to slip behind the car and go look at Pam's cabinet door. The same officer that had calmed his partner looked up and saw the couple.

"Hey, is that you Ezra?"

Ezra stopped, frozen for the second time that night. How did this officer know his name?

"Phil's told us all about you, Ez. One of these days we're gonna catch up with you, you know that, right?"

Ezra was speechless, aware of Pam's stare.

Then the cop looked at Pam. "And I see you're with Stanley. Hey, Stanley, you're looking real good tonight. Where'd you get the dress? You steal that too? You need another ride? Whatcha doing with the Ahmo, here, you gonna have him look at your cabinet door?"

"Oh, hi, officer." Pam's voice was now very husky. "No, no, me and Ezra are —"

"It's Ezra and I, Stanley, speak correctly."

"Sorry, officer, Ezra and I were just getting some fresh air and then we were going back inside. We were having such an excellent time, talking to our friends, when those two ruffians —" she nodded towards the back seat — "so rudely began scuffling

and just about ruined our evening." She —
he — turned towards her new friend, the carpenter with all the
yellow hair, and said, "Ezra, are you ready to go back inside,
darlin?"

Ezra yanked his arm away from Stanley's grasp, and
without a word, walked away, spitting and spitting, the sounds of
the guffawing officers growing increasingly faint with each long,
purposeful stride.

CHAPTER SIXTEEN

The front door to the apartment stuck sometimes, depending on the weather, and Ezra shouldered it open so hard the doorknob slammed into the drywall, again, making an even deeper dent. Ezra furiously kicked the door shut behind him, cracking one of the glass panes in the top half of the old, painted door.

"Phil, you here?" Ezra shouted. No response. "Hey," he shouted again, louder, the only response a rapid one-two-three foot stomp from the neighbor upstairs. He rushed to the bathroom, brushed his teeth for ten minutes, and then gargled mouthwash for another ten. Finally finished, he leaned on the porcelain sink and tried to look in the mirror, shaking his head, unable to meet his own gaze.

He walked into the short hallway that was the foyer to the screened back porch, Ezra's room. The door to the porch was slightly ajar, and the light was on. Ezra could see the bed was disheveled, not neatly made like he always left it, the way his mother liked it. He apprehensively nudged the door open with his highly polished left boot, huge hands curled into fists, blood thumping in his head. There was a note in the middle of the bed, crudely scrawled as if the writer was hurried:

IOU $6500. I'll be back in a week or so.
-- P

"That sonofabitch," he muttered. He reached under the mattress but he already knew his "bank" had been robbed. He had told no-one of the money, but his cokehead cousin had put it together. Ezra always carried $500 with him, a security blanket, and fingered the money belt he wore inside his pants, ten fifty dollar bills, laying flat. "I'm gonna kill him."

Phil had also laid out the brochures, "Crossing Into Canada" and "North American Bus Routes," on Ezra's bed from their normal place on the bed stand, as if taunting him, daring him to go. Ezra picked them up, looked at his watch — 12:30 Saturday morning — glanced at the bus schedule, no need, really, he had memorized it, stuffed a quick grab of clothes in a new leather bag he had bought, ripped the price tag off, and headed towards the front door. He could still make the 1:00.

On the run again. Just into Canada, just across the border, still on the bridge, Lake Erie immense on his left, he decided to be Ryan. Ryan Miller.

CHAPTER SEVENTEEN

Toronto 1973

Michael Knowles was trying to wrap up paperwork at the end of another long day, and was mildly distracted by the staccato rhythm of gnarled knuckles pounding the board in the next room. He had constructed the board himself, one inch thick solid oak, about ten inches wide and two feet tall, wrapped tightly with 3/8 inch thick hemp rope. It was mounted flat on the wall, the middle of the hemp rope board four and a half feet from the floor, hemp shiny and worn from years of knuckle-pounding. It was not one of the "sissy boards" sold at the Karate supply houses. Michael ran an Okinawan Karate school, a dojo, in northwest Toronto, and had developed a reputation for turning out competition champions.

Michael had been an Army brat, and had studied with the old masters in Okinawa. He had no use for the afterschool alternative to volleyball that Karate had become in most schools. It was even worse in the States, and he had moved to Toronto fifteen years ago to establish a "real" Karate school. Here the workout floor was hard, painted concrete, and if you couldn't take it, well, there was that pink flowery school over on 8th Avenue. You could get the tips of your white belt dipped in yellow dye by the end of the first week, he would say. But if you decided to leave, don't come back; the front door only swings one way. "We've created a generation of losers with high self esteem," he often would say, "giving medals just for showing up."

The student on the board was Ryan, another American who had defied all expectations with his drive and determination. And yet — something just didn't click. Michael didn't know much about Ryan except that he was from the Philadelphia area, and he thought he remembered Ryan mentioning once that he still had some family there. Ryan wasn't prone to talking much about himself, and in the tradition of Karate training and particularly in Michael's dojo, no one asked questions. Ryan had enrolled himself in every competition he could, and won most. He seemed to be on a mission to become the best, driving himself to extremes.

When Ryan first entered the front door on a cold, gray, rainy Friday morning three years ago, Michael almost sent him back out that same door. Ryan was probably in his early twenties at the time, the karate master thought, and looked like a poster child for the hippy movement. He was about six feet tall, muscular and broad at the shoulders, and the only reason Michael let him stay that first day was because of the obvious physical shape he was in.

Michael always watched how new students coming through his front door handled themselves, and this new fellow appeared to have a very comfortable center of gravity and balance. His thick blond hair was tied in a ponytail, and he had a simple leather band around his head. The young man met Michael's look with an unwavering return gaze, and his eyes were the kind of blue that no doubt was prized by the authors of *The Final Solution*. He wore a shiny, long sleeved shirt, and an old, black leather jacket that had seen better days. When Michael finally invited him onto the workout area, he unwittingly joined Michael with his shoes on, not barefoot, missing the most obvious protocol.

"Put your shoes over there with the others," Michael instructed him, and when Ryan had removed them he returned to the edge of the colored concrete and almost stepped back inside the workout area with his socks on. "The socks too," Michael patiently instructed.

The two other students working out on the heavy bag at the far end of the room became invisible; Michael's reputation for impatience was legendary. They had never seen a newbie survive the "shoes on the mat" test.

Finally Ryan was standing, barefoot, in front of this master of the martial arts, the man who had won more international kick boxing competitions than any other living person. Ezra had searched him out precisely because of that legend, and now here he was, former Amish, standing barefoot on hard concrete with his faded blue jeans and wide-collar paisley shirt, determined to bury his past forever, even his hated name.

"Try to hit me," Michael instructed.

Ryan took a quick, left-handed, half-hearted poke at Michael's right pectoral area. Michael neither blinked nor tried to block the thrust and simply said, "You can't hurt me there." Oh, yeah, duh, thought Ryan, I'm supposed to be hurting my opponent. And so it went, Michael uncharacteristically patient with this eager but amazingly incompetent and uninformed wannabe.

"Okay, be here tomorrow at 3:00 and we'll see how it goes," he told Ryan. There was no need to shower because they had not worked up any kind of sweat. "I'll be here," Ryan promised.

The rope board was the last item on Ryan's workout regime, right after the free weights, and he knew he needed to wrap up so Mr. Bowles could close. Once a new student joined the school, Michael became "Mr. Knowles," or "*Sensei*," or "Sir."

Ryan looked around the dojo and smiled to himself at all the improvements he had done to the place since he first started coming here. He had replaced the old fluorescent interior lights with state-of-the-art halogens. The storefront exterior finally looked like a world renowned school of champion fighters, with the elaborate carvings of fighting eagles Ryan had imported from Okinawa. Mr. Knowles probably could never have afforded those on his own, but the discipline and focus Ryan had learned at the dojo had enriched his life immensely, financially and spiritually, and he almost felt obligated to give some back.

And yet —

Ryan emerged from the locker room dressed impeccably, every still damp hair of his damp blond hair perfectly styled. He walked over to Mr. Knowles to bid him good night.

"You here tomorrow?" Mr. Knowles asked.

"No sir, I asked Jim to take the noon class."

Ryan had been teaching a Thursday noon class, "Beginning Karate," but had meetings with city officials tomorrow.

"OK, we'll see you Friday then."

Ryan bowed in the tradition of respect taught in all dojos, and backed out of the room Mr. Knowles was sitting in.

It was several months later. Ryan had tested for his black belt — how many times? He had lost count. Every time, the panel of other black belts had turned him down, in spite of his generosity and hard work, and he finally went to Mr. Knowles to ask him why.

"*Sensei*, do you have any suggestions for me? I have worked my butt off. I know the maneuvers cold. Why are you unwilling to award the black?"

The dojo owner continued working on the paperwork he had started, and after a minute scooted his chair back and looked up. Ryan seemed to have a bit of an attitude, he thought. It was highly unusual, unacceptable, for a white belt, even one that had been coming for years and had done so much for the school, to question the *Sensei*. And you never spoke before being spoken to when addressing a higher rank belt. But once again, the dojo owner ignored protocol and answered the young man.

"It's hard to put into words, son," he started slowly, "and that is part of the problem. Yes, you are very technically skilled, and yes, you are a big help with the school. But something is missing. You still don't have that instinct to defend yourself, to take it to your opponent. This isn't a game, this is serious business, and you're not there yet. I am not willing to award you black, because I think in a real battle you would be in trouble. It comes from here," he continued, touching his heart, "and some people just don't have that instinct."

Ryan said nothing, staring back at the man, the arrogant owner of the dojo, the greedy trainer that sure didn't mind taking his gifts, and said nothing. Finally, after a long moment, he replied, "Thank you *Sensei*," bowed, spun and left. You never turn your back on a higher rank. But he did, nostrils flaring, and walked out the door.

He never returned.

Ryan owned two vehicles, a new Porsche 911 and a ten year old Ford half ton pickup. The Porsche usually stayed in the garage, which was fine with Ryan, the pickup was his favorite anyway. Although it was nothing to look at, with more than a few patches of body filler, Ryan had replaced the old engine with a new 7.4 liter V8 powerhouse, and the rest of the truck was mechanically perfect. He had resisted putting loud mufflers on it, preferring the low growl the dual stock mufflers produced. He drove the pickup tonight, as usual, and slid onto the torn, vinyl front bench seat, turned the key, and the huge engine snarled to life. It was dark, and as he pulled away from the curb in front of the dojo for the last time, the windshield wipers seemed to keep pace with Bachman Turner Overdrive's "You Ain't Seen Nothin' Yet."

Ryan headed towards the edge of town, to his farm in the country, changed his mind, and pulled into a gas station. He backed into an adjacent alley, and then pulled out into traffic. He decided to go back to his office, he was a little restless, and so guided his truck west on Canadian Avenue towards downtown, keeping pace with the other rain streaked vehicles. Ryan parked a couple of blocks from his office, indulging himself in a recurring, childish fantasy of expertly warding off would-be muggers, skillfully disarming the attackers. He would show Mr. Knowles what he was made of.

To his disappointment, and relief, the walk was uneventful, and Ryan turned the key in the lock of the huge, leaded glass entry door, and shoved it open with his knee. The door closed behind him, and he walked the short distance to his office, the motion-activated lights turning on in soldier-like succession.

The building was the latest in a string of successful ventures Ryan had developed in this his adopted town. He entered the outer office, and allowed himself a moment of quiet pride and gratitude. Life was good, he smiled, and he had earned every penny of it.

Ryan's office was behind the reception area, and accessible through a short hardwood spiral staircase with floor to ceiling aquariums on both sides, giving the impression to visitors of entering through the sea. It always got an appreciative comment. Ryan's desk was a huge, curved, walnut masterpiece that he had designed and built himself. The aquarium continued around behind Ryan's desk, and on to the far side of the large office. But that arrangement had proved too distracting, so Ryan designed matching walnut furniture in front of the curved glass to partially obscure the colorful, backlit sea life.

Ryan tossed his battered black leather jacket on the couch and walked the few short steps to his overstuffed black leather desk chair, and slowly lowered his lithe frame into his throne. The young, successful, businessman glanced at the photos of his first project, five fix up houses he had purchased with money he had earned working as a carpenter. He kept them sandwiched between the tooled leather desk top and the glass cover. He had done most of the work on the houses himself, often after a long day on his regular job, and on weekends, and had sold them at a nice profit. Next had been a small development by the river, and now this four story office building in the heart of downtown.

He worked long, hard hours to achieve all this, honest hours, but his kind of success still drew detractors, enemies.

Building permits had been delayed, and now the anonymous phone calls.

Ryan slowly pulled the large drawer on the left side of his mammoth desk open, reached inside and pulled a worn manila folder out. He gently, tenderly laid a yellowed newspaper clipping on his desk and read again about the Amish family that had lost their home to fire. It was a short article inside the second section of the *Philadelphia Inquirer*, one of several newspapers he subscribed to. There were no photos, just the story. After a moment, he returned the article to the folder, dropping it flat in the drawer, in its proper place next to the stacks of unopened letters all marked "Return to Sender." He picked up the rubber-banded bundle, tapped it several times with a calloused finger, and then returned those as well and closed the drawer.

Ryan glanced at his watch and felt his throat tighten. At exactly 9:38, his desk phone rang and the first of five buttons on the front of the phone lit up, just like it had done every night for the last two weeks. Answer it or let the answering machine get it? After several seconds, Ryan picked up the black handle and answered simply, "Ryan." And exactly as had happened every night for the last fourteen days, there was no response, only the faint sound of murmuring, country music in the background, an occasional hoarse laugh, and the unmistakable sound of breathing. At first, Ryan had shouted angrily into the phone, but now he simply laid it down on the desk and waited for the light to go out when the caller hung up. Ryan had thought about going to the police, but —"We don't call the police," his father always said. "They're for the English, not us."

It was warm in his opulent office, almost too warm, but he was shivering.

CHAPTER EIGHTEEN

Ryan slowly returned the black handle to its cradle on the desk phone, and sat motionless. Finally, he rose and turned out all the lights but the ones that illuminated the walk ways, and made his way to the front door. He slipped into his soft black leather jacket, put on his stingy-brim black leather hat and stepped out onto the sidewalk, the front door automatically closing and latching behind him. He was still a bit jittery from the call, and jumped at the cat that streaked past. Laughing nervously, he turned right towards the spot he had parked his truck, and stopped with a jolt, jumped back flat against the building.

His truck was now sandwiched in between two other cars: a black Mercedes in front and an equally black station wagon behind, so close their bumpers were jammed up against the truck. Even in the dim light of the street lamp behind the station wagon, he could see that both autos had dark tinted windows, and could just make out the four figures inside the station wagon. He glanced back at the Mercedes, and, yes, there were people in there too. Both car engines were idling, the exhaust creating a stream of white moist air that rose out of their tailpipes, up to the top of the light dome created by the street lamp and disappeared into the black sky. The parking lights, the outlines of the cars, and the exhaust smoke shimmered eerily off of the wet sidewalk. The headlights from an occasional passing vehicle cast dancing shadows off of the buildings, then pranced away in the opposite direction.

Ryan ducked into the alley between his building and the adjacent small park that office workers used for lunch and smoke breaks. Ryan carefully picked his way through the five sleeping bodies curled up near the steaming underground heat grate, like small beached whales. A rat indignantly scurried out of his way, squeaking its displeasure. He kept a cautious eye on the vehicles through the wrought iron fence that ran along the front of the park, next to the sidewalk.

He had good cover right up to the north end of the park, where he would have to slip out of its dark protection and cross the sidewalk at the brightest point, directly under the street light, behind the station wagon. When he reached that point, still in the dark, he paused for a minute, and then with a deep breath, walked quickly across and moved towards the front passenger side of the idling station wagon, reaching for the door handle. The instant he moved into the light, he heard commotion and shouting inside, and the car rocked gently. He had almost reached the car when the driver slammed the transmission into reverse, cutting the wheels to the right. In the panic to leave, the car jumped the curb and slammed into the light pole. He quickly shoved it back into drive, spun the front wheels to the left, and nearly hit Ryan as he fishtailed out of the parking spot, clipping the left rear bumper and fender of Ryan's truck. The Mercedes had already left in a rush of whining tires and roaring diesel engine, and then they were both gone.

Adrenaline-spiked blood pumping through his veins, for an instant Ryan thought about giving chase. But there was no way he was going to be able to catch them, and if he did, then what, he wondered. "Maybe you're afraid," he scolded. Chest heaving, fists clenched, he stared at the black hole at the end of the street, and then slowly turned around to make sure he was alone. Not a soul. He hadn't been able to make out the license plate in the dim light, but had noticed a D with a circle around it on the Mercedes, the kind he had seen on the trunks of other European cars.

His breathing slowly returned to normal, and he stood there, unable to make a decision. He took a quick look under his truck — he wasn't sure why. Seeing nothing unusual, he opened the door and slumped behind the steering wheel. His right hand shook, badly, taking three attempts to insert the ignition key. He glanced in the rear view mirror, caught a glimpse of the worry-lined face under his black hat. He turned the key, started the powerful engine and gunned it several times. Worried and angry, he popped the clutch, fishtailing away from the curb, head swiveling from right to left, keeping a sharp lookout for the two vehicles. He crisscrossed the downtown area for a few minutes, like a spider weaving a web, then pulled onto Canadian Avenue and headed west to the freeway that led out of town, still on the lookout.

"What the hell did *they* want?" he wondered aloud. "What's going on?"

Ryan drove slowly up to the elaborate stone and metal front entry gate to his horse farm. The twenty minute drive had calmed him considerably. He felt the tension leave his face, and began to wonder if he was overreacting. He always felt safer inside the compound, and climbed out of the idling truck and rolled the gate open on its long track. He drove through, parked the truck again, and slid the huge metal wrought iron gate closed. He normally did not lock it, but tonight, wrapped the galvanized chain around the metal post end of the gate and snapped the lock shut.

Ryan approached his house, and his two chocolate Labradors came bounding out to meet him, wagging as if he had been gone for a year. He parked the truck in the three-bay garage, next to the Porsche, and climbed out. He went up the short flight of wide, wooden steps to the house, suddenly weary, and across the creaking front porch.

Ryan fussed over the two Labradors for a minute, and then went inside, double-checked all the locks, took a quick shower and fell exhausted into bed. He tossed and turned all night, sleep fitful from the evening's ominous closing.

Ryan bolted awake. The stable hands' slamming truck doors coincided perfectly to the rapid gunfire of his latest dream, and he sat up with a start. Groggily, thick-tongued, stupidly, he slowly realized he had been dreaming and laid back down. He

109

slowly calmed, and felt the day seep into his body. He began playing back the last month's events, trying to make sense of them. He had always been logical, and was certain his wits would win again.

"Okay, Ez — Ryan, you can figure this out. Lassiter was plenty pissed when you bought that property out from under him, but he's not the kind to send goons after you. Is he? Naw. Karate? Hard fought competitions, sure, but that was just part of the game. He heard *Sensei* barking, 'This is just a game to you, and that's your problem!' And the training was specifically to *NOT* take it personal. The twins? They've always been trouble, but not this. Not malicious. And those boys in a Mercedes?" He laughed. "They've never been able to hang on to anything."

He hadn't seen the twins for years and doubted they even knew where he was. And yet, his gut told him they were involved, and his gut had been a very reliable sentry. Keep your eyes open, he told himself, and swung his legs over the side of the oversized bed onto the cold wooden floor. He had kept the creature comforts to a minimum in the house; cold wooden floors hitting warm feet helped him to focus in the mornings.

Ryan descended the wooden staircase inside the rear of the house, barefoot, and subconsciously glanced at the double lock on the rear door at the bottom of the stairs. Both deadbolts were still locked, and the chair back still jammed under the door knob. Ryan headed to the kitchen to make coffee and a quick bite to eat, floor creaking.

Ryan saw Karen pull up in her new black Mercedes, and caught his breath. It was identical to the one last night. She swung the car around the cobblestone turnaround in front of his house, and he could see there was no damage to the front right fender, and no "D" in a circle painted on the trunk. "You're getting paranoid, Ezra," he laughed self consciously.

Karen was a very good rider, very pretty, beautiful, actually, and way too friendly with this "handsome horse breeder," and he grimaced slightly. He quickly finished his toast, poured another cup of coffee, and stepped onto the front porch.

Karen was married to a very successful litigation attorney that Ryan knew only slightly from social functions. She had a nice gray Dutch Warmblood mare boarded at his farm, waiting to be bred to Reimer, his champion stallion, and her coarse description of the upcoming event always turned Ryan's neck and ears and cheeks scarlet. He was perfectly comfortable with the operations of a horse breeding, but one didn't openly *TALK* about the specifics, one went about one's tasks with clinical detachment, he mused.

Karen had another woman with her this morning, and as they approached, Ryan found himself staring at the new rider, out of character for him. The woman had a lightly starched snow-white blouse on under an open, black suede jacket, and the front buttons strained slightly to cover her full, supple form. She had the usual tight black riding pants on, with the leather seat sewn on the backside, and was wearing the knee-high, perfectly shined black *König* German boots favored by the upper crust riders. She had already put her black leather riding gloves on, it was a bit chilly, and she had the prettiest long wavy black hair Ryan could remember ever seeing, hair dancing hypnotically in the early morning sun. The women drew closer, and he saw that she wore a small silver cross on a dainty silver chain around her neck. Her olive complexion was perfect, he thought to himself, and she had small permanent laugh lines around her mouth. Her eyes were wide and inquisitive. She made a heart-stopping figure, and for a moment everything seemed to slow down for the gentleman farmer.

Karen didn't miss any of this, of course, and as the two of them approached Ryan, she said, "Ryan, this is my friend Theresa. We are going to ride Alexa if that's OK with you." Ryan extended his right hand, spilling a bit of coffee from the cup in his left hand and stammered, "Mad to gleet you," immediately feeling the color start creeping up his neck. Theresa smiled, dark brown eyes twinkling, took off her right riding glove, and as she extended her hand, softly said, "Mad to gleet you, too." The three horse people all laughed, some with and some at, and Ryan turned even redder. Karen effortlessly moved into the awkward silence that followed, talking too fast about her dogs and the excitement of her mare getting to finally "be a horse" with Ryan's stallion. When she finally turned towards the barn, still merrily talking away, Theresa caught Ryan's glance and rolled her eyes and shook her head slightly, bemused. Ryan smiled back, started to relax, and at the first chance he had, interrupted Karen's non-stop dialogue with a, "Sure, that would be fine if you want to ride her. Just be sure to ride where the stallion can't see."

"You studs are all alike", Karen smirked, and sashayed off with her friend Theresa, the lawyer's wife laughing loudly, her friend slowly shaking her head. Theresa walked with the casual, confident, straight walk of wealth and good manners.

Ryan stood for a minute, absently wiping the drying coffee from his left hand, eyes following the increasingly smaller images of the two women, unlikely friends, approaching the barn. "Smooth," he told himself. "You need to give seminars on how to make good first impressions." Ryan busied himself with something, anything that would prevent him running into the two women, at least for a little while. He let himself into the equipment building, and after checking and rechecking the oil and fluid levels in the two tractors, finally decided to return to the barn, to check on the riders. It was his place, after all.

On the other side of the barn, in the arena, Theresa was riding the mare. It was apparent she was a very accomplished rider. Her long black hair bobbed and streamed behind her, and Ryan noticed that the mare moved better than he had ever seen her move. Theresa was relaxed and confident, sitting straight, and the mare responded perfectly. He was so impressed that he forgot about his earlier performance and found himself walking out to take a closer look.

"Where did she learn to ride?" he asked. Karen didn't look away from her mare and friend and said, "I don't know. I haven't known her very long and she only said she had been riding for a couple of years." Karen was uncharacteristically subdued, her acknowledgement of her new friend's skill. "I need to ask some more questions."

When Theresa was finished riding, she brought the mare over to where they were standing, dismounted effortlessly, and matter-of-factly said, "She's a nice horse." Ryan took the reins and Karen blurted, "OK, let's have it. You have been riding more than a 'couple of years.' Where did you train?" Theresa smiled slightly and said, "I was fortunate enough to ride with the German Olympic hopefuls for two summers. My father had some business in Europe and sent me there." The Germans are world renowned for their horsemanship, and usually take top honors in international competitions.

"Well that explains that," her friend commented. "The only other person I've seen ride like that is Ryan."

Theresa insisted on removing the saddle and bridle herself, rinsed off the mare with warm water, and only reluctantly allowed the stable hands to clean the tack and put it up.

"What are you doing?" Karen asked. Karen had casually handed off her steaming mount to the closest hand.

"Every good horse person should take complete care of their horse," Theresa replied.

The two women hung around for a couple more hours, and finally left without saying goodbye to Ryan.

"You gonna look him up?" Karen asked.

Theresa smiled at her new friend. "Maybe. Why?"

"You seemed more than casually interested in his breeding program, and I thought —"

"You know, Karen, this crass —"

"Oh, well, excuse meeee, Miss Never-Been-Touched-In-Her-Life. I'm the queen of flirt — I know what they all say — but you almost ran into that big Maple tree in Ryan's front yard, your eyes were so busy. Okay, okay, I'll tone it down. It's just —" her tone softened — "I haven't seen Ryan look back at a woman in years. What a catch he would be. You gonna pretend you're not interested?"

"Karen, would you mind keeping your mind on driving? I don't care to have a car in my lap. Didn't you see that parked car back there?" She stared out the side window for a little, then, "Yeah, okay, he's attractive. It's been a while for me, too."

Ryan liked Saturdays. He could handle any city business with a phone call, if it needed attention at all. As soon as the two horse women disappeared down the drive, Ryan turned to the barn and spent the rest of the day checking breeding schedules, counting the supplies, fussing over the details, relaxing on his farm. The tree shadows lengthened, beginning their glacial creep across the pasture. The stable hands and trainer slipped away, this was just a job, and they had families. Ryan swept up the last of the loose hay in the barn aisle, and finally walked out the front barn door towards the house, tired and looking forward to a quiet evening and good night's sleep. He trudged slowly up the front steps to the porch, and slowly lowered his tired frame onto the swing's worn oak slats, the two dogs tussling for his affection, knocking the swing into a swaying, rotating motion. Smiling slightly, Ryan said, "Jeb, Ned, go lie down," and the two Labradors obediently went to their respective blankets.

The county road that bordered his farm on the far southern side was still visible, dimly, and the tired horseman disinterestedly watched slow cars drive past every few minutes. People often stopped and watched the horses from the road, and the traffic tonight was particularly light.

The late afternoon light continued to fade, and at first he didn't pay any attention to the car that had stopped, someone obviously looking at the horses, until he noticed that it appeared to be the same make as the Mercedes parked in front of his truck last night. Both dogs sensed his increasing alertness. When he rose to go in and get the powerful field glasses he kept inside the front door, they both rose to a sitting position, whining slightly, not sure if they were permitted to leave their blankets. By the

114

time Ryan stepped back outside, they were both up and looking as intently as their master at whatever it was that got his attention. Ryan scanned the road, much closer through the Nikon's, but the black car was gone. Twilight had taken over, and Ryan stood quietly for a minute before going inside, absently scratching Jeb's ears.

Ryan was putting the last of the hand washed dishes up when the wall phone rang. He glanced at the clock, a little after nine, and muttered, "You're early tonight you SOB." He grabbed the white phone from its hook, the handset slipped out of his wet hand, the headset bobbing up and down on the straining cord, like slow motion fishing. He finally placed the uncooperative phone to his ear and mouth and growled, "I know who you are." He heard Karen's raucous laugh on the other end, "I bet you wish you knew me, don't you, you hunk?" Great, more Karen, he thought to himself. "Karen, sorry about that, I thought it was someone else." She laughed again, and immediately started her incessant chatter. She was tiresome enough during the day when she was sober, Ryan thought, but she had obviously been drinking and was even coarser than usual.

"I could *NOT* get that woman to shut up," she slurred into the phone.

"What woman?"

"'What woman'," she mimicked. "That pretty Italian with me this morning, you idiot. I have never heard anyone go on about you like that, 'What gorgeous blue eyes, what a wonderful farm, what delightful dogs.' I'm surprised she didn't start talking about those tight black Levis you always wear!"

Ryan recognized good manners, nowhere to be found in this conversation, and somehow knew Theresa had said little of all this, and certainly wouldn't have implied anything sexual. He wanted nothing so much as to end this embarrassing call.

"Hey, Karen, How's your husband doing? I haven't talked to him since he took on that big construction case."

Karen was not to be deterred, rambling on and on about how taken her Italian friend had been, Ryan increasingly embarrassed. Part way through her latest diatribe, Ryan heard the familiar "beep, beep" signaling another call.

"Hang on a sec, I've got another call," he told her, relieved, and pressed the button in the middle of the headset, then released it. Karen had completely distracted him with her talk of Theresa, and he had briefly forgotten about these nightly phone calls.

"Hello," he said into the phone. Nothing. Damn, he thought, here we go again. "Hello," he repeated, enough off balance from the lack of sleep and distraction of Karen's talk that he wasn't thinking as clearly as usual. "We're coming to get you, Country," a muffled voice said, and there was that hoarse laugh in the background.

Ryan froze, ten thousand volts coursing through his rigid body. No one had called him Country since — when? Grade school? All the old memories came flooding back of the derision, abuse, torment of his childhood. Could he never escape his past? Who *was* this? Why were they harassing him? Something was very familiar about the voice and the laughter, but he couldn't quite put his finger on who or what or where. Ryan slammed the phone back in its wall hung cradle, completely forgetting about his sodden friend on the other line.

He stood there for a minute, trying to regain his composure, not succeeding. A flood of horrible and mixed memories and emotions flooded his brain, old Scripture verse mixed with real estate jargon mixed with horse talk.

"You're going to Hell, Ezra," the little voice in his head shouted at him.

CHAPTER NINETEEN

The sweet melody of Beethoven's *Pathetique* filled the well appointed townhome Theresa owned in downtown Toronto. She had been playing her baby grand for over an hour and it was getting late. She leaned back on the shiny black piano bench listening to the last notes echo softly off of the pale lavender-shaded walls and mostly bare oak floors, covered here and there with fine Persian rugs. The melody from the vibrating strings gradually faded to nothing, her slightly heavy breathing the only remaining sound. The scented candles she always burned filled the room with their magic aroma, and at times it seemed as if the flickering flames danced in tempo to the music. She rose from her seat and slowly looked around, dainty nose deeply inhaling the faint cinnamon candle scent.

The lavish loft was solid, airtight, with the only outside noise the occasional passing of a car from the street, a muffled *swoosh*. The Italian beauty smiled in satisfaction. There had been some kind of incident on the street last night in front of the small park that her townhome overlooked. She thought she had heard a small crash, but when she looked out the only thing visible was a man wearing a hat getting into an older truck.

She pulled the drapes, smiled at her paranoia, and poured another glass of wine.

The loft was in a trendy area of town, and the only problem she had, besides that awful park, was the four story office building that had been built diagonal to her building, across the intersection. It blocked the admittedly peak-a-boo view of Lake Superior from her fifth story balcony. She knew the owner only by reputation, an odd fellow from the States she was told.

Theresa glanced at her Rolex. "After midnight again," she admonished herself. It had been an interesting day, she smiled to herself. She knew her mouth was in high gear on the ride back into town with Karen, but there was something about Ryan that had excited her. She couldn't remember feeling that giddy since high school.

Tomorrow was going to be a busy day, getting ready to leave for Philly for another week. She always pampered her pets, and when her gelding came up lame, she sent the horse to a renowned research facility near Philadelphia that specialized in that type of injury. The gelding seemed to be responding to the treatment program without her, but she felt this need to be there, to help.

Karen said Ryan's farm also did rehab, and she made a mental note to inquire into that. The prospect of seeing Ryan on a daily basis was exciting, and she knew herself well enough to know she would pursue that. Karen had also told her that Ryan had entered a horse in the upcoming Devon horse show just outside of Philadelphia, and had given her a program with the location of his barn circled in red.

She drifted off to sleep, smile lines lapping against full lips, like ripples on a peaceful pond.

Theresa lay in her soft king-sized bed the next morning far longer than she should have, hugging the blond headed pillow, lazily enjoying the soft melody of a Mozart piece softly playing on her music alarm. She drowsily glanced at the clock, and with a loud "Holy crap!" sat straight up and bolted from her bed. She glanced at her naked, finely toned body in the floor mirror in the corner of the massive bedroom. With a satisfied half smile, she glided across the overlapping Persian rugs into the master bath, and danced the cold-foot jig on the marble floor, hopping onto the small rug in front of her vanity.

Theresa picked up her makeup, glanced again at her watch, and then put it back down. She turned her head from side to side, mildly satisfied at the dark-eyed complexion and eyebrows that provided the luxury of either wearing makeup or not. After her morning ritual in front of the bathroom mirror, she went into the carpeted walk-in closet and began pulling outfits off of their hangers, tossing them into the leather luggage for the trip. The long closet was lined with Ralph Laurens and Pradas, mostly some combination of black and white that she had been told accentuated her complexion and hair color.

When she had everything out by the elevator that opened directly into her foyer she buzzed down for Frank, the doorman.

"Frank, this is Theresa," she said into the intercom. "Would you mind calling a cab for the airport and let me know when it arrives?"

"Yes, ma'am, right away," the wall speaker answered.

Late, as usual, the dark-haired young trust-fund-baby hurried through Toronto International Airport, oblivious to the glances and outright stares she always drew from the male travelers. She checked her one huge piece of luggage, over-tipping the attendant, and craned her neck to see how long the ticket lines were. She was on the 10:27 flight into Philadelphia International, and the lines were mercifully short. She arrived at the gate in plenty of time, for her "Seven minutes to spare this morning, ma'am," the middle-aged, balding, short gate attendant said evenly, neither friendly nor unfriendly. She rode first class, and slid into the plush leather of her favorite seat, 2A, her choice when available. The obnoxious, overly friendly businessman she sat next to on her last trip was not on the flight this morning, she noted with relief. The man next to her was preoccupied with putting the finishing touches on a presentation, cutting and pasting colored strips, brow furrowed. Fifteen minutes into the flight, the red "No Smoking" sign went blank, and cigarette smoke soon wafted up from the back of the plane.

The ride into Philly was uneventful, and the jet touched down at 2:55, slightly ahead of schedule. The trek through customs was short, too, and she was soon on her way to the apartment in her rented Continental, eagerly anticipating the visit to see her horse, see how he was coming along. She pulled into the covered semi-circle unloading area in front of the apartment building, and pulled up behind a new Jaguar. The young doorman

119

she particularly liked came hurrying over to help with the bulky, heavy leather suitcase.

"Good to see you again, ma'am."

"You too."

"You here for the show?"

"You bet."

The young man put her heavy luggage on a dolly and followed her into the elevator. She was soon comfortably settled into her third floor apartment, a nice place to stay while in Philadelphia, she smiled. Every time she visited, she ended up leaving more and more items in the apartment, and absently thought about how much of a hassle it was going to be when it came time to move all that stuff back to Toronto.

The front page of the *Philadelphia Inquirer* was dominated with coverage of the ongoing Devon horse show, one of the oldest, most prestigious shows in the country. The article took pains to point that out. competitions ranged from ancient carriage pulls to hunter/jumper. Theresa had eagerly anticipated this particular trip to Philadelphia, because of the show — and now Ryan. She planned to see as many of the events as possible, particularly the dressage competition. She began the task of neatly organizing her wardrobe, smiling and humming.

CHAPTER TWENTY

Sleep didn't come easy for Ryan again that night. He heard a thousand sinister noises, floors creaking, wind moaning in the tree branches, and drifted in and out of fitful, non-restive semi-sleep. His eyes opened for good as the first hint of early morning gray nudged the dark out of the eastern sky. Exhausted, Ryan lay there for several long minutes, trying without much success to make sense out of this unknown intrusion into his ordered life.

"Maybe you're making too much of these phone calls. No one has been hurt, no shots have been fired, nothing's been broken. So you got a few anonymous phone calls, big deal. *Country?* You live in the country, maybe the guys at the office are yanking your chain. Not my idea of fun, but those guys can be jerks. So how do you explain the scene in front of the office building, you naïve fool?" That one stumped him. "Coincidence? Not likely." Fully awake, Ryan's mind re-entered the tight circle of non-productive thought that had yielded nothing useful yet.

Alternately angry then confused then worried, he finally drawled, "Well, Country, maybe you had better get your lazy ass out of bed and do something useful. Something *is* going on, but laying here worrying about it isn't going to solve anything." The horseman had developed this habit of talking to himself from years of living alone, and it seemed to give him some comfort. "Tomorrow is the big day and you need to at least show up."

Ryan climbed out of bed, twisted his stereo knob on, and the strains of Donna Fargo's "The Happiest Girl in the Whole USA" filled his bedroom. For an instant, he saw Theresa on stage, microphone gripped in her dainty right hand, singing to him, smiling.

Ryan wasn't much of a traveler, and had booked a flight on a new regional discount airline, which was at least $35 cheaper than the big carriers. It was a no-frills way to fly, no doubt, but he preferred to spend money on tangible things, like cars. His secretary had tried to convince him to "fly in a little bit of luxury," but he had retorted, "I get there at the same time whether I spend the money for a high priced first class ticket or ride coach, so what's the difference?" So he road coach. Ryan grabbed his black leather bag, bulging with enough clothes and toiletries for a week. He patted the two Labs goodbye, sleep-stumbled down the steps, and headed for the airport.

It had been a long time since he had been to that American city, and he couldn't shake the feeling that there was no brotherly love waiting for him in Philadelphia.

CHAPTER TWENTY-ONE

Pennsylvania 1958

Samuel and Rachael looked eagerly forward to having their first child, and after several years of uncertainty, were delighted when the young bride was finally "with child." The pregnancy was extremely difficult, dangerous. Toward the end of an interminable nine months, eighteen year old Rachael was confined to bed. The doctor had sewn her shut, closed the end of the dark, wet passage to this world to prevent an early, probably fatal escape by the child. Labor was even more difficult, and then, after almost a day and a half of agonized labor, Emma emerged, howling her outrage, bringing a relieved half-smile to the exhausted midwife's creased face.

The old midwife stitched Rachael back up as best she could, but the result looked like something Frankenstein would have rejected. It was several days before one of the English neighbors could take Rachael to the hospital, but by then the awkward healing had begun and had to be redone. When the surgery was finally over, the doctor shook his head as he was leaving the operating room, and, uncharacteristically for him, scolded Samuel severely for not bringing his wife to the hospital when they first realized they were having problems during delivery.

Rachael recovered, more or less, in time, and basked in the attention she received from her husband and the community, and doted on the wiggly pink bundle, her daughter. In spite of the problems she had with delivery, she was satisfied and grateful. This was what life was all about, she remembered thinking: living God's will, raising a good Christian family, being part of a tight-knit, supportive community.

Samuel grew up on this same farm where they now lived, and when he married Rachael and joined the church, his father gave him these twenty acres on the back corner of the larger property. His father knew he liked this spot, wooded land with a pond out front and views across the farm overlooking the original homestead in the distance. Samuel often came out here as a young man to spend quiet, spiritual time, studying God's word and reflecting on the joys of living this simple, productive, satisfying life.

When Samuel and Rachael began courting, he often brought her out here in the open wagon behind two draft horses. They spent hours just talking, planning, hoping that it would be God's will for them to end up together. And maybe, just maybe, build a home and raise a family here in God's country. They dreamt and planned, placing round river-bottom rocks where the corners of the house would go, and lined the front walk with even more rocks. They often held hands, lost in the moment, but it never went beyond hand holding, not even a kiss. The Elders from both of their communities agreed that joining the church and being baptized had to be an informed, conscious choice, and to choose, one had to know the alternative. So both teenagers knew it was their choice to attend *Rumspringa*, go wild, sow their wild oats, live their life like the English, see what the rest of the world was like, to make this conscious choice, but they chose not to. It frankly never occurred to them to even consider it; why would any sane person do that, they wondered? They seldom even talked about the wild parties, but when it did come up, they agreed it was foolish, dangerous, and neither one had any desire to ruin a perfect life.

Years later they often reminisced about the house building party Samuel's father had arranged, and the memory of Amish neighbors swarming over the property. They built the house, the barn, the paddocks, the gravel drive; it was one of their fondest memories. Rachael had commented once it was too bad they didn't have any photos, and Samuel reminded her that the community forbade graven images. Besides, he almost scolded, here it is, look at it. Why did they need photos? Rachael wanted to say to send to family in other states, but Samuel was the head of the house, and she thought the comment would be out of line, disrespectful, so said nothing.

There could be no photo album, but the Elders said nothing about keeping a written account of their precious daughter's childhood, so Rachael wrote something in a large, black-cardboard covered journal every night. The writing was a strange mix of old German and English, mainly misspelled words with terrible grammar and out of place punctuation, and illustrated with drawings, lots of drawings. Each night, at bed time, her father put his daughter on his back, her legs dangling on either side of his arms. She held on to his neck, almost too tightly, sometimes grabbing his long beard, and together they took the precious book upstairs to her bed. After the stories about Jesus and right before the nightly prayer, he went over the story of her life, looking at the pictures her mother had drawn, and she squealed with delight.

And then her father kissed her on her forehead, telling her he loved her, and just stood there for a little, looking down at his princess pretending to be asleep. She was almost lost in the big bed, with its wrought iron headboard and matching footboard, the handmade quilt tucked under her sides the way she liked it. He turned slowly, not wanting to leave, socks almost silent on the polished wood floor, and as he reached the door, she always softly said, "I love you, Papa."

Rachael was raised on another large farm just across the county line, and there had always been good-natured chiding about which county was better. She knew Samuel since — well, forever, and remembered their two fathers joking about "your county" this, "my county" that, always ending up in roaring laughter and back slapping. There were a few religious differences between their communities, but nothing big. Rachael's Elders had

125

approved the use of telephones, provided they were in phone booths by the road, the phone company happy to oblige, Samuel's Elders did not. Her Elders said it was okay to use modern machinery, provided you pulled it to the field with horses, and it wasn't self propelled. The result was no doubt hysterical to the constant stream of English people driving by, craning their necks, trying to get a better look at these odd country people.

The Elders in Samuel's community tended to be more conservative, although they approved electrical generators for shop and farm equipment. Electricity was fine, they said, as long as it wasn't part of the government's power grid.

Samuel's father installed a huge diesel electric generator out back. It had two large batteries for starting the reluctant machine, next to the sawdust collection system. Two 250 gallon gravity flow fuel tanks stood on their tall metal legs, one on either side of the generator, one gasoline, for the lawn mowers and washing machine, one diesel for the generator. Sometimes the local fuel supply company would miss his farm, and it was easier to just take several five gallon containers with him to the grocery store. He was oblivious, or at least ignored, the open mouthed stares of the visiting city folks. To him, it was perfectly natural to fill the five gallon tanks at the gas pumps outside the store and put the now full cans in the back floor of the horse drawn buggy, head for home.

Samuel's father had one of the finest shops in the area, equipped with the latest woodworking machinery. His father didn't understand much about electricity, but had a cousin, no longer Amish, that worked as an electrician, and wired the entire shop to run off of the diesel powered generator. His father had a 12" table saw with twelve different kinds of blades, from big-toothed blades for ripping to fine-toothed ones for panel sawing, and dado blades for rabbiting. He had a five horsepower shaper, a powerful machine, with a hundred different carbide bits for making moldings. A powered electric lift moved the lumber down from the second floor storage area when he needed it. His father even had a belt driven sander, twelve inches wide and ten feet long. No one knew of another one like it, even in the commercial cabinet shops.

The shop was in constant use, both for the furniture and cabinetry he made for sale to the outside world, and the constant barn raising and home building within the community.

Wealth was a way of life. There were no TV's or stereos to buy, no fancy cars, no utility bills, the houses were always paid for, so there was always plenty of money from the crops, the furniture, the occasional outside job. Money was a tool, like a scythe or a scoop shovel, and if you took care of it, like any other tool, it was always there, ready to be used.

But true wealth was in the heart, they all knew, living God's will, raising God-fearing families, and Samuel was wealthy there, too. Every action of every day, every thought of every day, regardless what tool he was using, supported and added to the ultimate goal; defeating the Devil and spending eternity in heaven. This time on earth was short, Samuel knew, and he was totally dedicated to living it in a manner that assured that he and his family would be together forever.

Emma was a delightful child, beautiful by any standard, with dark, curly hair, and long dark eyelashes shading exotic, liquid brown eyes. Early on, she had learned that if she acted surprised and said, "Oooh, oooh", while pointing at some new thing, it brought smiles to her parents' faces and hugs to her. Even as a very young child, she always wanted to help her mother: take the finished cornbread out of the oven, carry dirty clothes to the basement, sweep the floor. She learned quickly what "hot" meant, taking the usual parental instructions or admonitions happily, eagerly. She always wanted to help her mother mix the ingredients, both of them giggling at spilled flour and dropped eggs. She loved the miniature apron her mother made for her, and stood on the three legged oak stool her "Papa" had made for her in her "Grandpapa's" huge shop. She especially liked cleaning up the bowls and spatulas and egg beaters right after the latest baked good was carefully slipped into the oven, batter all over her smiling face.

She often heard "Cleanliness is next to Godliness," and while she didn't really understand what it meant, her mother was always scrubbing, sweeping, washing. Emma loved the smell of sun-baked clothing as it came off of the clothesline, and would bury her face in the basket, inhaling deeply. The kerosene lamps were replaced with scented oil lamps, and the symphonic smells of fresh baked bread, scented oil and the drying herbs hanging from the ceiling racks were a delight to all that entered.

Rachael never complained about the work, always willingly carrying the large loads of laundry to the basement, hand scrubbing against the washboard. But things were especially happy around the house the day Rachael's father brought a new, gasoline-engine-powered washer, the "Automatic" to his daughter.

Samuel helped Rachael's father carry the new machine down the outside stairs, under the double doors that lay flat, covering the storm entrance to the cellar. They carefully ran the metal, flexible exhaust pipe to the east side of the house, where prevailing winds would usually carry the exhaust away from the garden and clothesline. "Watch the wind, son," her father said, "and be sure to check the connections on this exhaust every week. The fumes can kill you." Samuel knew all this, of course, but never minded hearing what his father-in-law had to say.

Emma loved to wear her bonnet, and would delight at changing her little dresses several times a day. First the blue one, then the purple one, then the green one, all a well washed out version of color, and her mother indulged her. She even learned how to handle the straight pins that held her dress together, and never questioned *why* straight pins and not buttons or zippers, like she had seen on the other girls' dresses in town.

Samuel and Rebecca long ago decided that Emma would attend the church school, not the public one. They weren't being overprotective, they agreed, it was for her benefit. No point in exposing her to the ugliness of the world. Besides, she excelled in the education that mattered, learning how to be a good wife, how to look after her future husband, and above all, how to love her Lord Jesus Christ. So let's get this education out of the way, they said, unnecessary, but required to keep peace with the English. She can attend the church school, but always come straight home. And Emma didn't mind.

She heard so many stories about the English world that frankly she was a little apprehensive about it anyway. She studied just hard enough to move to the next section, agreeing with her parents that formal education was of little use, and could be dangerous, preferring to come straight home after class. She flew in the front door, untied bonnet strings almost straight out behind her, wooden screen door slamming behind her, and with a rushed, "Sorry Mama," she raced upstairs, tossed the books on the bed and as quickly ran back down.

"Mama may I go feed the goats?" she asked as she tore back through the kitchen, and rushed out the back door without waiting for the inevitable "Sure." The goats were a recent addition to the farm, and Samuel was experimenting with goats' milk and cheese. At first she turned up her nose at this new, pungent provision, but came to like it, and loved the goats like the brothers and sisters she didn't have. She asked her father one night why she didn't have any sisters, and her father solemnly told her that they would love for her to have sisters, and brothers, but it appeared not to be God's will. He didn't tell her about the trip to the doctor, fifteen miles both ways in horse drawn buggy on the dangerous highway, and the silent, totally silent, trip back, nothing really to say. The doctor told them there wouldn't be any more children, that the scarring had permanently damaged the uterus lining. They didn't understand some of the medical words, but understood perfectly the part about no more children.

Samuel was ashamed at his reaction, blaming his wife. God had said to go forth and multiply, and now this suddenly strange woman bouncing along beside him couldn't. She was deficient. Rebecca tried to hold her grief back, failed, and hot tears spilled down her cheeks, unknown to her husband, grimly gripping the reins and staring straight ahead, cold, detached. "Where is your faith?" she silently asked Samuel. Either we believe in God's plan or we don't.

And so the schism began.

CHAPTER TWENTY-TWO

Pennsylvania 1974

"I don't know why you're being so stubborn," Ezekiel scowled at Emma, straddling his bike, his left foot on the ground and looking over his shoulder at the sixteen year old Amish girl. She had also stopped. They had ridden their bikes down to Mike's Store at the corner of CR172 and the US highway, and were returning, saddle bags now full. "I just don't want to, Zeke," she pouted. "Those kids just get crazy and drunk and stoned and I just don't want to."

The annual *Rumspringa* was planned for the fall, and teenagers from several states were eagerly anticipating this annual ritual, this "running around" period in their lives intended to show them the outside world, let them make a choice about joining the church or leaving. It was a risky practice, the Elders knew, with underage drinking and drug use. The local law enforcement generally took a hands-off policy, preferring to let these strange people police themselves. A flawed policy.

"Mother, Zeke wants me to go to the Miller farm in September." She tried to get her mother to open up, to express an opinion, to no avail. "You know the church says you can't join until you know the choices," her mother replied, "and we can't tell you whether to go or not. That has to be your decision."

Emma poured a tall glass of iced tea, adding ice from the fancy, propane powered refrigerator/icemaker, and went outside, carefully closing the screen door behind her, looking for her father. Emma and her father were very close, best friends, maybe he would tell her what to do.

"Hey, Papa, how's it going?" she asked. Samuel was behind the barn, splitting wood for the coming winter, his usual Saturday morning activity. He stopped to rest and carefully set the double-bladed ax next to the splitting stump, took his straw hat off and wiped the glisten from his forehead with his blue, sweat streaked shirtsleeve.

"It's going good, Em, going good. I think the woods will last two more winters, but I need to get back over to Lehman's and look at that oil furnace again. How is that bike holding up?"

Samuel had fastened clear plastic runners on Emma's bike to keep her billowing skirt from tangling in the chain. "It works fine, Papa. I can do the pirouette now, have you seen me do it?" Emma was a magician on her bike, to her parents' worry, but they seldom said anything.

"I have seen, yes."

"Mama says I should go to *Rumspringa* this fall," she started.

Father and daughter liked to tease each other, but this was not one of those moments. "You know the church says you can't join until you know the choices —"

"I know perfectly well what the church says. I don't want to go but Zeke wants me to go, all my friends want me to go, you want me to go, Mama wants me to go, I guess I'll just go then."

Samuel wanted desperately to tell his baby girl not to go, *please don't go*, but bit his lip. "The choice has to be yours," he said quietly.

The Elders said over and over that the church has no jurisdiction until a soul makes a formal declaration of its faith and joins the brethren. Then, only then, does the church have the right to guide, to control, to keep them on the straight and narrow, defeating the Devil, that raging, all consuming beast, so they can all spend eternity together in the presence of God Almighty. Only an adult, "Not a child, you have to be sixteen," can declare his or her faith. Samuel hadn't needed to go wild to know he wanted to join, to stay with his friends and family, but it had been his decision, no one had counseled him to stay away. In that grand tradition of non-direction, he was also silent now, and would not try to sway his daughter.

"Did you go to *Rumspringa*, Papa?" She knew the answer but wanted to hear it again.

"You know I didn't, Em, but that was me, this is you. How can you make the choices you need to make if you always wonder what it's like out there?" This was all about choice, free will.

"But I don't want to know, I have already made up my mind!" Her voice was pinched, slightly higher.

"Emma, we have had this discussion many times —" Samuel's voice also began to show the signs of strain, she dared not sass, and the muscles in his temple began to pulse as he tightened and relaxed his jaw muscles. The girl was getting dangerously close to disrespect. "If you have made up your mind, so be it, but don't be a-coming out here asking me to be for making this decision for you."

By now Emma's face was bright red. She wasn't used to her father scolding her, and shouted "Fine! Great! Good! I'll go, get drunk, get stoned, smoke cigarettes, get pregnant, then will you be happy?"

Samuel completely lost his patience and ordered her, commanded her, to go up to her room, now. The sixteen year old girl, his baby girl, the one that had brought so much joy to this household, spun on her new white sneakers and stomped off towards the front porch, stormed inside, deliberately slammed the screen door, noisily climbed the stairs, and kicked her bedroom door shut.

CHAPTER TWENTY-THREE

Preparations for the fall event were massive. The organizers, which included one of the Elders, although he would not attend, decided to pay for a live band this year. That meant a generator, bigger than last year's which only had to run the lights, and after a lot of deliberation they decided to rent one rather than borrow one from one of the church members. Sometimes these parties lasted into the wee hours of the following morning, and no one felt like they could be without their generator for that long.

The Miller farm was the choice for this year's *Rumspringa* again; it had worked well last year. Teenage neighbor told teenage neighbor, and word of the eagerly anticipated affair spread like an out-of-control prairie fire. There would be over two hundred revelers this year, and everyone agreed it would be the best ever. The church members seldom talked about it, and when they did the talk ranged from a bit of residual envy to "Why did I ever do that" remorse.

Once Emma decided to go, she threw herself into the preparations whole-heartedly. Zeke was smugly ecstatic, hell, he had scarcely stolen a kiss from this lush peach, and his well rehearsed fantasies spun out of control. He had already had her a hundred times, in his mind, spending way too much time in the bathroom or in the barn, by himself. He was careful to not be overly eager; he knew she could turn on a dime, this mercurial maiden, instant reversal, and so he was the picture of patient support.

"I know what you're thinking," she often said, and he would reply in total sincerity, "Not at all, Em, not at all." This young girl, who had never even had any of the fermented cider that the kids snuck, would be his, all right, he just had to be patient. He had pushed for more than a kiss on a couple of occasions, but her immediate rebuff made it clear that wasn't going to happen. And so he was patient. And schemed. And would have told her anything, lungs and vocal chords directed by hot hormones. Thirty days was not long to wait. His mouth went dry at the thought of slowly removing that vanity cloth on the front of her dress that failed miserably to hide her growing breasts, and running his hands all over her young body. Maybe he would rip it off, but those blasted straight pins were a problem. Slowly, that would be best. Very slowly. Try as he might to return to the task at hand, his seventeen year old instincts had other ideas, and he would have to excuse himself to hide the obvious, returning after a couple of minutes, face slightly red from the cold water, and was able to sit again.

He busied himself with his agreed-upon tasks for the party: go to town in the open wagon Friday morning, get the generator, make sure the five gallon fuel tanks were all filled with diesel, check the engine oil, make sure there was plenty of extra oil, test run it, take it out to the farm, carefully roll it down the wagon ramps onto the specially prepared gravel area, and run the electrical cords to the band area and the lights. There was a lot of discussion about the lights, were they really necessary, the boys against them, the girls for them, and finally they decided to have them, but made sure there was plenty of dark area as well. The band came out right after noon to set up under the tent, and the lights were all tested at the same time. He asked the rental yard if the generator was powerful enough, and the guy had smirked and said, "I thought you people liked the dark." Zeke had been on the verge of a retort, caught himself, paid in cash and left.

The ride back was uneventful enough, and despite the insistence of the bay gelding to turn right, back to its barn, Zeke insisted the horse and wagon turn left, down the road to the Miller farm. The main event was still two days off, but there were already a number of buggies parked in an area a quarter mile from the party site, some horses tied to hitching rails, some ground tied. The horses didn't like the loud noise, the bright lights, and were confused and unhappy with the break in their routine. Bad enough to bring them out here late at night, but there was no point tying them too close to the din; there would be some out of control rides as it was. The boys drew straws to see who would do equine duty, tending the animals, making sure they had hay and water. They were always disappointed when their short straw came up, always trying to bribe a younger boy to take their spot, always failing. These affairs usually lasted all night and the country farmers took care of their animals, especially the horses, so they made them as comfortable as possible.

Zeke drove through the parking area, the area that would team with activity a couple short days from now, and pulled back on the long reins, one hundred yards from the stage. The bay gelding obediently slowed to a stop, and after setting the buggy's hand brake, Zeke stepped down, a study in casual cool. He said "Hi" to James, "Haven't seen you in a while," and to Mark, "Good to see you again," a nod to another young Amish fellow he had seen around but couldn't remember his name. His face was flushed with the excitement of this big event, and try as he might to be calm and mature, his sentences came out fast and choppy. Most of the boys had dropped the traditional clothing and donned jeans and T-Shirts. Baseball caps replaced straw hats, work boots were shoved into the trunks of the buggies and new black leather shoes shuffled across dirt and gravel.

The band manager was there, a little impatient at the incompetence of these folks, and took charge. "You, there," he shouted at Zeke, "get that generator off of that wagon and let's get this show on the road. Why can't you have electricity like normal people?" he muttered, not waiting for an answer. Zeke and a couple of friends carefully guided the generator down the ramps, struggling with the huge, heavy piece of machinery until it was in place. One of the older boys from a neighboring, more liberal Amish community worked as an electrician, and took control of the various heavy cords to the stage and floodlights. The generator started with no problem, cold-diesel-knocking soon settling into the chest-thumping-rhythm of the machine as it warmed to its task. The band manager was soon satisfied his equipment worked. Amplified base echoed off of the surrounding hills, louder than the generator. The manager left in a cloud of dust, his high powered Plymouth Duster bouncing over the wagon wheel ruts, alarming horses on either side, squealed onto the paved road and disappeared into the night.

Night was approaching, and the boys lingered. Some refreshments had shown up early, out from under buggy seats, and the experienced revelers of years past suddenly had a lot of new friends crowding around. Zeke had heard the stories, but had never seen a bong or cigarettes rolled by hand. He thought he knew what kind of green tobacco was in the clear plastic baggies, but he wasn't sure. The veterans knew from experience that it was best to ease into this world, and so they used the old, weak weed for the "newbie" joints, saving the best, more potent stuff for themselves, later. "Let's wait 'til the juveniles are safely home and tucked into bed," they snickered.

Friday was the kind of day that fall legends are made of: trees in their resplendent fall colors, crimson reds, shining golds, leaves flitting downward through crisp air, swirling behind urgent hooves and spinning buggy wheels. The horses snorted blasts of steam into the early evening cold air, keeping time with their pounding hooves. Drivers' cheeks were rouge with no effort. It was an amazing site. Mostly bay horses pulled almost identical buggies, some two-seaters, some four-seaters, all rushing to this legendary look at the Devil's playground. This methodical madness was intended to scare Hell out of young Amish teenagers, children really, adults by definition only, bring them back into the fold. Hundreds of them, from all directions, merged seamlessly at the entrance to their Woodstock, a steady stream, like molten black lava pouring into the huge field. The band had already started, and the nervous horses were causing problems, used to a steady hand, not the distracted, jerky hands of tonight. They reared, kicked, screamed, and their inattentive drivers were forced to come back to the present, talk them back under control, soothing words, drowned by the piercing lyrics to Jimmy Hendrix' "Foxy Lady."

For the most part, the boys all looked like the English boys over the hills, closer to town, but the girls were still dressed in their pinned-up pastel dresses and bonnets, and shawls wrapped around shoulders against the cold. It was almost too cold, the boys agreed. They all had only one thing on their minds. This was their first shot at the up-til-now forbidden booty, that precious commodity, the "only thing." But first they had to party, had to drink, had to act cool, smoke like it was no big deal, get high. The nervous energy was everywhere, the too-shrill laughter, the too-cool posturing by the shivering boys.

The predators were there, too. Older boys and young men that weren't going to make it back into the fold. "Jerk-overs," they were called, a derisive term the locals used for the kids that got jerked over into mainstream society. They were completely lost, trying to figure it all out, learning on the fly, making mistakes, some costly. Some of them drove too fast in souped-up cars they had only recently learned how to drive. Some laughed too hard, drank too much, and some, like the twins, fought at the drop of a hat at any perceived slight. The twins were there, of course, the twins were always there. This was their main client base. They were the suppliers of the magical dust, that chemical entry into adulthood. They came in their Pontiac GTO, the GTO so well known to the local authorities. They parked on the other side of the road, parked so they could make a quick exit. "You never know," they told each other.

The big parties on the Miller farm were never raided. Who knew why. There were certainly plenty of raids at the smaller, private parties in the trailer houses used by the *Rumspringa* spillover, English trailers. The trailers were converted to speed parties, and were frequented by young men and women still "running around," still deciding on the path they would choose. The "official" *Rumspringas* were tolerated by the English system, but it was an uneasy, fragile tolerance. If they wanted to destroy themselves on private property, destroy old Miller's farm, the thinking went, look the other way. But the English trailers on the outskirts of town were a different story. Many of the young men living in the trailer houses had done short jail time, overnight, sobering up time, but were never prosecuted. They had to suffer the ass-chewing administered by the judge, sitting in a strange courtroom with heads pounding and stomachs churning, and act contrite, no, actually be contrite. Some cried, none were defiant, and they always got off: "Go home, don't let me see you in here again." But there was something just plain wrong with arresting a young woman dressed in religious clothing and prayer bonnet, even if she was obviously stoned. So the deputies always delivered the girls back home, "Here, put her to bed."

The Indians had their peyote, the Amish had their coke and speed. It was part of their strange and mysterious lifestyle and religion, and as long as no one else got hurt, just leave them alone.

CHAPTER TWENTY-FOUR

In spite of her misgivings, Emma had to admit she was having a good time. Nervous and excited at the same time, she would have preferred to stick close to her girlfriends, hoping that Zeke wouldn't even show. Or that he would.

She looked absolutely gorgeous, with her neatly ironed violet dress and vanity panel pressed to perfection. Her white bonnet framed her lovely face, glowing cheeks flushed pink with cold and excitement. She wore her best black Converse high top basketball shoes, anticipating a full night of athletics, and as her feet jigged to "Hey, you, get off of my cloud," blasting from the makeshift stage, the new shoes would peek out from under her long, swirling, pleated dress for an instant and then duck back under cover.

She resolved not do anything stupid. Okay, she was here, maybe she would drink a little beer, but nothing stupid. Just a peek at the Devil's playground. No coke, no speed, no pot, certainly no hard liquor, and, *AND*, Zeke was dreaming if he expected her to just lie down and give it up. Not tonight. She wasn't fooled with his assurances that he didn't even want that. It wasn't going to be that easy, she resolved, not with her. So she partied, not too hard, starting to relax, even enjoying herself. Her girlfriends were disappearing one at a time, into the dark, but that was fine, that was their decision. She was perfectly content to stay right here, right in front of these excruciatingly loud speakers, too loud to hear or speak, and dance.

She saw Zeke making his way through the gyrating crowd towards her, and she stopped and stared. Was this really him? This boy had a smart haircut, was wearing perfectly faded blue jeans and a very nice black leather jacket with matching leather hat. He looked amazing! Who did he know that could have helped dress him in such perfect fashion? He slowly made his way over to her, and she could feel her resolve begin to seep out, drain away. He had two small glasses of something, it looked like

140

Coca-Cola. The bass was so loud it made the top of the dark liquid ripple, vibrate, effervesce. "Rum and Coke," he mouthed, and she thought maybe she could try a little of it, just a little. Without another word, it was futile with the blasting music, just a quick hug of his long left arm around her shoulders, he held his glass up for a toast. His mouth moved with some simple little saying, and although she couldn't hear a word, he sure looked cute, she thought, and put the cold mixture to her lips and took her first sip. The rum burned on the way down, and in spite of her most determined effort not to, she began to cough and cough, and Zeke, in spite of *himself*, started laughing. She started laughing with him, and soon they had finished these drinks and he was off for more. It wasn't so cold anymore, between the dancing and the rum, and now she was really beginning to relax, have a good time. In fact, she progressed from the nervous wall flower to the life of the party in one quick night.

Early night became late night, here comes midnight, and beer and rum and whiskey soon stepped aside for the powder and smoke. The bongs and pipes and mirrors and razors came out. Someone said there were needles over behind the big tent, but most of these kids wanted nothing to do with the needles, so they smoked and snorted and drank. The music tempo had slowed, and the drunk lead singer slurred through a softer, off-key "Help Me Make It Through the Night." Slow dancing couples were everywhere, stepping all over each others' untrained, cold and stoned feet, staggering off behind the tent, into the woods, into the back seats of the buggies.

Emma's formerly quick and determined brain had been replaced by unfamiliar mush, and the usually firm ground was determined to move out from under her feet. She leaned on Zeke to keep from staggering, and when he handed her the bong for the last time, she inhaled as if it were oxygen, as if somehow it could save her.

The blond twin was the first to discover them. Emma was on the ground, motionless, and Zeke was leaning against the huge oak tree they used to climb as kids. The twin's brain had gone fuzzy, too, from the powder, but the sight of this young girl lying motionless on the ground did not alarm him. It was common, it always happened. Zeke was not well and soon staggered off behind some trees, returning in a minute, wiping his mouth with the back of his hand.

The band was on break.

"You better take her home, Zeke."

"I can't."

"Why not?"

Zeke looked at his older friend, looked at him like, "Are you stupid?"

"Yeah, okay, alright, I'll take her, I know her old man, he'll be plenty pissed if she doesn't get back tonight." He leaned over and shook her shoulder. "Come on, Em, get up, time to go home, party's over." He shook her again, harder, still nothing. The first glimmer of alarm snuck into Zeke's brain, through the haze of misfiring synapses. He kneeled beside the twin, lost his balance and fell against the tree. He crawled over to the inert young Amish girl and shook her hard, jerking her bonnet loose to lie beside her on the now-freezing ground. "I don't think she's breathing," he told Zeke.

The twin put his ear to her chest, the chest that Zeke had so coveted just hours earlier, and stood up quickly. "She's not. I'm getting the hell out of here." And he was gone, running hard, swallowed by the night. Zeke, suddenly very sober, if still queasy, also stood. He took a tentative staggering step, almost fell, turned and looked back at the lifeless girl on the ground, and burst into tears. He turned away, for the last time, and made his groping way through moaning couples on the ground, smoking junkies leaning on their cars, and found his rig.

Zeke untied the filly, climbed into the single seat buggy, turned the horse towards the main road, and slumped forward. The filly knew the way home, was anxious, and took off at a strong trot, bouncing the young Amish boy around in the cab. He felt nauseous again, unfastened the two latches at the bottom of the push-out windshield, cold blasting his still hairless, sweating face, calming his stomach. Almost distractedly, he saw the speeding car and a figure dart into the headlights' glare, tires squalling, twin headlight beams flashing in his eyes, and then pointing up, into the thick sky. The buggy in front of Zeke stopped quickly, and Zeke's filly almost ran into the back of it, skidding to a stop.

Shouts of, "What happened?" and, "Who was it?" filled the air. One of the teenagers running by shouted, "Ezra, Ezra Neuenschwander almost got hit," "Where is he now?" and "He ran off," "The driver's alright, I think."

What the hell is Ezra doing out here? Zeke would recall wondering later. He hasn't been around for years.

The Elders discouraged too many trips to the doctor, "God will take care of the details," so there would have been no way of knowing about Emma's faulty left ventricle. *Cocaine-induced myocardial infarction,* the coroner's report said. But to these simple country folks, these God-fearing farmers and carpenters, these family oriented purveyors of the good life, it was simpler than that: it was God's will.

Except to her father.

CHAPTER TWENTY-FIVE

Samuel didn't really expect Emma to be home that night. He had hoped, secretly, that she would, but the custom was to stay away, sometimes for days. So when heavy eyelids overcame worry, he slipped into a restive sleep, sitting in the bent-willow rocker his uncle Abram had made for them when Emma was born. His balding head slumped forward, crushing the mass of beard hair onto his chest, gnarled, worn hands folded in prayer. The little time-bird at the top of the walnut grandfather clock mocked him all night, the "cukoo" sounding more like "yoohoo", then "yoohoo, yoohoo" then "yoohoo, yoohoo, yoohoo." Each time the bird stirred, the worried, exhausted father shifted to an equally uncomfortable position, chin eventually drifting back down onto his chest until the bird popped out again, cheerily announcing the ever-later hour.

Dawn had just peeked over the eastern hills, pink with a promise of afternoon snow flurries, when a weary Samuel was wakened for good by the sounds of his wife's shoes sneaking through the kitchen. He stirred, making the familiar early morning grunting noise she knew so well. She walked up and laid a hand on his shoulder, a once common gesture. "She will be fine," she tried to convince both of them. "She is a good girl, and has a very good head on her. She will be fine." Samuel didn't shrug off the hand, his usual reaction, and just sat there with his sore muscles for a minute, not saying a word.

"Would you like me to tend to the chores?" she asked softly. The farmer slowly got out of the chair, and her hand fell back to her side. In a very low voice he said, "Just busy yourself in the kitchen. I'll take care of the animals like I always do."

Rachael still loved this now-distant person she had married so happily all those years ago, and turned to the kitchen to "busy herself" and to hide the pain in her eyes. She would never give up, she had promised herself, never settle for this loveless existence. But there was plenty of time to try to rebuild

144

that life. So she walked to the kitchen, lit the propane burner, and worried about their daughter, the only glue left in this marriage, this house.

A thousand tragedies danced in Samuel's head. He had heard all the stories, the kids that overdid it, the kids that left to never return. "Not my Em," he would chide himself, "not my Em. She didn't even want to go. Maybe I should have told her the truth, that I didn't want her to go, to hell with the church. But she's such a good girl and Zeke is okay, they're probably just sleeping it off somewhere."

And so it went, the tired farmer's mind spinning out of control, wrestling it back, furiously chopping wood and mucking stalls, too tired to work but too unsettled not to. Tomorrow was Sunday, Emma would be back soon. They could all get a good night's rest, go to the Sunday morning worship service like they had these last sixteen years. There would be Emma, sitting up straight beside her mother with all the other women and children, and Samuel would sit with the men, trying his best to not let his pride show, or even, for that manner, glance at his family.

It was a little unusual to have unannounced visitors on Saturday, especially early morning. Not wildly unusual, but out of the norm. The single-horse black buggy was moving slowly, a trot, yes, but a slow trot, the light snow flurries barely swirling behind the slow moving rig. The windshield had been lowered to ward off the crisp autumn air, and Rachael couldn't see who was inside, the glass steamed up from moist breath against cold glass. Whoever it was would be a big person, she thought, and sitting on one side; the buggy listed to the left.

The black horse, an old gelding, slowed to a walk and finally came to a stop in front of the house. A large man stepped backwards out of the carriage, the buggy leaning and creaking and groaning in protest as he stepped on the little metal step halfway to the ground. He stepped onto the cold snowy grass and the buggy sprung back upright, relieved of the off-center weight. The big man turned towards the hitching rail and draped the reigns over the top, and she recognized Bishop Yoder.

The old Bishop, long flowing gray beard ruffling in the day's cold swirl, head covered with his traditional black hat, overcoat collar turned up against the chill, slowly walked towards the house, bent to the brisk air. Bishop Yoder never stopped by to ask, "How's it going? How's the family?" No, this Bishop was the most dedicated of God's servants, and when he showed up, clutching worn Bible, it wasn't going to be good news. Rachael felt her knees tremble, and clutched the door casing with her left hand to steady herself as she slowly opened the front door.

"Bishop, what brings you here today?" She was frightened.

"May I come in, child?" he asked softly, sternly. She stepped aside, and as he entered the immaculate home, removed his hat and asked if he should take off his shoes.

"That won't be necessary. Can I get you something hot to drink?"

He said, "No, thank you. Where is Samuel?"

"He is out behind the barn. He didn't hear you?"

The old bishop started to say, "I don't think —" when Samuel swept through the rear door, noisily banging it shut behind him. He had seen the Bishop approach the house, and dropping everything ran to the back door, through the little enclosed back porch he had added to keep the work clothes out of the house, and into the kitchen, stopping at the door to the main part of the house.

The Bishop's thinning gray hair was plastered against his head, lily-white skin above the hat line, permanently burned cheeks below; he, too, worked the fields. He was sternly religious; there was no aspect of this man's world that did not further the religious lives of his flock, and it fell on him to deliver this type of news. He told Emma's story, in his eloquent Pennsylvania Dutch, spattered with English words like "cocaine" and "speed", how their daughter had gone to be with her Lord. He knew it would be hard for a while, he told them, kindly, that was only natural. He understood they were human, after all, but it was God's will.

146

His disciplined delivery didn't ease the shock at all, not at all.

As he went on and on, telling the story of this young woman's life, which they knew better than he did and barely heard, his voice remained calm, the same way it did every Sunday delivering the weekly sermon. "The Devil is everywhere, behind every tree, under every napkin, and it is our duty to protect ourselves and our families from this beast," he said simply. "Sometimes we fail."

They hadn't even made it out of the foyer area before the old Bishop had begun, such was the urgency of knowing, and telling, and Rachael slowly sank to the floor, totally oblivious to the lack of modesty of her position. She no longer heard the words, only the noise, and she started to weep, the kind of quiet, hollow weeping a woman does when she has no control over anything, nothing left to live for. She knew in her heart that this was God's will, everything was part of His plan, but she didn't understand. "It is not our place to understand," she had heard so often. "It is our place to trust, to place our lives in His hands."

Samuel had no visible reaction to the news, no tears, no questions, no trembling lip, nothing. He listened to the long, detailed explanation, expressionless. When the Bishop finally wore himself out, Emma's father slowly walked to the front door, carefully stepping around the slumped figure of his wife on the floor and opened it for the Bishop to leave. The Bishop opened his mouth, thought better of it, put his hat back on his pious head and stepped over the threshold onto the front porch. He made his way down the now snow covered porch steps, steadying himself on the slippery railing, and walked towards the buggy. A cottontail, starkly brown against the white snow, sat up on its hind legs, and its long ears could hear the sounds of the weeping mother and the light crunch of new, dry snow under religious boots.

Samuel didn't wait for the Bishop to descend the steps. He didn't wave goodbye. He didn't watch the buggy slowly

147

disappear down the long, tree lined lane to the county road, dual buggy tracks and hoof prints left in the snow. By the time the old preacher reached his buggy and climbed inside, Samuel had already disappeared into the bedroom, tracking mud, and began to change his clothes. He slowly but deliberately removed his work jacket, work pants and shirt and put them all in the hamper kept in the bottom of the closet. He still said nothing. He put on fresh work clothes, the new ones he had bought just last week, the ones that still had the tags on them. He reached for the small cardboard suitcase on the top shelf, the black, starting-to-fade one his family used when visiting *freundschaft* overnight. The emotionless former father filled the case with several days' change of clothing, fresh socks and underwear, and then, hesitating ever so slightly, put his hunting knife in the bottom, the one with the six inch blade, the one he used to skin the deer, rabbits and squirrels he hunted. He turned to leave, turned back to the closet, reached in the bottom of the drawer, and lifted a stack of bills, lots of bills, and shoved them in among the clothes.

When he came back out of the bedroom, his wife was already cleaning up where Samuel had tracked snow and mud into the house, dirt he was always so careful to leave outside. She had scraped up most of it, and was pumping water into the metal bucket to mop the remaining dirt film. They didn't look at each other, not once, and when Samuel left, out the back door, she may as well have been invisible.

The craziest thing Samuel did when he was sixteen was to learn to drive a car, eighteen years ago. Driving came natural to him, and the instructor commented it was a shame to see that kind of gift wasted on him; everyone knew he was going to join the church, and then there would be no more driving. But in the meantime, when he was sixteen and then seventeen, Samuel drove everywhere. He even ran a couple of stock car races, never winning but always putting in a respectable performance.

His father bought him a brand new 1956 short-bed stepside Chevy pickup. The truck had a huge 350 cubic inch V-8 engine with dual carbs sticking up through the hood, positraction, four on the floor, rear tire "slicks" and it was fast, very fast. *Stepside Sam* his English buddies called him. He parked the candy-apple red car in the front yard of his parents' home every night, under a huge oak tree, and they didn't mind; he lived at home his entire *Rumspringa* and always came in at a decent time and never smelled of alcohol or smoke. He tried smoking cigarettes for about a week, couldn't understand why "anyone would want for to inhale that vile smoke," didn't like the way it made his truck cab smell, quit and banned anyone else from smoking in the truck.

There was never any question about his joining the church, he talked about it openly; everyone knew his driving was just a phase.

Something snapped in Samuel's brain when he heard his daughter was dead. His faith had been gradually cooling, anyway, over the years, like a kettle sitting on a turned off stove, and it finally went cold, stone cold. He didn't have a well defined plan, no plan really, he just knew he had to avenge his daughter's incomprehensible end.

The car he bought was an everyman's car, a two-year-old black Pinto, in pretty good shape, and seemed reliable enough, he thought, and he paid cash for it. He tried to buy one from the car lot in the third town over. He remembered the lot for its cheap prices. He rode all that way, in the cold, on his bicycle, precariously balancing his suitcase across the handlebars. But there were too many questions and too much paperwork, "Where's your driver's license?" So he bought one out of the community newspaper he found when he stopped to warm up at a café in town.

149

The man who sold the car to him had questions in his eyes, but didn't ask them out loud, and hand-wrote out a bill of sale and handed it to the bearded farmer. He had expected to come way off his asking price. He had argued with his wife about how much to ask, and set a deliberately high price to allow for those negotiations. But the fellow seemed to be in a hurry and paid in cash, so better to count one's blessings and send him on his way, he told her. He had satisfied his legal requirement, he added, so his conscious was clear. Besides, there was something wrong with the Amish man, maybe he is crazy. Samuel tried to put his bicycle in the trunk, then in the back seat, and finally just left it in the man's driveway and drove off.

Samuel's next stop was almost half way to Philadelphia, at a small barber and hair styling shop. He could feel the mood change the minute he stepped through the glass door. That was exactly why the mop and wild beard had to go. The shop was busy, by now it was Saturday evening, and he sat in the uncomfortable chair for an hour, waiting his turn, leafing through the magazines. The magazines were filled with lurid photos and debased stories of who was sleeping with whom, children born out of wedlock, fighting, and drug use. Five years ago, maybe even a year ago, Samuel would have noticed the Devil's hand in the magazines, but now, absently leafing through them, he seemed oblivious. His turn finally came, and when he left the shop, he was just another clean shaven man, dressed in drab work clothes.

The gauge on the Pinto's dash said it was time for fuel, so Sam stopped to gas up. When he emerged from the nasty bathroom at the convenience store, no one he knew would have recognized him. The colorless clothing was gone, wrapped up in a bundle under his arm. He now wore bright blue Wrangler jeans, a nice denim long sleeved shirt with pearl covered snaps, a brown leather jacket with wool collar, Nike shoes, and a bright red baseball cap with a white "P" embroidered on the front. It was the only hat left on the rack, and the attendant said it didn't really mean anything. He thought about not wearing anything on his head, but it seemed just too odd, after all these years. Besides, the strange man looking back at him from the mirror had a band of tan around his eyes, kind of like a tan raccoon, pale skin above the eyebrows and pale skin under the mouth, where the beard had been. At least the hat hid the top half.

He tossed his old work clothes in the trunk, and pulled into traffic.

Samuel pulled up to a seedy motel just before midnight. He was relieved to see the vacancy sign lit up, and paid cash for a room for a week. The desk clerk had seen dozens of these country workers, trying to blend, and didn't even yawn. "No smoking in the room, no drinking in the room, no whores, *try* to not trash it," he intoned. Samuel mumbled his agreement, and let himself into the small, dirty room, setting the small suitcase in the corner. He hung the new jacket on a metal coat hanger, fumbled with the TV and finally figured out how to make it work. It came on with a blast and he immediately turned it off when the wall started pounding and a loud, "Turn that damn thing off!" came shouting through the thin wall.

Samuel pulled the filthy bed cover down to the foot of the bed, on second thought, kicked it off on the floor, and lay down on the fresh sheets, sheets that smelled like too hot dryer, almost scorched. And chlorine. These almost weren't sheets, he thought, certainly not bearing any resemblance to the fresh, sun dried, always ironed wonderful sheets his wife fussed over. For the first time that devastating day, Samuel had nothing to do but think, and for the first time, a tear spilled from the outside corner of his eye, down his tanned cheek across pale white skin usually covered with bushy beard, onto the scorched pillow case. Just one tear, and then his resolve returned, and with tightly clenched teeth, he drifted off into fitful sleep, chasing Amish drug dealers, beating them senseless. But they always got away, and the chase began again.

He never could kill them, in those dreams.

CHAPTER TWENTY-SIX

Bobbie was a punk, pretending to live the Amish way with his plain clothes, suspenders and church-sanctioned haircut. But he was a punk; everyone knew it. Trying to live with a foot in both worlds. Samuel never had liked him, although up until now had done his Christian best to welcome him back into the church.

Samuel went on a mini-missionary trip to Philadelphia with two other church members to try to bring the young, errant man back into the church. Mr. Herzog didn't even charge for the trip. Was that just a month ago? He had no trouble finding the young man again. His tent was pitched on the outskirts of town, this time for a very different reason.

"Hey, Bobbie," Samuel said as the surprised teenager pushed the canvas flap aside and climbed out. "I'm looking for to Ezra. I guess you be knowing why." Samuel's throat was tight and he talked in a high-pitched tone, anticipating a fight.

"Screw you, you ignorant —" was as far as Bobbie got before the angry farmer literally picked him up and slammed him upside down into the nearby Maple tree, knocking a few leaves loose into the air, drifting down past the two men.

"*Schraube nicht mit mir, weil ich nicht mehr Pflege,*" Samuel hissed. "Where do they get the drugs for *Rumspringa?*"

Bobbie had never been so surprised in his young life. These — his — people, these *easy marks* never did that, no matter the circumstances. It was God's will, they always said, these ignorant people. His vision finally cleared enough to look up at the wild, angry man leaning over him, a furious glower on his face, and decided to give it up, tell him what he wanted to know.

"Everyone knows where the drugs come from, Samuel," he began hesitantly. "Don't you?"

"Of course, but I want to talk to Ezra," he lied. "Where is he?"

"Ezra? Ezra who?" Bobbie was confused. "Nuenschwander? What's he got to do with —" he started to say, but Samuel had drawn his huge fist back, and he quickly added, "I don't think Ezra has anything to do with —" Samuel reached down and grabbed his hair, yanked it hard.

"Look, I heard Ezra moved to Canada somewhere. He changed his name to Ryan, Ryan Miller. Dunno why. He runs a horse business of some kind, and I heard he was going to be at some big horse show here in Philly this year. Devan, Davin, something like that." He gently pulled his hair from the man's still-knotted fist. "You want the twins. I seen 'em workin' construction on the south side, some development called The Downs, I think. They've been getting their stuff from Jonathon, but the last time I saw them they had found a cheaper supplier. You know the twins, always trying to go on the cheap."

"They still be driving the GTO?" Samuel remembered their car.

"Far as I know, Lord knows they could both drive Caddies. I guess it's their way of blending." Bobbie laughed.

Samuel stepped back from the crumpled punk, and stood up completely. "You're going to Hell, Bobbie."

"Yeah, well keep my seat warm." Sensing the immediate danger was over, Bobbie slowly stood up, regaining some of his attitude. "See ya there," he retorted over his shoulder, watching as Samuel strode quickly to his car.

It was past quitting time when Samuel made his way down the littered street of the housing development, weaving to avoid scattered piles of lumber and trash. There were a few men hanging around, and a couple of women dressed in almost nothing, in spite of the cold. The afternoon light had begun to move over for the evening dusk. The streetlights began to glow, softly at first with their quiet cracking and hissing, then buzzing, then growing silent as they began to burn brightly, casting their eerie glow down the street. Three men stood beside their motorcycles, a block from where Samuel stopped the car. He sat and watched them. Maybe they know the twins, he thought, or Ezra. In spite of what Bobbie had just told him, he had heard Ezra was at Emma's *Rumspringa*, handing out powder, pocketing money. The men appeared to be in no hurry to leave, and were handing a funny looking cigarette back and forth.

Samuel slowly opened the door to his car, winced slightly as the dome light came on, reached over his shoulder and flipped it to the off position, flooding the car in darkness. One of the men looked his direction, gestured to one of the other men, who also looked, and the two of them shared a laugh. Samuel gently closed the driver side car door, and walked hesitantly towards the workers.

"Hey, wazzup dude?" one of the bikers asked.

"Not much, not much," the farmer-come-city man replied.

"What brings you to our great city, my man? Lookin' for a little action, a little pussy? You just missed the nuns." The second biker guffawed, a low, hoarse laugh created by too much booze, too much smoke, too little sleep, finishing up with a coughing fit. "You crazy-ass country people think you kin jes' change clothes and drive into town in a car and no one's gonna notice?"

Another round of laughing, leg slapping.

Samuel could feel his neck redden, but said nothing for a minute. "I just got into town this morning and I'm looking for some work, wondered if they were hiring," he lied. The three bikers laughed again, but not so hard; at least this one wasn't going to make up a story.

"Dunno, Country, dunno. Do we look like we be in charge of da hirin'?" he asked in an exaggerated accent. "Didja notice it's quitten' time? Why doncha take that big steed of yourn down yonder and ride it back in the mornin'. Mebbe you'll find someone den."

"Yes, you are probably correct," Samuel replied in his clipped speech. After a pause, he tentatively continued, "I have a couple of cousins working here, I think, brothers, twins in fact, although they don't look like twins. They drive a 1964 GTO, bright red, and the last I heard they were working here. Do you know them, maybe where for I could be finding them?"

This time the three construction workers leaning on their bikes didn't laugh. So this country bumpkin knew the twins; that shed new light on things. The third biker, the one with the leather saddlebags on his Harley, spoke for the first time.

"So you know the twins, eh?"

"Yes. Do they work here?"

The third biker glanced at his friends and said, "Saw 'em this morning, worked their typical half a day, not sure how they get away with that, guess they know people in low places." His two friends grinned. If this funny speaking person knew the twins, well, that was different, business is business.

"Do you know where to I could find them? Tonight? I need to ask them something and it can't wait until tomorrow."

"Hey, ask me, I can probably answer your question for less than the twins charge," he said, reaching inside one of the saddle bags, hand emerging holding a small plastic bag.

Samuel wasn't sure what he was talking about.

"No thanks, really, it concerns for a family matter."

By now the three smokers had tired of this game, whatever it was, and any respect this ill-spoken country fool had gained disappeared with his decline of the offer. It was fun if there was profit involved. Now it was simply annoying.

"Try the Kountry Klub. Even if they aren't there, you're sure to find someone else you can talk to. We're all family."

The men were still chuckling when Samuel reached his car, and he opened the car door and slid onto the cold, grey, vinyl seat. The little four cylinder engine hummed to life, and Samuel made a U-turn, not enough power to spin the tires even in a sharp turn.

The twins were nervous. The smaller one, the dark-haired one, the one that never drove, was especially nervous. "That crazy bitch did it to herself," he said.

155

"Shut up, just shut up," his brother snapped. This had been going on since they first heard about Emma. Every so often he had a pang of guilt, supplying these innocents with all kinds of drugs and booze. But, he would add, that was their religion, and if he and his brother didn't supply them, someone else would.

"Crazy bitch," the small brother muttered before slumping against the passenger side door, glumly looking in his side view mirror. Both twins had heard about Emma killing herself. Maybe she did it on purpose, they had wondered. They had heard about Samuel leaving Rachael in the house by herself, had heard about the haircut and the car purchase; they had "friends" everywhere up and down the well traveled road between Philly and the parties, and had heard all about it. They even knew what kind of car Samuel bought, and saw it on every street corner, always in their rear view mirror, a ghost, gone when they looked again.

"Jon's looking for us," the driver, the blond twin, added. "He may not be happy."

At this, the smaller twin became even more depressed. "I told you that was a bad idea. I told you. But no, you have to always be right, always squeeze a little more. And now look, look what you did. For what, a little more money? I told you that was a bad idea. And Ezra's in town. Is he looking for us too? Why do you suppose he wants to be called Ryan now?"

The joke had gone too far, the twin driving the car knew. Calling Ryan, hanging up, giving Jon his address and phone number. Jon had even convinced the German fellow to send a couple of his boys up to Canada to rough Ryan up, telling the German that Ryan was a big drug dealer and wanted to come back to Philly.

"Jon doesn't know anything. All he said was, 'You haven't bought anything for a while, what's up with that?' I told him we were just taking a break, not to worry, and he was fine, so quit whining already. 'Sides, he's too preoccupied with *Ryan* to worry too much about us.'"

"You didn't talk to him, I did, and he is *not* fine. He knows. He knows." After a short pause, the dark haired twin continued, "You know, sometimes —"

His bother cut him off, "Don't even start with that shit tonight. I don't want to hear about it."

When things got a little tough, just a little crazy, his weak brother always started in on maybe they should move back home, forget this life, maybe they *were* going to Hell, the church would always take them back, no matter what, and he was in no mood to listen to that drivel. But this time things were different, things may have gotten out of control.

The twin behind the wheel had to admit his brother was probably right. He had been a little nervous the first couple of times they bought from the muscular young man with no expression, the one that drove a fancy black Continental. He had a pronounced German accent, different than theirs, European, and the twin had heard him speaking German into a payphone, not close enough to catch the conversation, but close enough to understand a few words. He thought he heard "Eshra," and "Jonathon," but at the time wrote it off to being paranoid. The phone call he got from his buddy at the Kountry Klub warning him about Jon unnerved him, but he had no intention of letting his brother know that. They went way back with Jon, way back to middle school. Jon would understand, it wasn't too late to turn this all around, make it like it was. But then what about the German? He didn't know the German at all, other than by reputation, but reputations were always an exaggeration, weren't they? He had told a few stories about himself and his twin, gross lies, but that was this world they had fallen into.

Where did the truth end and the fantasy begin?

Jon pulled his truck slowly into the gravel parking lot at the Kountry Klub. He usually tried to avoid the potholes, but tonight drove through several of them, preoccupied with the business at hand. He circled several times, looking for the twins' car, didn't see it, so went inside.

"Hey, Kirby," he nodded to one of his drinking buddies walking towards him on the front porch. "You seen the twins?" Kirby shook his head no, and walked through the front door beside his friend. The loud country band had just finished their first set, and the players were climbing out from behind the net put up in front of the stage to catch any thrown beer bottles. Someone had started feeding dimes to the jukebox.

Jon and his buddy sat down at the bar and ordered a couple of Sly Fox beers, their favorite local beer, the one on tap. Jon was in a bad mood, and even in this club, when Jon was in a bad mood it was better to leave him alone. So Kirby just sat there, sipping his beer, saying nothing.

"I'm gonna kick their ass so hard they'll get arrested for speeding in Chicago," he growled. Kirby had heard all about the twins' betrayal, and would have preferred to talk about something else.

"Yeah, they deserve that and then some," he agreed instead.

CHAPTER TWENTY-SEVEN

Devon Horse Show

Ryan pulled up on the side of Building Ten and shut off the motor. He locked the car door and walked around to the front of the two stalls he had been assigned for the show. His trainer, grooming the filly with the star on her forehead, looked up and smiled. "How's it going, Boss?"

"Good, and yourself?" Ryan replied.

Ryan had entered his horses in three events, and this afternoon was the first one. The two horsemen had been in many competitions together, but this was *Devon*, the Wimbledon of horse shows, and they were both trying to be calm, hide their edginess. Ryan ran his hand across the filly's right shoulder and down her front leg, gently feeling around the fetlock. The young horse obligingly raised her hoof, almost placing it in his hand. He felt some more, then placed the foot back on the ground and looked at his trainer. "I can't feel anything. What do you think?" The joint had been hot and swollen a few months earlier.

"She doesn't favor that leg at all, even after a brisk workout. I think she's sound, ready to go. What do you think?" The trainer had a habit of always deferring to Ryan, letting him make the final decisions.

"Yeah, I think so. Let's see how she does this afternoon."

The ride down from Toronto had helped clear Ryan's mind. He didn't know what, if any, danger he was in, but for now at least, that was far away from his thoughts. There were more immediate issues to be dealt with. Ryan and his trainer decided it would be best if the trainer took the fillies into the arena, not Ryan, to get them used to the place.

The two men were deep in conversation, walking back from their initial inspection of the big show barn, when Ryan knocked the lady down. It was a blind corner, where the corners of two barns almost came together, creating a narrow pass, too narrow for horses but a perfect shortcut for two-leggers. The water hose for the barn was on the south side and the stable hands had been careless about spilling water when they filled their buckets. At the point of contact, her left foot slid out from under her and she threw her right foot straight in front, like kicking a field goal, trying in vain to regain her balance. Ryan instinctively reached down and caught the flash of white pants with his left arm. At exactly the same time, he slid into the mud, and on the way down, the screaming woman managed to grab the trainer's windbreaker, and all three went down in a squealing, thrashing mass of arms and muddy legs.

"I'm so sorry, are you OK?" Ryan managed to get out as the three of them staggered back to their feet, three very muddy people.

She was laughing. "Yes, I'm fine, thanks so much for that little help. I don't think I could have gotten this much mud without it."

Embarrassed, Ryan managed, "Well, I, uh — I just wanted to make sure — I was just — wait, is that you?"

The woman stopped her futile effort to brush the wet, sticky mud off of her recently immaculate white pants, looked up, immediately smiled and said warmly, "Ryan! I didn't know you were here! What a pleasant surprise!" She moved closer as if to hug him. He was so startled that he took a step back.

"Theresa?" was all he could muster. "Theresa?"

The trainer had heard about Theresa, and wasn't buying any of this fake surprise. He had work to do, and if the rich folk wanted to stand around, muddy from top to bottom, and act like this was a coincidence, well — that was up to them, but excuse me, I have work to do, and he was off. "Phony bullshit," he muttered to himself and slogged off, scraping mud from his clothes; one more chore to add to this already crowded day.

"I am so sorry, man; it's good to see you. We have a bathroom if you would like to —" His genuineness made up for

160

his inarticulate delivery, but Theresa didn't mind, didn't mind at all, and just smiled and let him sputter. Finally, it was her turn.

"Ryan, thank you very much for the offer to let me use your bathroom, but I think I will go back to my apartment and get cleaned up proper. I actually have towels and a clean change of clothes there." She had seen the facilities they provided for the stable-hands. She took his hands in hers, mud squeezing out. "Why don't we get together later tonight, if you have time, maybe catch dinner somewhere?" She had been patiently waiting for Ryan, "This guy," to call her, and he hadn't, so it was time to turn it up a bit.

Ryan had turned slightly red from her teasing, but was also happy to see her, he had to admit to himself. He should have called, had been meaning to, but so many things were happening — the lame excuses never left his thoughts. "That sounds like a lot of fun, but I can't tonight, I'm sorry." Why did he say that, he wondered, he didn't have a thing to do.

Disappointed, but outwardly fine, she started to say, "Of course, the show is coming —" when he interrupted, pulling a small, spiral bound notepad out of his muddy pocket.

"Tell you what, give me your phone number, do you have one here? Where are you staying? Let me see if I can move some things around. Dinner sounds nice." He quickly scribbled the number.

"Call me then," she said over her shoulder, walking away, white pants and suede jacket decorated with the dirty, sloppy goo.

Theresa had tossed an old blanket in the trunk of the rental car, force of habit. Old blankets had as many uses as a Swiss Army knife, her father had taught her. She went back to the car that she had parked in the box office owners' area, ignoring the stares. She opened the trunk, put the blanket on the perfectly white leather seat, slid in, started the engine and headed for her apartment. She smiled to herself, pleased that her planning had paid off. Not that she was obsessed with Ryan, okay, a little obsessed, but there was something about him. Was she intrigued because he hadn't called? Maybe. A little. Every other man she'd ever met couldn't wait to call, wine her, dine her, try to separate her from her panties. Maybe he really didn't want to get to know her, she wondered, maybe he was shy, maybe he didn't like women, maybe — maybe — she grabbed her head with both hands, quieting the voices.

The brochure that Devon sends to all the box office holders lay on the leather passenger seat, still open to the participants' page, and Ryan's name was circled. Her great grandfather had been in the right place at the right time, and had been one of the fortunate few to own one of the highly coveted air-conditioned and heated sky boxes, one of the best, in the middle. She never met her great grandfather, but saw the photos. He was a handsome man, tall and always smiling, and always wore black with a plain, black broad-brimmed felt hat. He wore an oversized buckle on his belt, he had been to Texas once, bought the buckle. He cut a striking figure, and from the stories, would have been a good person to know. No one was quite sure how he made his money, but now the sky box was hers, and she never missed a chance to use it. She loved Devon.

She had already decided not to invite Ryan up there, to the opulent box. Not this time.

The young heiress was so preoccupied with her plans, with Ryan, mind racing, that she didn't even notice the black Lincoln that pulled out of the parking lot at Devon, three cars back, and followed her to her apartment. She didn't notice as the car drove slowly past her as she pulled up to the curb and parked. She didn't notice it slowly pull around the corner, reappear behind her, and pull into the parking spot several spots back.

Ryan was genuinely surprised to run into Theresa. He thought of her often, and idly wondered why he was reluctant to call. The last woman he dated — what was her name, was it two years ago now? She suffocated him, like ever-present heavy air, the moist, unstable air that's hard to breathe right before a rapidly

162

approaching thunderstorm. She called him "my little project." At first the sex had been great, steamy, exhausting, then it became a duty, and finally, the arm holding, the baby wouldn't respond. She wasn't surprised or overly bothered when he finally helped her move her things out to the trunk of her car.

And so he became oblivious to the looks, the attention he always got when women were around. They were all the same, they all wanted something, they all had an agenda. And so he hadn't called Theresa. But he couldn't get her out of his mind.

Ryan did his best to clean up in the little stable-hand bathroom, the room just barely large enough to turn around in, and emerged respectable. The only change of clothes he had was work clothes that he always kept for just this sort of emergency. Horse people learned early on that if you are around horses and horse facilities, you will, sooner or later, need a change of clothes.

He pulled the still damp notebook out of his pocket, and looked at the scrawled *Theresa* and the phone number written beside it. "What *is* it about this woman, Ez — Ryan?" he asked himself. "She's a beauty, an exotic, all right, but look around, there are a million beautiful, exotic, women. She loves horses, sure, but there's hundreds of handsome women right here right now that love horses." He looked in the direction she had disappeared. "She smells good, is that it?"

Distracted as he was, he knew nothing of the man with the new baseball cap, a bright red baseball cap with a white "P" embroidered on the front, the man with the determined, haunted look in his eyes, watching him, watching every move.

The burly biker parked his big Harley on the sidewalk, right next to the rusty, clunky heat pump that barely heated Samuel's room. The biker had long ago replaced the mufflers with straight chrome pipes, and the staccato *"potato-potato-potato,"* distinctively Harley, twisted loud with tattooed hand, threatened to break the window less than three feet away from Samuel's head. In his fitful sleep, Samuel was delivering a new washing machine to Emma's basement when it morphed into a Harley bumpily roaring up her basement stairs, and the real Harley yanked him back into this world.

The farmer lay there for a while, his racing heart beginning to settle. It was Sunday, and a dozen brilliant sunbeams snuck through holes in the undulating curtain, dancing on his chest and pants. He could have easily reached the pull cord, flooded the room with light, but his arm wouldn't obey. His mind drifted back home, to the image of hundreds of black-clad men driving their shawled wives and blanketed children in their black buggies to — which house was the service at this morning? He couldn't remember. It was too far away to remember. He briefly thought about his wife, and quickly put the thought aside. Too much of a distraction; he would deal with that later.

It took two attempts to crawl out of bed, a miserable mattress that could tell a thousand stories, a berth that sank in the middle, like the hammock in his front yard that hung between the giant maple trees. Samuel stumbled over to the little kitchenette and brushed the crumbs of the previous occupant off of the countertop. It was pocked with cigarette burns. He rinsed out the coffee pot and began a fresh brew, as fresh as the burned pot could offer. Samuel had never been a big coffee drinker. He felt all drugs, even caffeine, were unnecessary, maybe even an affront to God, the only stimulant a person really needed. But this morning he needed caffeine, as much as he could get. He drank the black liquid slowly, careful not to burn his thick, swollen tongue. He hadn't thought about the overnight stubble, and then, remembering where he was, smiled ever so slightly at the prospect of showing up outside, in this wretched place, freshly scrubbed.

Samuel didn't really have a plan. Overnight his resolve had slackened, like water seeping out of a wet sponge. He vaguely intended to find the twins — and then what? He opened the grimy curtains and looked out at the small crowd leaning around the parked Harleys, the men in their leathers, the users, the construction workers, and wondered again — then what?

Ezra — Ryan, was in Devon this year, he heard. He needed to find him. Devon was all over the newspaper, and Samuel struggled to comprehend the unfamiliar words. Thankfully, they had included a map, showing the main entrance and the worker entrance. He had also picked up a brochure the night before, and circled Ryan's name and his barn number. The map in the brochure was puzzlingly vague, and he was glad the newspaper had a better one. Samuel knew better than to drive up to the front entrance, his old car would just draw unwanted attention, so he set out to find the worker entrance. On the way, he stopped for a breakfast, one of the fast food places, choked down half of the greasy burger and soggy bun before throwing the rest away. How could people eat this, he coughed? His mind again drifted to Rachael, her fine breakfasts and warm, tidy home. He longed to talk to her, but that would have to wait.

Samuel found the back entrance without too much trouble. While waiting in line to turn left into the workers' parking area, left turn signals blinking out of sync, several cars passed going the opposite direction. One of the cars was driven by a beautiful, smiling, black-haired goddess, and several cars behind her, a black Lincoln, an expressionless, muscular young man behind the wheel. Samuel took no note of either car.

The guard at the gate demanded his permit, "No one gets in without a permit," but after a couple of minutes of back and forth and impatient horn-honking, motioned him on in. He certainly looked like a worker, the guard mused. Why else would he be here? "Bring the permit back as soon as you find your boss!" he yelled after him, jotting his plate numbers down.

"That has to be him," Samuel told himself several times. The man was the same age that Ezra would be, and looked like what he supposed he would look like after all these years. He hadn't known him well back home, but they did know each other, and that was certainly him. Ezra appeared to be covered in mud, but that happened if you worked around livestock. Samuel had been covered in mud many times, and could just imagine the wrangle with the horse right before Ryan must have slipped and fallen. Samuel could barely see the horses, they were under the shade of the overhang, but he wouldn't know the horses anyway. Samuel watched, watched the man go through the door at the end of the stalls and emerge with a clean change of clothes. He watched as the man walked away, disappeared, and didn't go after him.

CHAPTER TWENTY-EIGHT

The twins often partook of their own product but never,
well, seldom, to excess; it was better to keep some semblance of a
clear head, they agreed. Their main income was from the
Rumspringa parties, but as with any burgeoning business, they
needed to expand, to broaden their customer base. And so they
began looking for other outlets. Even though they had developed
some skill at dealing with the wholesalers, the bikers, they had
little experience with other buyers, regular junkies. The country
parties, the *Rumspringas*, were unique; where else could they find
dozens, hundreds, of naïve users, innocent children, never
quibbling price, and most importantly, the cops pretty much took
a hands-off attitude.? It was amazing, a bonanza. How could they
replicate that?

"Maybe we need to go to Florida," the dark haired twin
mused out loud, "and see where they're getting their stuff down
there. Winter's coming, and it would be nice to not freeze my ass
off for once. We could fill the trunk and head out next week.
What do you think?"

His brother thought it would be too risky. They didn't
know anyone in Florida, and besides, all the stories made it sound
like a drug dealer free-for-all. They would probably just get hurt,
or worse, dead. "Let's try the school kids in the city, like we
talked. You know how crazy kids are anymore. They'll try
anything."

They talked about hanging out at the playgrounds after
school but the dark haired twin wasn't willing to sell drugs to little
kids. His brother protested, again, that wasn't what he meant.
And so they agreed, for the tenth time, that they would target the
middle schools. After all, that's when they got their start, using,
and it had worked out well for them.

167

Jimmy joined the Lancaster County sheriff's department within two weeks of leaving the Army. He had been an MP, and loved cracking heads. He had always been one of the trouble makers in high school, and his parents were relieved when he decided to join up, right out of high school. The Army would make him or break him, they hoped, and sure enough, four years later he had emerged with a better attitude. He even apologized to his parents for all the trouble he caused.

In his three years of employment with the county, the biggest problem he dealt with was the drugs. Drugs were everywhere. Early on he had busted everyone for the slightest infraction, but soon began selective enforcement like everyone else on the force. They were understaffed, and there was too much drug use to bust every user, so he focused on the hard core junkies and, of course, the dealers.

The Amish were hands off, he learned.

"Jimmie, some detective from Philly wants to talk to someone about a couple of guys they're watching. They think they may be from here. You got time to talk to 'im?"

Jimmie was in the office filing reports and almost said no, those detectives were usually pompous and condescending. On the other hand, he might have a bit of fun, so he picked up the phone on his desk.

"Is this the sheriff?" the detective asked.

"No, this is one of the deputies."

"Is your sheriff around?" the voice asked.

"No, he ain't," the deputy answered, doing his best country hick impersonation. "Kin Ah hep you?"

After a slightly too-long pause, the weary sounding detective began. "We've been watching three guys that appear, from their plates, to be from your neck of the woods. Would you mind running them for me and let me know if you recognize them? They've been dealing, and it looks like something bigger is up."

Jimmy wrote down the license plates, and after a slight pause, said, "I don't need to run these. The first one belongs to brothers, twins, but not identical. What do you call that, when twins aren't identical? Fraternizing?" He chuckled at his own wit. "The second plate belongs to a fella named Jonathon. He's a bad ass. We've been watching these three for a while too. What are they up to? We don't see much of 'em any more. The brothers mainly show up around *Rumspringa*. Hardly ever see Jon anymore."

"*Rumspringa*, what the hell is that?" The detective had visions of these bumpkins bobbing for apples.

"You ever been out of the city, detective?"

"Yeah, once, but I got something on my shoe so I came right back home."

Here we go with this, Jimmy said to himself, and could feel the red on his neck starting to spread. He almost hung up the phone, but decided against it, and continued. "Yeah, well, I guess if I had the choice of living with all your rapists and murderers or out here in the country, with all the various things one could step in, I'd hightail it back, too." Without pausing long enough to let the detective retort, he went on. "We have a very fundamental religious group out here called the Amish. They live a very strict life with no electricity, no running water, make almost everything by hand, and are a very productive, God-fearing community."

The detective had heard of them and had seen the brochures. "So what? They make furniture, don't they?"

"Yes, they make furniture," the deputy acknowledged wearily. That's all these damn city people bother to remember, just the sound bite. "And they farm, and work in factories, and in stores, and get stuff on their shoes, and they build houses and barns, and they raise fine families, even if they are a bit strange. They are almost never any trouble, and for the most part, you couldn't ask for a better bunch of neighbors."

"For the most part?"

"They have this weird belief, based on their religion, that you can't join the church unless you have been exposed to, and even experience, the evils of the world. So, when their sons *and* daughters turn sixteen, they are allowed to go wild, run around, what they call *Rumspringa*. Can you imagine deliberately sending your daughter out to get drunk, do drugs, to get laid, when she turns sixteen, all in the name of getting religious?"

The deputy had a two year old daughter and he intended to do everything he could to *protect* her from the ugly side of life.

"The Amish know how to party. These parties usually have other Amish in from other states. It's not uncommon to see several hundred show up. The party, marking the beginning of *Rumspringa*, is by invitation only. They always pick a spot on one of the farms in the middle of their community, so we never get called about the noise or nothing."

The phone was silent again, for the better part of thirty seconds, and as the deputy was about to hang up, again, the detective said, "Tell me about the brothers, twins you said?" His voice was even, controlled.

"Not identical twins. *Fraternizing* twins. They are always together, but the blond haired one is the leader. He is ambitious, but a little slow, so they will never be more than two-bit dealers. His brother is scared of his own shadow, and the biggest danger he poses if he's ever brought in, is pissing himself. The third guy is worth watching. His name is Jonathon, and he's a bad one. The twins are wannabees, but Jon is going places. The last I heard, he joined the Raven's. I'm a little surprised he still has that same car 'cause we all know it by sight. The biggest trouble the twins have is Jonathon. He has always used them to run his errands, and if someone is going down, he wants it to be them. The twins are idiots."

"You know all this from watching them, Deputy? You have ESP or something?"

"I went to school with all three of them. The twins dropped out after the eighth grade, and Jon dropped out his junior year. He was trouble then, smart trouble, but always put the twins out front to take the fall."

Another long pause. "I have to tell you, I don't believe this stuff about the Amish being into drugs. Everyone knows their story, reads the brochures, visits their furniture stores. There are a couple of Amish furniture stores here in Philly. I love their stuff, and I find the *Rums* — whatever you call it, parties, hard to believe. Why, I don't know, but if this were even partly true, why wouldn't we see the arrest records? If they have these massive parties, according to you, where are the busts? Why don't we read about those?"

This was always the reaction the sheriff's department got from the city detectives; what was the point in going on?

"We do things different out here, Detective. The Amish influence brings an incredible amount of tourist money to the area. What do you think would happen to that tourist traffic if the headlines started running stories about rampant drug use? Besides, about 95% of the youngsters eventually join the church, so if they get drunk or stoned, we just look the other way. We have plenty of other calls."

"I'm sure getting stranded cats out of trees can be very time consuming." No response. "So you're telling me these three citizens we've been watching are old friends of yours. Two of them are a little retarded, but the third one is worth my time. And you're telling me that their main customer base is Amish sixteen year olds? All this cocaine is coming back out to the country, the peaceful countryside where I want to retire, and that as long as the drugs stay with the Amish, that you just let it slide? Do I have it right, Deputy?"

"We call it Amish snow."

"I think you are full of shit, Deputy. I don't know what your game is, but I plan to write a formal complaint, 'Impeding an investigation,' so expect to have this conversation with your Sheriff." The detective slammed the phone so hard it was a wonder it didn't break. His partner glanced up, only casually listening to one side of the conversation.

"What's up?"

"I got some retard deputy that claims the three boys are dealing in Amish snow."

"Whaddya mean?"

"He says the biker, his name's Jon, Jonathon, is buying speed and coke and the other two, it turns out they are twins, are selling it to the Amish for some strange religious ritual they go through when they turn sixteen. I hate calling out there. We always get this crap."

His partner rolled his eyes and went back to filing reports, reports about drug trafficking that appeared to be going to the country, but they were still trying to find out where in the country.

Samuel drove slowly back towards the motel, confused and conflicted. He had become "English for a day" for what purpose? Knife the twins for dealing? Why not the Bishops for condoning it? Why not himself for letting Emma go?

He had never been so weary in his life, and almost turned onto the freeway leading home, where he knew Rachael would be waiting, to the familiar, the safe, the place with no Emma. And so he didn't turn, he kept on going, just driving, trying to make sense of something, anything. He pulled into a café, a nice one, it appeared. He didn't notice the Harley parked at the other end, walked in and slumped into the first booth and ordered coffee. He absently stirred in five of the little creamers that the waitress brought. She came by his table, a little too often, with refills, and was tempted by his good looks to strike up a conversation. His troubled slouch stopped her, though, and she merely smiled politely, carefully pouring the coffee.

The troubled man, the weary man with the clipped accent, sat there for about an hour, and then left, tossing a couple of quarters on the table, not enough for a tip, got in his little black car and drove slowly off. He had calloused hands, she noticed, probably not an executive, and no doubt she would never see him again. Just as well, for in spite of his fit physique and pretty brown eyes, he had problems and the last thing she needed was more problems. So she wiped the table, and went to the next table, absently checking out the biker sitting there. He had a hard look about him, hard enough to temporarily unnerve the usually steely waitress. He had noticed the strange man that had come in, too, the troubled man, and disinterestedly watched as the man drank four cups of nasty coffee.

"What's your name, sweetie?" She seemed interested, the way any man interested her.

"Jon. Yours?"

"Susie, but *you* can call me Honey."

Jon wasn't particularly fussy about women, as long as they weren't too far over the hill, they all had the equipment he was looking for, but this one was a toss-back, reject. "Well, Susie, I gotta go, so keep the change." He stood, grabbed his black leather jacket, tossed a $10 on the table, and walked out.

Susie paid his bill, pocketed the change, and walked over to the next table. A man with a new pickup had just sat down. "What's your name, Sweetie?"

CHAPTER TWENTY-NINE

Ryan sat on one of the bales of hay in front of the stall, and reached up to pet the horse nuzzling the top of his head. He had been there since early morning, and realized he had not even taken time to eat lunch. He glanced at his watch: 5:30. The fillies had done pretty well in their first show, but nothing spectacular, so Ryan and the trainer had a long talk about what could be done to improve their performance.

"I think maybe the driver is a little too much in their mouths," Ryan commented. "We both noticed that before, have you said anything to her?" They had chosen this particular driver partly because of her exotic appearance up on the buggy seat, and hoped she would have a lighter touch than the men drivers they had tried. The fillies were very soft-mouthed and Ryan and the trainer both knew they did better with a lighter touch.

The trainer wouldn't look at Ryan, then said, "Maybe you can handle this job better than I can, huh? I can clear my stuff out in five minutes!"

Ryan had hired this man less than a year ago, but still had not gotten used to his temperamental outbursts. He chose to ignore this comment, although it took an effort. He suspected there was something between the trainer and the driver, none of his business until it affected their performances.

"She is a little heavy handed. You were the one that told me. I'm just asking what you thought after today's show."

There was an uncomfortable pause, and the trainer finally said, "Yeah, probably so, I'll talk to her."

"Okay, good. I'm going to call it a night. Is there anything you need a hand with?"

The trainer was about to pop off again, thought better of it, this was a good gig, and said, "No, thanks, we — I've got it handled."

Ryan gathered his clothes, caked with now-dry mud, and headed for his car. He started the car, put in gear, paused, and turned it back off. He climbed back out, walked to the row of payphones, and pulled the notebook out of his pocket. He looked at where he had written "Theresa." He didn't even know her last name, dropped two dimes into the pay slot, and dialed the number, slowly, watching the dial return to its upright position between numbers. It rang once, and he quickly hung up. He walked away from the open pay phone, reached for the car key, paused in mid air, and returned to the payphone. He found her number again, and this time he could hear her phone ring, his hand sweaty on the black phone handle.

She wasn't home, but she had a recorder.

"Hi, this is Theresa, leave me a message and I'll call you right back." His mouth went dry at the sound of her voice, and he could almost smell her beautiful hair.

"Hi, this is Ryan. It's about a fifteen before the six, and, I — uh — was, uh thinking — wondering, if maybe, if you weren't doing anything — too busy — maybe later we could get togeth — I mean maybe go to dinner or something?" He almost hung up, and then added his phone and room number at the hotel.

He returned the handle to its cradle, and put his head against the cold glass.

"Great. Hate those answering machines." Shaking his head at his fumbling, this time he did start the car, and pulled out of the parking lot, headed for his hotel, wondering if she would even call him back. "What does she want with me anyway? She's obviously sophisticated, well off, educated, upper crust, and I'm — well, look at yourself, man. Sure, you made a little money, but other than that, what is there? You know horses? She's probably just playing. Hopefully she won't even call back."

Ryan wished he had never called, never met her.

Theresa was happy, humming to herself, excitedly anticipating an evening with this handsome, gentle man, who would hopefully, finally, call her. "Jeez, what does a woman have to do to get a phone call, send an invitation?" she wondered to herself, smiling.

And so, when she stepped out of her car, she didn't even see the muscular, expressionless young man that snuck up behind and grabbed her, one gloved hand and jacketed arm around her waist, the other gloved hand roughly clamped over her mouth, effortlessly lifting her off her feet. With seemingly no effort, he walked back to the Lincoln, and roughly shoved her into the back seat, where she slammed up against a man sitting on the other side. The man with the gloves slid in beside her, and she became the center of a human sandwich. The stench of old cigar smoke, pounding adrenaline and her already churning stomach almost caused her to throw up. But it passed, and she sat there, startled and stunned, as the car roared away from the curb and down the tree lined street.

The driver slipped the huge black luxury car out onto the main street. Theresa looked at the man sitting beside her, the one she had slammed into. He had not said a word, and she watched the passing headlights and store front lights dance on his face. He was in his fifties, and was wearing a fine, wool, German driving hat, a large wool muffler, and dark sunglasses with black plastic frames. He wore a black trench coat over dark gabardine pants. They had been riding for about five minutes, not a word spoken, and finally, without looking at her, the man said, "You and Eshra meet later?"

He had a very thick German accent, and she didn't understand what he said. She looked at the man's face, but he was still staring straight ahead, expressionless. "I'm sorry, I didn't understand that," she said as evenly as she could. If she was afraid, he wasn't going to know.

"Are you meeting Eshra tonight?"

This time she understood the question, but didn't recognize who she was supposed to be meeting. "I don't know an Eshra," she responded.

He took his sunglasses off, and turned and looked directly at Theresa. It gave her a chill. "I know all about you, Theresa, and

I know all about Eshra." He was talking slowly, carefully pronouncing every word. "I watched you at Devon. Do you think I am stupit?"

He paused, and lit another cigar.

"You and Eshra can do whatever you want in Toronto. The trade up there is none of my concern. I sent some boys up to see what was going on, and as long as you keep your business out of Philadelphia, no one cares. But this business of coming into my city will not be tolerated. Pretending to come to the horse show, pretending to have a horse in rehab, Eshra pretending to be interested in the shows with his horses, I know all about that. The only reason you are still alive is because of the respect I have for your father, but I will not tolerate coming into my town." He had started to get agitated.

Theresa couldn't have been more confused, but decided against arguing with this man, so she said nothing, just sat and tried to make some sense of this man's comments. He obviously had her confused with someone else, and she didn't even know an Eshra. Her mind was still spinning when they pulled up alongside her car, the door still ajar and the dome light still on. "Leave town, and do not come back," he snarled.

She had barely climbed out of the car when it squealed off. She instinctively threw herself out of the way, and banged her right knee into her car, the knee still caked in dry mud. She stood there for a second, rubbing her bruised knee, head spinning, looking around, no one in sight, and closed the door to her car.

Theresa limped up to her apartment, not sure what she was going to do. She had always been level-headed, logical, so maybe when she had a chance to think things through, they would make more sense, she hoped. She turned the key in the apartment door, heart still pounding from the ride in the car, opened the door, stepped in, and looked around. Everything was exactly as she had left it — as far as she could tell. Thirty minutes ago, this was her home away from home, warm, comfortable, and now it was cold and uninviting, maybe even dangerous.

Theresa slowly walked, limped, around her apartment, looking in every room, behind every door, even under the bed. She crept into the kitchen, and opened a few of the lower cabinet doors, checking everywhere. She finally satisfied herself there was no one besides her. The red message light on her answering machine was blinking, and as she apprehensively rewound the tape, her heartbeat wound back up. Her well manicured finger poised momentarily above the "Play" button, then slowly descended and pressed down.

Relief flooded her tense body as she heard the familiar voice "Hi, this is Ryan. It's about a fifteen before the six, and, I — uh — was, uh thinking — wondering, if maybe, if you weren't doing anything — too busy — maybe later we could get togeth — I mean maybe go to dinner or something?" She jotted down his number.

She walked into her bedroom, across the deep carpet, and into the master bathroom, debating whether to call Ryan. She laid her purse and car keys on the marble vanity top, and slowly began removing her mud-caked clothes. She winced when she pulled her pants off over the sore knee, and glanced down at the swelling and the crumbled mud falling on the marble floor. She dropped her dirty designer clothes into the laundry bag left by the staff for the weekly laundry service. Terrycloth robe draped over her shoulders, she limped back out to the kitchen, rummaged in the freezer, and sat at the kitchen table, bag of frozen peas to sore knee.

"Okay," she started talking to herself, "number one, you're not dead. You're not even hurt, at least not intentionally. So let's rule out that whoever this fella is, he doesn't want either of those. Number two, he thinks Ryan is Eshra. If he saw us at Devon, which he says he did, or someone says they did, it would take very little digging to figure out that I was with Ryan, not this Eshra. So either he is stupid, which it appears he is not, or his information is coming from somewhere else, and that source is either stupid or is feeding him misinformation. Third, why this reference to my father?"

178

She thought about calling her father, ask him what the hell was going on, decided against it, and continued talking to herself. "Maybe Ryan knows this man. Maybe he knows who Eshra is? I need to call him."

She slowly began to wonder how Ryan could be involved in this, and as she mulled the various clues over in her mind, she became irritated. Ryan was in it, all right. He had to be. She picked up her phone and dialed his direct room number. After the fourth ring, his voice came on saying, "This is Ryan, leave me a message."

"Ryan, this is Theresa, it's about 8:00 and I need to talk to you. You will not believe what has happened to me. Call me right away." She wondered if the tension in her voice came through.

Samuel had already heard about the Kountry Klub, that infamous hell hole, the Devil's den, and had been able to find it on the city map, although he couldn't read a lot of the words. But he could match up the name in the yellow pages to the city map he had bought, and he knew generally where he was. The front desk clerk had not been helpful, he wasn't about to help anyone find that place, so Samuel headed out on his own. By now, the determination to seek revenge had been replaced by a sense of longing, sorrow, and he had all but decided to abandon this quest and return to his wife, to his life. He still wanted to talk to the twins first, and Ezra, if he could find them. He wanted to explain to them how they were ruining lives, just look at his own. And so he drove off, planning in his mind to head back to the country first thing in the morning.

He pulled out on the main drag, traffic was heavy, and was generally, almost casually heading towards where he thought the Klub was. He noticed the red GTO several car lengths ahead, in the same lane he was in, stopped in traffic, waiting for the light to change. Was that them? Was that the twins? As the traffic pulled ahead, towards the now green light, Samuel swerved his car sharply into the right lane, cutting off the lady in the Porsche. She laid on her horn, he slammed the accelerator pedal to the floor, and the car hummed ahead. The adrenaline hit the blood stream, and Samuel suddenly longed for his step-side, the 350 tuned for max power, but instead, the sewing machine on wheels hummed a little louder, and gradually closed the distance between the cars.

The twin on the passenger side, the nervous one, heard the horn blare, and leaned forward to look in his side view mirror just as the little black car that cut the Porsche off lurched into the other lane. His mirror was blurry with drizzle, and he couldn't make out who was in the car that had nearly pulled alongside.

"It's Jon," he screeched at his brother, "He's gonna kill us!"

His brother peered in the rear view mirror, through the rain distorted rear window, but couldn't make out what his brother was looking at. He turned to look over his shoulder, still couldn't tell. Holy shit, maybe it was Jon, and maybe he was going to kill them! He quickly turned back around, stomped the gas pedal, huge engine roaring, wheels squalling, and never even saw the traffic light turn red again. The last sounds he heard were his brother screaming, the skidding tires of the big truck trying to stop, the deafening crash of two tons of truck slamming into one ton of red Pontiac, and then nothing, not even the rapidly approaching sirens.

As distracted as Ryan was with the fumbled message he just left, he still glanced in his rear view mirror as he headed back to his hotel, a habit that he had formed in Toronto. The traffic was heavy. Devon was always a big draw, but he didn't notice anything out of the ordinary. On the way back to the hotel, Ryan remembered a couple of things he needed, and pulled into a convenience store. He absently made his way up and down the aisles, distracted with visions of black-haired Theresa dancing in his mind. He decided if he didn't have a message from her when he returned to his room, he would call again. He paid the cashier, and quickly walked back to his car, resolved to find this woman, whatever her intentions.

He backed out of the space in front of the brightly lit store, too quickly, anxious to return to the hotel. He had already begun to rehearse his next call to this woman, determined not to make a fool of himself for the second time. "Hi, Theresa, this is Ryan — Hello, this is Ryan — Hi, this is Ryan, is this Theresa?" Worse.

He needed to turn left across four lanes of traffic, close to a traffic light, and after a quick glance to the right, started pulling into the street, then glanced back to the left. He slammed on the brakes to keep from pulling into the path of the small black speeding car that had just crazily changed lanes. The car behind him, also anxious to leave the parking lot, almost crashed into the back of his car. Shaken, he looked up in time to see another car, a red car, rocket into the just-changed-to-red traffic light, and the big, two-ton dually truck accelerate from the side street, crashing with a thunderous slam into the passenger side of the car.

Drivers of half a dozen cars, just stopped for the red light, immediately jumped out and ran towards the burning car, one of them brandishing a fire extinguisher. Ryan hesitated, not sure if he should run over also, the young girl driver behind him blaring her horn impatiently. He finally turned sharply right, back through the parking lot onto a side street, and headed for his hotel. He didn't see the small black car u-turn and careen across all four lanes of traffic, narrowly avoiding another accident, and speed off down the big street, out of sight.

CHAPTER THIRTY

Shit! Ryan thought to himself, the image of the horrendous crash seared onto his mind. No one could survive that. Out of habit, out of a lifetime of habit, he wondered briefly where the man's soul would go.

Did he really believe that any more, he wondered absently.

Ryan was back on the main drag, six or seven blocks from the accident. Traffic was heavy, and he pulled off to the side of the road along with most of the other cars for the approaching police and fire trucks. A few drivers kept on going, oblivious, uncaring. "We'll read about this one in the paper," he said to the air in his car. "It's a bad one."

Ryan pulled back into traffic, mind wandering. His car seemed to have auto-pilot, turning first down one tree-lined boulevard, then another, and finally into his hotel's parking lot. He sat in the car watching the businessmen walking to and from the hotel entrance, like the swaying of a clock's pendulum, oblivious to his plight.

The small, spare hotel room was dark and cold. Ryan turned the thermostat up but kept his jacket on, waiting for the heat to warm the dimly lit room. He wandered to the window, looking down at the parking lot, for what, he didn't know. He glanced at the phone, partially hidden behind the lamp on the night stand, and didn't notice the red message light flashing.

Maybe this woman was just like all the other English women after all. His father had often said the English women were of the Devil, they all cheated on their husbands. What a myopic view of the world that old fool had, he laughed. But it wasn't just his father. That sentiment was institutionalized, all the Amish men believed it. It was doctrine. It isn't that Amish women have any different drives and desires than the English women, they just never have the opportunity. At least, after *Rumspringa*.

Ryan was still astounded how those years of brainwashing formed indelible imprints in one's beliefs, hard to erase, years later, even when one knows better. And yet he found himself returning to that old, groundless position about women, like a stretched suspender snapping back into place on his back. He worked hard, over the years, to treat and view women as equals. One day, he hoped, he wouldn't have to catch himself and force a more appropriate response. One day it would be natural, automatic, the first reaction, not the forced reaction.

Ryan's room phone rang. He quickly walked to the phone, nearly knocking the lamp over in the dark, and in that instant realized he had a message. Maybe she *had* called? Maybe this was the English woman again? "Damn it man, don't screw this up. She may be the brightest thing that has happened to you, ever."

"Ryan," he answered, trying, failing to keep his voice even.

"Why didn't you call me back?" she asked, irritation seeping through the line.

Ryan felt his blood pressure rise. Old reaction.

"I didn't see the message light. I just got back," he responded coolly. "Where are you?"

"I'm in my apartment, nursing a sore knee. What's going on, Ryan? I don't know why you didn't call me back. Who do you know from Germany or some other damn place that would want to scare me? Huh? What's going on?"

Ryan's head felt like it was about to explode. He had just witnessed a man, maybe two, surely killed. Now this woman, with her evidently over-active imagination, was too excited and agitated to make any sense, and it was directed at him. He thought about hanging up, but that little voice in the back of his head kept telling him to cool it, get the facts.

"Okay, slow down — "

"I am going slowly. I'm upset, and I think it involves you. I was abducted tonight, almost killed." She spoke very slowly, very deliberately, yet her voice was shaky. "Some asshole grabbed me outside of my apartment, on the street, and shoved me in the back seat of his car. Another man with a thick German accent and smelling like stale cigars asked me about Eshra, and told me to get out of town. He said he knew all about me and Eshra and wouldn't tolerate us coming to *his* town and horning in on *his* business. Do you know an Eshra who lives in Toronto and has come to Philly? He thinks *you* are Eshra. What is going on?"

Ryan felt his throat tighten, the room suddenly hot and stifling, sweaty. What *was* going on? And now she was in the middle of it, this woman whose scent and elegance simultaneously made his heart swell and his knees buckle.

"Theresa," he began slowly, softly, "I'm so sorry. Are you okay? Did you call an ambulance? Did you call the police? Are you hurt?"

The truth was she hadn't even thought about calling anyone but Ryan. Pissed as she was, her instinct had been to call him first. It was, for some inexplicable reason, imperative that she talk to him, be with him.

"My knee is just sore. I iced it and the swelling is already going down." She was calmer. "And, frankly, I didn't even think about calling the cops. Strange, isn't it? Maybe I should call them?"

Ryan heard the *beep-beep* signaling another call, and thought briefly about answering it.

"Are you there?" she asked.

"Yes." He decided not to tell her about the missed call. This time Ryan had to ask if she was still there, and after a pause, she answered that she was.

"Alright, there's nothing we can do about it tonight," she continued. "I'm going to get off the phone, have a hot bath, and try to get a good night's sleep. I'm not going to call the cops, at least not tonight, until I have time to think this through. If *Mr. German* wanted me hurt or dead, we wouldn't be talking, I'm sure. He also said he knows my father, so I will call him in the morning to see what he knows. I don't know what is going on, but I have a feeling there may be more to this than you are letting on. I want you to tell me everything, and be honest with me, but not tonight."

The line went dead.

Ryan was relieved that she was off the phone, but also confused. At the same time, he was finally determined to get to the bottom of all this. The phone calls had been going on too long, and now this woman that he couldn't get off his mind was involved. He needed to find the twins. His gut told him somehow they were in the middle.

Ryan called the front desk. The operator said he had two messages. "Some lady named Tracy, or Trisha, or something, said you had better call her back, right now. She sounded pretty upset. And you got 'nother one just now, some cop, says his name is Williams, says there's been an accident and you need to call him right away." She gave him both phone numbers and her opinion that he was going to have the most trouble with Tracy, she was plenty upset. She was laughing when he hung up.

In spite of the very efficient electric heater, the hotel room was suddenly cold again. Ryan sat on the edge of the bed for a minute, trying to collect his wits, failed, and reached for the phone.

"Front desk," the sergeant answered.

"Patrolman Williams, please," Ryan replied.

"One moment."

The line clicked and hummed, then, "Patrolman Williams."

"Hello, this is Ryan Miller, you just called a minute ago about an accident?"

The patrolman explained to Ryan that two young men had been involved in an accident a little while ago, a bad one, and the surviving man was babbling about his brother being dead. The survivor had been taken to Lutheran Memorial, and had asked for Ryan, and had this phone number written on the cover of a horse show pamphlet. The survivor? Could this be the same accident he had witnessed? Ryan explained where he was and asked for directions to the hospital.

The hospital was about ten minutes away, and his mind was spinning more than ever on the drive over, a million thoughts competing for attention. The patrolman had refused to give him any more details, urging him to go to the hospital right away.

Ryan pushed through the double glass doors to the emergency room, and rushed up to the admittance desk. The two

185

women in line in front of him were arguing with the tired, bored, indifferent middle aged woman behind the counter. The admittance procedure could not be changed, she was explaining to the first woman, look around, hold your horses, everyone has an emergency, she was just doing her job. The brightly lit room was packed: crying children, scared looking parents, the smell of disinfectant permeating the air. The busy ER staffers were doing their best to attend to their wards, but the flow coming in the door was more than they could handle. It was a Friday night. The worst cases were hustled off behind stainless steel swinging doors with cross hatched safety glass on the top, and the less critical placed on gurneys in the hallways.

Ryan's turn finally came, and he told the disinterested woman the story, explaining that his cousin had been brought in, probably less than ten minutes ago, and was asking for him. She flipped through the stack of admittance paperwork in front of her, said she couldn't find him, but feel free to look in the hallways. She probably just hadn't had time to do the paperwork yet. Ryan turned slowly away, and picking his way through sick and bleeding Philadelphia citizens, headed down the closest hallway, his stomach objecting to the strange smells and sounds. After about five minutes, he found his cousin, flat on his back, a needle with a clear tube sticking in his arm, white-taped in place, the tube connected to a clear plastic bag hanging from a stainless steel hook above his head.

His face was the color of the beige walls.

Ryan walked up to his cousin, lying on the stretcher, broken, and put a hand on his lower arm. The cousin looked up, slowly, and said simply, thickly, "Ezra."

The two men just looked at each other, temporarily wordless.

"Where is your brother?" Ryan finally asked.

The surviving twin turned his face towards the hallway wall, away from his cousin, and said nothing.

"He's gone, isn't he?" Ryan already knew the answer, but needed to hear it.

His cousin nodded ever so slightly.

"What happened?"

The twin said nothing for a couple of minutes, and then slowly looked back at his cousin standing over him, and started talking, slowly, painfully. "Ezra, you have always been there, even when we didn't deserve it. This all started years ago, part of *Rumspringa*, but you know all that. We were just having fun, making a little money, raising a little hell. You know the drill; everyone gets crazy during those times."

Ryan, Ezra, said nothing, kept his hand on his cousin's arm.

"My brother and me came to Philly, you know, looking for work, seeing if we could make some extra dough dealing, you know, nose candy, ice. But Jonathon wanted to keep us down, under his goddam thumb." He tried to swallow and continued. "An' speakin' of Jonathon, I'm sorry for the phone calls, man, that was supposed to be a joke. Jon asked where you was, and we was giggling an' crazy, laughin', guess we was stoned, so we gave him your number up in Canada. You called me onetime, remember, and left your phone number, said you was in Toronto? Maybe you forgot. Anyways, I called you back and got this recording that said you was Ryan Miller, so I put it together that you had changed your name. I guess Jon told this German fella that you was this big dealer in Toronto, and was coming to Philly to kick his ass, run him out of town. Jon's been braggin' how he tripped your wire. He was just sorry he couldn't be there to see it. The German went fuckin' nuts, said maybe he would even take a horse or two out. Jonathon had explained how much you loved those horses. So it was a gift, Jonathon said, when they heard you was coming to Philly-town. Jonathon decided to include your new girlfriend in his plan, and goaded the German into grabbing her, convincing him she was part of all this. Evidently the German knows her Daddy, some old business connection, and that's prob'ly the only reason she ain't popped."

The twin paused long enough that Ryan leaned over, saw he was still breathing. The twin looked up and continued. "We made a mistake. Bad mistake. We thought it'd serve Jonathon right, the goddam prick, if we bought our inventory somewhere else. So we found this German guy, one of our clients had heard about him. He didn't like Jonathon neither, so it didn't take no convincing at all to get him to start selling to us. I think he liked us. We always done what we said, too. Anyways, one of our other clients told us Jonathon was super-pissed, and we got to worrying about maybe we made a big mistake. So I called the German this afternoon, and told him you and Jonathon went way back, how you had been enemies since grade school, how much Jon hated you, and that Jon was just trying to get him to get you and maybe get rid of the German at the same time. I don't know." He raised his non-needle arm and brushed tears back with his stained Robin-egg-blue gown sleeve. "I don't know if the German believed me. I don't know, maybe he did." By now the twin was openly weeping, tears running down acne-scarred cheeks, onto the tiny hospital pillow.

"I killed my brother," he cried softly. "I killed him sure as if I'd shot him."

Ezra was stunned. Jonathon, Germans, the twins, his own cousins, Theresa, what the hell was going on? "Where is Jonathon now, tonight?" Ryan asked his cousin.

The twin just lay there, on the gurney, motionless, wordless. There appeared to be no signs of life at all, no blinking, no breathing, nothing. Ryan was just about to go get someone when his cousin, the bigger twin, the planner, the schemer, the brighter of the twins, slowly looked over at him and said, "He's always at the Kountry Klub. It's a biker place. *Auf Wiedersehen,* Ezra."

Ryan slowly turned from the still warm body that was, an instant ago his cousin, now a gradually cooling corpse. Ryan stood, feeling hollow and empty. He didn't see the man in the corner, watching him, dressed in new jeans, a nice denim long sleeved shirt with pearl covered snaps, a nice brown leather jacket, Nike shoes, and a bright red baseball cap with a white "P" embroidered on the front.

CHAPTER THIRTY-ONE

Ryan drove slowly past the Kountry Klub, down to the end of the chuckhole-filled gravel street, splashing muddy water up under his white rental car with each teeth-jarring drop into the murky holes. He made a slow U-turn at the first intersection, a four-way stop, and slowly returned to the dancehall. He pulled into the west edge of the lot, the furthest distance from the front door, beside the dumpster. The neon cowboy and his date dancing over the entrance shimmered in the muddy pools of water dotting the unpaved parking lot. There were the usual half a dozen people outside, taking a break from the chaos and noise and smoky-thick air inside.

It was 11:30 on a Friday night, and the party was in full swing. Two construction workers, morphed into cowboys for the night, were earnestly positing the benefits of spending the night to their skeptical dates. One of the girls giggled and said okay, and the couple staggered off to his recently scrubbed pickup. He opened her door with a flourish, tossed his too-big hat in the back on top of his tools, started the truck and rumbled off to consummate their newfound relationship. The other girl kept shaking her head no, and when her "cowboy" became a little too insistent, pulled loose from his grip, shouted something at him, stomped back inside, and hugged the first cowboy she came to. Her frustrated date shuffled off to his old Bondo-pocked van, kicked the front left tire, and rattled down the road to spend the frustrated night alone.

Ryan sat in his car, the cool of the evening and muffled music gradually creeping into the silent vehicle.

Ryan finally decided to go inside the dancehall. He had on black jeans and a soft black leather jacket, just like the one his mother had given him all those years ago. He climbed out of his car, carefully avoiding one of the pools of muddy water dotting the parking lot.

189

He had been past the Kountry Klub a couple of times, and had casually thought about how rough it looked. He wouldn't like it, he knew, with its low, rusty corrugated metal roof and clapboard siding, the wood front porch with hand hewn posts and rails, trying to look like a western saloon. The parking lot was full tonight, with all varieties of high handlebar Harleys, pickups new and old, some actual work trucks, and an occasional car. No one knew for sure who owned the place, but the burly man behind the bar, completely covered with wild, multi-colored tattoos, kept some semblance of order. He went by Tiny.

Ryan slowly walked the distance between his car and the front entrance, swinging saloon doors, wincing slightly at the ear-splitting volume of the off-key country band trying to sing "Help me make it through the night." He stepped up on the front porch, and slowly, cautiously, made his way inside.

Ryan stood inside the door for a minute, eyes adjusting to the dimness, smoke and haze. A few of the men glanced his way, took no interest, new workers came and went all the time, and went back to their liquid courage. The bar was to his immediate left, a long, mahogany, hand-carved antique, the finish worn and stained from years of abuse. The wall behind the bar was plastered with a variety of mirrors, lit and unlit, and there were over two hundred bottles of hard liquor, whiskey, tequila, and vodka, lining every glass shelf.

The low ceiling sloped from front to rear, seven feet tall at the front door down to six feet at the rear. The ceiling was partly covered with corrugated metal roofing, screwed and nailed onto the water stained ceiling from the inside. The leaking water ran down between the ceiling and these metal panels into gutters running along the inside of the rear wall. The gutters emptied into downspouts that disappeared through the bottom of the walls, the busted out holes sealed off with moldy pink insulation.

Tiny was behind the bar with the two women barmaids, all busily pouring and serving drinks, tossing glasses and bottles back and forth to the whistles and cheers of their audience. Tiny and the two women all had long, double pigtails, and they had practiced tossing their heads in unison, six long pigtails swinging together, like synchronized swimmers. The closest barmaid saw Ryan, smiled broadly, winked and blew him a kiss, and went back to work. Half a dozen patrons sat or leaned against the bar, posing, sipping their beer or whiskey, trying to talk above the din of the band and shouted conversations. A grizzled biker leaned his shaggy head forward so the woman hanging onto his arm could talk directly in his ear, rolled his head back with a loud guffaw, and ordered another drink. At almost midnight there must have been fifty revelers still having a good time. Construction was slow on Saturdays, half the workers didn't even bother to show up for work, and this was why they pounded nails all week, magical Friday night.

Ryan sauntered up to an opening in the sea of flesh leaning on the bar, and ordered a Sprite. Drink in hand, he turned around and leaned backwards on the bar top, hooking one heal of his black cowboy boots on the brass foot rail behind him, a study in casual indifference. He had never been comfortable in honkytonks, and was especially alert this night. He wondered if he would recognize Jonathon after all these years, but when he spotted him, in a booth at the back, there was no doubt. He suddenly felt cold, his hands grew icy, his breathing shallow and rapid. He stood up rigidly from his spot on the bar, and found himself staring at his old nemesis, the bully who was totally oblivious to this intent man at the bar. Jonathon was having a good time with his groupies, laughing and smoking.

Ryan put his half-empty glass on the bar top, edged towards the booth, slowly making his way past the late night couples. They were dancing, wrapped around one another, swaying in slow rhythm to the music, feet shuffling on the cornmeal and peanut shell covered wooden dance floor. Ryan had no plan, no idea what he planned to say or do. He stood at the end of the booth for a minute, and finally shouted "Jonathon!" as loudly as he could. The shout was snatched by the deafening music and dancing and loud conversations, and Jon didn't even look up.

"Jonathon!" he yelled again, and finally one of the women, the one closest to the end, looked up from her giggling and nudged the man on her right, leaned over and said something in his ear. Jonathon looked at his date, followed her thumb gesture up at the black-leather clad man standing there, the man with the grim look on his face, and motioned "what" with his hands and mouth. Finally, a look of recognition seeped over the biker's face, mirth replaced with just a flash of surprise, maybe even a little shock, and then broke into a broad grin. "Country," he said, mouthed, the sound of his voice overtaken before it even left the table. He leaned over and said something to the woman next to him and she slid out of the seat and slithered past Ryan, still giggling, rubbing against him on her way out. Jonathon slid out next, and stood up, still grinning broadly, ending up directly in front of Ryan, an inch from his nose.

"Whatcha want, son?" Same Jonathon, older and fatter. His large beer belly slammed into Ryan, shoving him backwards, off balance. Even in this smoke and beer soaked putrid air the man's breathe would have brought a mule to its knees, and as Ryan involuntarily took a step back, he caught his heel on the table leg and had to catch himself with his left hand. Jonathon broke into a laugh. This was his old buddy, the Ezra that had been so much fun to have around, and with a smirk he took a step forward. Before Ryan could react, he was yanked from behind, almost jerked off his feet. It was Tiny — there was going to be no fighting in his place. Tiny was twice as big as Ryan, and had no trouble dragging him across the floor, to the wild cheering of the crowd, and tossed him out the front door, sending him sprawling on the wet, muddy gravel.

"You wanna fight, do it out here. Better yet, get your sorry ass off my property." Ryan could barely understand him for the loud music blasting past the huge man, nearly filling the open door, but his intent was crystal clear. As Tiny turned to go back inside, Jonathon slipped past him, Mr. Cool himself, said something to Tiny who nodded "okay," and walked over to where Ryan was brushing himself off.

192

"What took you so long?" he asked. "I been messin' with you for a long time. You Ahmoh's sure are stupid. Too much inbreeding, eh, whatdya think, Country? Isn't that what you say up there in Canader, huh, *EH*?"

Ryan had lived this moment a thousand times. It would be over in a second, the spin kick to the left would take his old tormentor out in a split second. He wouldn't even see it coming. It was always the spin kick, his best move, his most practiced move that would end it before it started. But now that he was here, all the training flew out the window, and with a rage-soaked bellow, he threw himself straight at this evil man, head down, no discipline, no finesse, just straight in. Ryan never even saw the other biker, the one with the curled up fist, and when it crashed down on the base of his neck, pitching him forward even faster, his face couldn't have presented a better target for Jonathon's knee, the knee that caught him square on the nose, splattering all three men with his blood. Ryan went down in a crumpled heap, legs and arms jerking like the rabbits they used to shoot when he was a kid, and then he lay there, motionless.

His first conscious memory was of being dragged across the muddy gravel, away from the noise and the lights, out towards his car, onto the field next door. The two bikers unceremoniously dropped the black clad body like a sack of potatoes where they stopped, and stood back and lit their cigarettes simultaneously. They leaned back against the tree at the corner of the field, at least partially hid from passing traffic, and sucked on their smokes, still animated, their breathing slowly returning to normal.

"What are you going to do with him?" the second biker asked the drug dealer.

"See that big dumpster over there?" He motioned with his free thumb. "He's going to have a very long sleep with the other garbage."

Ryan looked up, head throbbing, one eye swollen shut, as the bully, his old nemesis, pulled the knife from his pocket, pressed the button and the gleaming blade snapped into place. The feeling was beginning to return to his hands and feet. He could actually control the movement of his fingers again, and he readied himself to kick, bite, scratch, throw mud, whatever it took.

Just as Jonathon started to bend over to "End this silliness, get rid of this stupid nuisance," bright headlights flipped on, flooding the three men, Ryan's car, the tree, the field, and part of the road in brilliant light. Jonathon looked at the source of the lights, squinted, angrily shouted, "what the hell —" He folded the knife back into his pocket and started walking menacingly towards the car. As he approached the car, he stopped, dead in his tracks. He knew that car. That car shouldn't be here. That car was never here. His biker buddy had disappeared, it was one thing to have some fun in the dark, but this wasn't his gig, this was Jonathon's, so he was gone, and Jonathon was there by himself.

The big black Lincoln didn't move, just sat their idling, prying the dark with bright lights. Jonathon hesitated for a minute, looked back at his prey, and decided to call it a night. There would always be another time. This country fool would be back, he didn't have a clue who he was up against. He walked quickly over to his bike, the one closest to the front door, coughed it to roaring life, and spun gravel onto Tiny's front porch as he made his hurried exit.

The Lincoln sat and idled for another couple of minutes, then dimmed lights to low beam and backed slowly out of the spot it had occupied, and moved towards the paved road, turned left and disappeared around the corner.

Ryan lay still, rage mixed with humiliation, throbbing pain mixed with determination. He finally pulled himself to his hands and knees, fell over onto his left side, and lay still once again, head throbbing in time with his pounding heart. After what seemed an eternity, he tried again, was able to remain steady on his hands and knees, and finally pulled one knee up under his torso. In an agonizing effort, he finally stood upright, looking like a toddler taking his first steps, almost falling, catching himself, and slowly, painfully, shuffled his way to his car. He dropped the keys once, head thumping again as he bent over to pick them up, found the door key, unlocked the door and fell in. He sat, slumped, the dome light on for all the world to see this defeated country boy.

His bleeding nose had slowed but not stopped, and the blood was both slippery and sticky on his hands, making it difficult to drive. He drove very slowly, fuzzy-brained, and wondered if he would make it back to his hotel. There were a few close calls, horns blaring too loudly in his pain wracked brain, but eventually he made it into the hotel parking lot. It was late, very late, so he decided to use the rear entrance, up the back elevator, to avoid the questioning looks. He left a few bloody smears on the elevator's control panel, sure to raise some eyebrows in the morning. He finally found his room, struggled with the slippery key, and staggered inside.

His mind had finally begun to clear, and he knew he wasn't going to like his mirror tonight. He decided to clean up in the kitchenette first, and trudged over to the little stainless steel sink, tracking mud and blood on the floor. He grabbed a wad of paper towels, and began the tedious, delicate task of cleaning the mud and gravel and caked blood from his face. He finally finished with his face, and gingerly removed the torn leather jacket, dropping it on the vinyl tiled floor. His right arm was starting to bruise where he had evidently hit something on one of his trips to the ground, and he winced as he touched it gently. He decided against trying to wash his hair in this little sink, and mustered the courage to go to the bathroom, finally ready to assess the damage. He made his way across the carpeted floor of the living room, now dressed only in his black T-shirt, boxers and socks, and stumbled into the bathroom. As carefully as he had been cleaning himself up, trying to make himself somewhat presentable to himself, the man staring back looked shocked. His nose was obviously broken, blood still slowly seeping out the bottom onto his upper lip, and his eyes were slowly turning black. He barely recognized the man in the mirror, and for just a second, the room swam again.

"Well, Country, you may as well try to get some rest. Can't go back to the hospital. Too many questions. Man, you were awesome tonight."

He cleaned up the little blood on his upper lip, carefully avoiding touching his huge nose, and walked into the bedroom, exhausted and hurting, when the room phone rang.

CHAPTER THIRTY-TWO

Samuel had been driving aimlessly around Philly for an hour, going nowhere. His little sewing machine car finally sputtered and coughed, jarring the family man back to this world. With a final, futile whine, the little engine quit, fuel tank drained, coasting to a stop beside the road. Samuel stared straight ahead at nothing, finally switched the key off, and slowly got out of the car. He could see bright lights beaming into the sky, backlighting the bare trees several blocks away, closer to the highway, and walked slowly towards them.

He had known the twins since their birth, a happy affair, any time you add to your family. He thought of their father, odd-man-out in the company of odd people, but even he showed signs of joy on that wondrous day, awed by God's gift, twin boys.

Joy. Now there was a word he hadn't thought of for a while. Joy came from inside you, right? Isn't that what the church teaches? Who are we, mere mortals, to question God's will? There is a bigger plan, always a bigger plan. We were placed here on earth for mysterious reasons, temporary inhabitants in an evil, wicked place. Only through self denial and discipline can we leave this place with peace, reach the eternal prize, confront and conquer the Devil, and with God's help, ascend into heaven, spend eternity with the Lord. But what if your only daughter is taken? And what about the twins? Did they deserve this? A bloody end? They were good boys, a little misguided, sure, but good boys. Everyone hoped they would come back home some day.

The weary, confused, angry, sad, unhappy man slowly made his way towards the lights of the highway, and he thought of Ezra. Ezra, always steady, always willing to help, successful, even-tempered. He needed to call Ezra. But Ezra has rejected the church's teachings, he argued with himself. "I need one of the Bishops. I need my Rachael. I need my Emma."

In the middle of the litter-pocked parking lot behind the late night store, Samuel dropped to his knees and for the first time since his baby girl left him, tried to pray. He really tried. He closed his eyes, clasped his hands over his head, reaching for the sky, and tried to pray in a loud voice. Pleaded with God to give him a sign, something, anything, please! And then he waited, but nothing happened. A sole car slowed to look at this spectacle, didn't like what they saw, and sped off. Samuel slowly rose to his feet. "Where are you?" he demanded of the sky. Empty. Nothing.

Samuel stumbled into the all night mini-mart. Lard-fried chicken simmered and bubbled in the oft-used tin pan behind the grease splattered display glass. He wasn't particularly hungry and yet ravenous at the same time, and ordered the two-piece special, two thighs, white meat was extra, a biscuit and soft drink. Samuel took his meal from the disinterested teenager behind the counter, slumped into the worn, hard, bent-Formica bench seat and slid the red and white grease-soaked chicken box to the center of the sullied table.

Slowly chewing the rubbery fowl, barely able to swallow, Samuel took a few sips of the flat Pepsi, and slowly, like the first light on an overcast morning, began to realize that today he would be going back home. He knew Rachael would take him back. Wouldn't she? Would she be waiting for him? What was he thinking, he shook his head, just leaving, leaving that poor, sad, wonderful, loyal woman at home alone to grieve for her daughter, and now her husband? And the church would take him back; that was one of the church's great strengths, no matter what, they would always take you back.

The realization had its calming effect. Anyone watching this frumpy farmer would have certainly seen the difference. The hard lines around his mouth and eyes began to soften, and staring eyes came back into focus, seeing once more.

Samuel tossed most of the meal in the overflowing trash can and walked outside, reaching for the first payphone in a row of three on the front of the building. It was late, he knew, but he needed to talk to Ezra, tell him he forgave him for Emma's death.

198

He had written the direct phone number to Ezra's hotel room on a piece of paper, the hotel's front desk attendant had been cooperative, and after a hesitation, dialed it.

"Hello?" Ezra sounded like he had a bad cold and was not at all happy, very tired.

Samuel couldn't talk. Try as he might, no words came. What was he thinking, why was he calling? He gently replaced the black receiver into its cradle.

Theresa couldn't sleep. She had completed her normal evening routine, meditative music and yoga followed by the usual herbal tea, but it didn't help. She had left three messages with the front desk at Ryan's hotel; she couldn't quite bring herself to call him directly. Let him call her back. In spite of what she had said, she needed, wanted, to talk to him again, now, tonight. Somehow she knew he wasn't the problem. So she slid back out of bed, wiggled into her house slippers, shrugged into her housecoat, went out into the kitchen, and put the still warm teapot back on the flame.

While the water slowly heated and bubbled to a boil, she sat at the kitchen bar, chin in cupped hands, elbows resting on the marble counter top, debating whether to call Ryan again, his room this time. It was almost three in the morning, he already had three messages asking, almost pleading, with him to call her, no matter the time, and he hadn't called. "Evidently he doesn't want to talk to you, at least not tonight. Wait 'til morning." No, it had to be tonight, right now.

The stainless teapot began its urgent whistling, and pouring the water, she decided, finally, to call his room, call direct. Maybe he hadn't gotten the messages? That had to be it, he simply hadn't gotten the messages, or surely he would have called. She reached for the phone and cautiously, slowly dialed the number to his room. Busy. Busy? Three o'clock in the morning and his phone was busy? Who was he talking to at three o'clock in the morning?

She stood up and began rapidly pacing, her robe billowing behind her, like wind whipped waves. This was not like her, letting a man keep her awake until the wee hours of the morning. She had known other men, but in general found them to be rather — simple? Was that the word? One dimensional? Self-absorbed? Whatever the description, they didn't particularly interest her, except in an occasional, pass-the-time sort of way, to be shooshed out the door as soon as was polite. A few of them had hovered for a couple of days, almost irritatingly so, but finally got the point and faded to black. Some were educated, some were rich, but they all lacked depth, sincerity.

Her mind drifted back to Ryan, smart, yet a little rough around the edges, and a small smile crept onto her face. What was it? Was it the thrill of the chase? He was one of only a handful of men that had not fawned all over this black-haired goddess. "You want what you can't have? No, probably not." She wasn't like that. She didn't want something just because she couldn't. What did she know of this man Ryan? Nothing, really, except that somehow, something in his world had bought her a ride with a sinister man with a thick accent that said he knew her father.

She couldn't get Ryan out of her head. What was his connection to the German? She felt a kinship with Ryan, a feeling she had never before experienced. Did this feeling blind her to a sinister side he may have? Somehow, she didn't think so.

She picked up the phone handset and spun the rotary dial again, impatient between numbers. This time it rang and rang, no answer. She slowly hung up and sat on her sofa in the dimly lit room, sipping her tea, now worried.

Ryan no sooner hung up the phone to the anonymous caller, the one he thought he had left in Toronto, when it rang again. His first inclination was to answer the phone and scream obscenities at this maniac, ask him where he was, "I want to meet you right now," but just the initial, jerky motion of reaching for the phone sent pain shooting into the base of his brain, and instead he unplugged the cord from the back of the phone and threw it on the floor. He slowly, painfully, stumbled over to the couch and curled into a fetal position.

CHAPTER THIRTY-THREE

Ryan is a demon of speed and accuracy, hitting Jonathon at will, slipping and turning away from his clumsy attempts to strike back, as if the bully was fighting in a bottle of thick syrup. Ryan's last brilliant move was a jumping spin kick, so accurate and so hard that the drug dealer's head was torn violently from his shoulders, and sent spinning past Tiny standing in the front door and onto the empty dance hall, splattering the hapless bartender with blood.

Hands clenched and sweating, Ryan woke with a jolt, both couch pillows knocked onto the floor. A rare, early morning autumn sun crept through the open curtain, shining into his black, swollen eyes. He turned away from the brilliant pain, and slowly came back to life, back from the fight, back into his room. Too fuzzy-brained to think, he lay there, and finally, after what must have been half an hour, slowly rose to a sitting position, head cradled in his hands, hands still faintly streaked with blood and mud. His thoughts were faint sparks this morning, random sparkles, making little or no sense.

Ever so carefully, Ryan rose from his thinking man position and slowly shuffled to the kitchenette, poured tap water into the cheap, metal coffee maker and put two packets of the hotel coffee in the top. The coffee maker slowly gurgled and sighed to hot life, and with unsteady hands, he poured the scalding liquid into his cup. He took an uncoordinated sip and jerked the cup away from his now-burned tongue and top of his mouth, spilling even more on the floor. Finally, between the strong coffee and the plain fact of being awake, his brain started to function, and he began playing events over in his mind.

The gray plastic end of the long phone cord was still unplugged, lying on the low-pile blue rug next to the nightstand. Ryan thought back over the past several months. Jonathon, with the unwitting help of the twins, had evidently taken his all-consuming hatred of all things Amish to a new level. Starting with the phone calls, disciplined phone calls every evening for, how long, two months, and then hatched this plan to involve the German, hoping to get Ryan killed? Was he that consumed? Evidently. And the twins, dedicated screw-ups, careening carelessly through life, knocking things over, finally smacking the wall, gone. At least the German knew he wasn't really here to take over more drug territory. Man, what a story line, and he obviously believed it. Or did the twin really tell the German that? Who knew what the truth was any more? Was the drug business really this crazy? And what of Theresa? She was shoved into this car, maybe the German's, and told to leave town with Eshra, an obvious reference to him. Theresa. Even through the muddled brain and bruised body, he could feel his heart swell at the thought of this woman.

Ryan had never had any contact with the police in his life. It was simply something he had never been exposed to. "It is not our way." How often had he heard that growing up? And he probably still wouldn't have involved the police except for her. He had always managed to take care of himself, but this had gotten out of hand, she could have been hurt badly. He decided he would call the central station, at least clue them on to Jonathon, let them check him out, hell, they probably know all about the Kountry Klub anyway.

Ryan walked back into the bedroom area, looked at the still unplugged phone cord, and remembered the second late night phone call he had not answered, and plugged the cord back in. The phone rang almost immediately. He let it ring a couple of times, and then warily picked it up.

"Hello?" He answered in his thick voice.

For a minute there was silence on the other end, and Ryan felt the color on his neck start to brighten. He was about to hang up on this maniac, it was out of character for Jonathon to be starting this early in the morning, when a woman said, "I'm sorry, I have the wrong number."

Ryan immediately recognized Theresa's voice, and said "Wait —" just as the line went dead. "Damn," he muttered. He badly wanted to see her, hold her, try to explain. Would she ever want to talk to him again? Man, I can't buy a break, he thought. He was about to return to the other room when he noticed the red message light blinking.

The detective was on the day shift for the month, and he walked into the busy precinct station, through the glass door to his office. He threw the morning paper on his desk, sending some unfinished reports to the floor. Section B of the paper had a small item about a fatal accident the night before over by the Kountry Klub, and he casually glanced through the article, didn't recognize any of the victims, and tossed it aside. He went for his second cup of coffee, and had just returned when the phone on his desk rang. It was the desk sergeant.

"I've got some drunk wants to talk to someone about drug trafficking. I can't hardly understand him, probably stoned out of his gourd. Can you imagine being wasted this early in the morning?"

The detective sighed and pushed the second button on the bottom of his phone, the one that was lit, the outside line button. They got so many tips it was ridiculous, most of them either revenge setups or just plain mean, getting the cops to make someone's life miserable, usually over a soured drug deal. But occasionally —

"Detective Swansen."

"Do you handle drug cases?"

No, I just play with myself all day, he wanted to respond. He had a bit of trouble understanding this person, probably a man, although you never knew. It sounded like he had a bad head cold and was talking through a towel. His words were pronounced well, the person was educated, but he thought he recognized the clipped, German-tinged manner of speaking that came from the surrounding country. These guys always called from pay phones, watching too much TV, as if they could or would trace every crank call that came in. Where do these idiots come from, he wondered tiredly.

"Uh, yeah, whatcha got?"

"Do you know a place called the Kountry Klub?"

The detective stopped shuffling the paperwork he had also been working on and listened a bit more closely. The Kountry Klub was arguably the busiest drug center in the city, and they had been interested in it for some time. "Yes, I do, why?"

"They deal drugs over there."

No shit, Sherlock. "And just how would you know that, my friend?"

Ryan could tell the conversation was not going well. It dawned on him that this detective probably got a dozen calls a day similar to this, and if he had any hope that the detective would even write this down, he was going to have to give him something more, something to get his attention. "I know a man named Jonathon. I don't know him well, but he has been bragging about having a cop in his pocket, that he's bulletproof, that he owns this town, that he can do whatever he wants and no one will touch him." Ryan paused, waiting to see if this fabricated, hopefully-true, story would get any attention.

"Go on." Any time a citizen called with allegations of a bad cop, it was worth listening to. These stories usually didn't go like this. Usually they wanted to tell about how bad so and so was, when would we go arrest his sorry butt, haul him off to jail. Dirty cop? Let's see if this scumbag has anything else.

Ryan gave a detailed description of Jonathon, including the license plate number on his Harley. He went on to talk about the German connection, how it looked like drugs were being funneled in from Europe, not the normal southern route. He had the plate number from the Lincoln, would the detective like that too? The detective said he would, and as he slowly hung up the phone, he finished the long note he had written to himself.

His partner was late this morning, and walked in as the detective made the last entry in his little notebook. "I just got a call from a fella, probably a junkie, but he says the guy we've been watching at the Kountry Klub is buying from some guy from Germany, and they've got a cop on the payroll."

His partner paused in mid motion, and slowly turned to look at his partner. "Did he mention Jon by name?"

"Yes."

"He says our man has been buying from some German guy. Remember that Lincoln that's been around, with the out of town plates? He says that is the big guy, the one we should be interested in. I think our caller got the shit beat out of him, I think he is from the country, and I think he knows a lot more about what's going on than he told me."

"That would be a first, huh?" his partner joked dryly.

"What we got going this afternoon? We got time to run over there later and see if our man is around? Maybe we'll get lucky."

"Let's do it. We need to check on the break-in over on 15th, but we can do that on the way over to the Klub."

Jonathon was in a dark mood. He had long ago made a policy of not dealing directly, keeping the twins between him and the buyers, and now those colossal fuck-ups had gotten busted up, dead. He debated with himself, finally deciding he would deal directly for the time being, a short time. He knew all the spots in town, he had kept close watch over the twins, and the middle school crowd shouldn't be much trouble. So he would deal direct, just for the time being, until he found new packers, new junkies.

He was worried about the German, too. Tiny had called. No one made Tiny nervous, but he sure sounded nervous when he told Jon about the young, huge, blond headed man that parked a black Lincoln right in front of the entrance, climbed out of the driver's side, and came into the Klub asking for Jon. Someone, probably one of the twins, had evidently told the old German that Jon had been using him to get to Ezra, and he would be beyond pissed. Jonathon had seen the old German angry one time, with a biker that hadn't paid, and he shuddered slightly at the memory.

He didn't know why he hated Ezra so much, and didn't spend much time trying to figure it out. He just hated him, probably simply because he was different. He hated all of those ignorant people, those "God-fearing," simple-minded foreigners living in the best part of the country.

It was late afternoon and school had been out for over an hour. Jonathon drove slowly towards the middle school on the west side of town, where the twins had bragged that they moved the most stuff. He had borrowed a friend's car, and had smeared mud on the license plates, obscuring the numbers. The few remaining kids were just hanging around, smoking, boys watching the girls, trying to catch a glimpse of what might be under those tight little miniskirts.

Jonathon circled the school for the second time, making pains to go several blocks into the adjacent neighborhood before returning for a second pass. As he drove slowly by, one of the boys motioned over his left shoulder with his thumb, evidently indicating he wanted to meet behind the school, by the metal swing set, next to the empty basketball court. Jonathon gave him a thumbs-up in return, and turned the opposite direction, back into the neighborhood, went several blocks, turned on another residential street, and eventually made his way to where the boy was standing, hands in his pockets.

Jonathon had been cautious, very cautious, on this his first foray into direct drug distribution. He idled slowly up to the sallow looking kid and cranked his window down, cool autumn air spilling onto his face. The young boy sauntered over to the open window, and looked in at the new face behind the wheel.

"Where's my man? Who the hell are you?"

"He got hung up. I'm his older brother. What the hell do you care?"

The boy was silent, eyes squinted, taking in the new driver. He wiped his constantly running nose on his shirt sleeve, and his pupils were dilated, like a cat's in the middle of the night. His hands twitched slightly.

"Maybe you da man? Huh? You da man?"

He was doing his best TV crime drama mimic, and Jonathon was in no mood for it.

"Listen, sonny, I got a lot of stops to make today, so if you got the jack I got the smack, capiche? Just cut the bullshit, okay? I got these nifty little plastic packets with $5 of white happiness snuggled inside, so if you want to be happy, pull that wad of cash out of your pocket, count it out, give it to me, take this and get the hell out of here. Or, if that is too much for your tiny brain, go home and sit on your mamma's lap, and cry to her about how mean someone treated you."

The boy's cheeks started to redden. He was about to make a smart remark back to this new distributor, this jerk, when they both were stunned at the big black car sliding to a stop on the loose gravel inches from Jonathon's car, blocking him in between the chain swings and the monkey bars. The boy no longer wanted anything, thought fleetingly of his mamma's lap, and dove between the car and the corner of the red brick school building, rolled immediately back onto his feet at a dead run. He could hear shouting and gunfire over his shoulder, but never paused to even look back.

Jonathon had made that most basic of mistakes: getting so involved in the business at hand that he forgot to keep an eye out, and now the German, that rabid assassin, had him cornered, had him boxed in, on his first delivery. He yanked the gearshift into reverse, slammed into the black car, grabbed the 9mm pistol on the seat beside him, jerked the car door open, and flung himself out of the door onto the loose gravel, rolling. If he was going down, the German was going down with him. He quickly rose to a half crouch, and began firing indiscriminately at the figure that had jumped out of the big black car, hitting him. He realized at that instant that it wasn't the German, and it wasn't a Lincoln, and the other man that jumped out was shouting something that sounded like "Police!" And then it went dark. And cold. Very cold.

     The two detectives grabbed their coat jackets. Shorter days meant cooler evenings, and they knew they would need them before the night was over. They headed down the back stairs of the precinct station, down to the parking garage, and made their way out the back ramp in the black Crown Victoria. It was one of the newer fleet cars, and they had chuckled on several occasions how it looked like the new Lincolns, weren't they hot shit? They were both in good moods; they had received commendation letters just that morning on their arrest and conviction rate. Behind the good natured ribbing about who they were blowing to get those letters, the other detectives clearly liked them. A couple of rookies even openly congratulated them.

     They pulled up to the bakery shop that had been robbed, avoiding the broken glass still lying on the sidewalk and in the street gutter, and stepped inside. They spent half an hour talking to the patrol officers, first to arrive on the scene, swapping jokes and stories in between noting details and gathering what information they could about the robbery. By the time they wrapped up it was late afternoon, probably still too early for any real action at the Kountry Klub, so they decided to swing by a couple of the schools. A few mothers had been complaining about drug activity after school.

     The first couple of schools they drove by were normal, if slightly disturbing: kids trying to be adults hanging around outside, smoking, pointing at the two cops driving slowly by. One of the kids flipped them off. Detective Swansen, driving, slammed to a stop and the kid immediately disappeared around the corner. The detectives slowly moved on, making their usual remarks about the sorry state of the nation's young.

     The shadows were growing longer, and the breeze diminished to almost nothing as they approached the last school, slowly driving by the front of the almost deserted red brick building.

"Let's get on over to the Klub," the shorter detective said to his partner behind the wheel.

"Okay. I'm gonna drive around back for a quick look and then we'll head over."

The detective sensed something. He could have turned right, to the east, but he instinctively wanted whatever western glare was left in the ruddy sky behind them when they approached the back of the school, and so turned left, then right, then right again. The big black car slowly rounded the corner, turning east on the beautiful, tree lined street that ran beside the playground. The gate was open through the six foot tall, galvanized, ugly chain link fence that imprisoned the children when they were out playing. The nose of the Crown Vic nudged past the open gate, and they saw the back end of a car sticking out around the corner of the old school, idling, the exhaust smoke disappearing upward from the tailpipe. Detective Swansen hit the brakes, slammed the car in reverse, backing down the street, jerked it back into drive, turned the steering wheel sharply, and whipped through the gate, roaring up behind the car. The detectives' car slid to a slightly sideways stop and the shocked boy that had been talking to the driver dove backwards, fell to the ground, immediately got up and sprinted off around the east end of the school.

The driver of the parked car violently rocketed his vehicle backwards, spewing gravel against the school, and crashed into the detectives' black cruiser so hard that Detective Swansen dropped his service revolver on the floor, and he bent over to retrieve it. His partner jumped out of the passenger side, gun in hand. The drug dealer leaped out of his idling car, fell to the ground, and as he sprang back to his feet started shooting, hitting the detective. Detective Swansen jumped out, shouted "Police!" crouched behind the nearly useless shield of the driver's car door, leaned around the edge, and with a single shot dropped the drug dealer, who crumpled without a sound where he stood.

210

CHAPTER THIRTY-FOUR

Samuel had made his way back to the motel, on foot, several hours earlier, and fell exhausted onto the bed, fully clothed. He was partially awakened when the motorcycle started up right outside his window. But it wasn't until the biker twisted the hand throttle on the right side handle bar, exacting a sudden, loud "brattt" from his bike, that the bleary eyed man from the country could be counted among the living once again. For a moment he just lay there, stupid, completely disoriented. Consciousness, unwelcome consciousness seeped into his being, and the events of the previous days came into focus.

But today was different, today he was going home.

Samuel hadn't showered in several days. There hadn't been time. But, this morning he would shower. He wanted his Rachael to have her same husband back, well, as close as he could get, considering the close cropped hair and shaved chin. He had kept his clothes, the plain black clothes that were so familiar, and even though they would be crumpled they were clean. He quickly slipped out of the clothes he had slept in for the past two nights, and walked briskly towards the bathroom, wearing his socks, protecting his bare feet from the filthy carpet.

The shower helped to clear his mind, and as he dried off he glanced at the coffee maker with the coffee stains running down the sides, smiled to himself and shook his head. He didn't need any stimulants this morning. He reached for the bag of clothes on the floor of the coat closet. He poured the drab clothing out on the bed sheets, and carefully smoothed out the garments before putting them on. When he had finished, he allowed himself one quick look in that portion of the cracked mirror hanging over the sink that still reflected images, and was satisfied with what he saw. He and Rachael didn't have mirrors in their house, even though the Bishops were silent on the issue, wanting to be careful not to encourage pride. But this was different. It was important to make sure his appearance wouldn't be too much of a shock when she saw him. His short-cropped hair was mostly camouflaged by the black hat. He would prepare her before he took it off. He had always worn his beard short so his shorn face didn't look that out of place, except for the stubble.

He tossed his English clothes in the trash.

Samuel stepped out of his room, and several of the men lounging for their early morning smoke stopped and stared, the usual kind of stare his kind got when they mingled with the English. He was determined not to notice, not this morning, and walked briskly down the street, retracing those ten blocks he walked last night, down to where the sewing machine car was still parked. The only damage was a broken off antenna. Most of the vandals had already gone to bed when he left it last night. He continued past the little car, towards the all night mini-mart with the greasy chicken. The attendant on duty was young and was reading the morning paper. He was middle-Eastern and not at all interested in his job. He glanced at Samuel waiting patiently at the counter, then continued reading. So Samuel turned and reached for one of the two red five gallon metal gas cans on the bottom shelf, across from the counter. He placed it on the scratched glass top and waited.

He was patient for a minute, then finally asked, "Might I could trouble you please for to allow me to pay you?"

The swarthy young man deliberately folded his newspaper and said, "It's not for sale."

Samuel calmly, patiently pointed to the $2.99 price tag. He was used to this treatment.

"When we only have two left, we rent them. We don't sell them."

Samuel held the young man's gaze, not blinking. "Okay, for sure, can I please rent it?"

"Yeah."

"Would you mind telling me, please, how much it does cost to rent it?"

"Fifty bucks."

Samuel stared, then reached into his front pocket, withdrew the wad of bills, and counted out fifty dollars. The attendant watched him, took the money, stuffed it in his pocket, and as Samuel turned to leave, said, "The gas is ten bucks." Samuel stopped. He had seen the price per gallon on the pump. It read $0.55, and even Samuel knew five gallons was not ten dollars. But he reached into his pocket again, and laid another ten on the counter. This one also disappeared into the young man's pocket.

"You know how to work the pump?" He was being insolent.

Samuel nodded yes, walked to the pump and filled the container. He lugged the full can back to the car, realized the container did not have a spout, and sloppily poured most of it into the car's tank. The little Pinto sputtered and coughed to life, and Samuel drove the two blocks back to the store. He entered the lot from the side street, and decided to fill up somewhere else. He returned the container to the attendant, wished him a good day, and left.

Samuel headed north on Government Boulevard to Green Street, turned left towards the Interstate, and merged with the sparse early morning traffic, away from the city. He decided to call Ezra, he was once again interested in the man's soul, and pulled into the first rest area. He walked into the new building, nodding at a man dressed in total black, his long curly hair hanging to his shoulders, walked to a wall pay phone, and dialed his old friend at the hotel. The hotel operator answered, and put him through to Ezra's room. The phone rang several times, and then went to the hotel's answering system. He didn't understand exactly when he was to start talking, but began anyway.

"Ezra, this is Samuel. My girl Emma is dead, killed of an overdose in *Rumspringa* last week. I should have told her to not go to that party. She didn't have to, and now I have to live with that. I will take it to my grave. I have been in the city, trying to find the demon that did this to my Emma, and have for sure found him and killed him and his evil twin. I didn't mean for it to happen,

213

but it did happen, and God's will cannot be denied. All this is part of His will, even if I for sure don't understand it." There was a long, shrill tone on the phone. Samuel pulled the receiver away from his face, looked at it, and then continued, "I am going to return to my house and plead for forgiveness from God Almighty and from my wife. I don't know if they will forgive me." He paused, then, "Come back home, Ezra. This is not our life. Come home and repent, join the church, you and I both know you are headed for Hell. You need for to come home, Ezra."

Samuel went on and on, a long, rambling pleading for the man's soul, not knowing that he had exceeded the message length allowed by the hotel. And so all Ryan heard was that the crazed man had been in the city, his Emma was dead, and he had killed the twins.

CHAPTER THIRTY-FIVE

Ryan called the front desk and listened to the operator read the messages Theresa had left several hours earlier. Well, that's good news, he thought, or maybe not, depending on how she reacts to this crazy story. He hung up the phone, but the red message light kept blinking.

"This is room 39 again. You just gave me my messages, but the light's still blinking. Can you turn it off?"

"One moment please." The operator was tired, indifferent. "Evidently the message machines are working again, just a minute, I'll connect you."

Ryan listened, then slowly replaced the receiver on his room phone, head spinning. There was Theresa, pleading with him to call her. Then Samuel, blaming himself for a traffic accident, not leaving a phone number, saying something about Emma being killed. For an instant, he thought about running off again, slinking away, a life-long knee jerk reaction. Go somewhere that no one could reach him. He grabbed his head with both hands, shook it hard.

He needed to talk to Theresa. It was still early, 8:33 the alarm clock stared at him, too early to call her. "No it's not; she called me at 3:00 this morning." He suddenly needed to talk to her, be with her, but with this face?

The phone only rang twice when her sleepy voice answered.

"Ryan! Where are you? I've been worried sick! What's wrong with your voice? Do you have a cold?"

"It's been a tough night." There was a short, awkward pause, and he continued. "I guess I have some explaining to do. Have you had breakfast yet? Are you hungry? Would you like to meet somewhere?"

"I would *love* to meet you. Any time, any place. In fact, why don't you come over here? I can scramble some eggs and heat the water. You prefer tea, right?" Coy was out the window, it was time for plain talk. But then she had always been a straight talker.

Ryan hesitated. He hadn't looked in the mirror this morning, but he knew it would be ugly. But he really needed to see Theresa, be with her. Somehow he knew it wouldn't matter, this woman was different.

"You know, that sounds wonderful," he said slowly. "Give me a little time to splash my face and I'll be over."

"Do you know where my apartment is?"

"Yes, I do."

She had never told him, so that meant he had gone to the trouble of finding out on his own, and the idea gave her a thrill, rush. Then she remembered the German and sobered, slightly. "Okay, see ya in a little. You can just ride the elevator up, the doorman won't mind."

He hesitated, then added, "Theresa, I had a run-in with an old nemesis last night, and he — uh — got the better of me. He had a friend that I didn't see, and — well, my face is pretty banged up. I don't want you to be frightened when you first see me — it — the face."

She was alarmed. "Ryan, how bad is it? Have you seen a doctor?"

"I haven't seen a doctor. I don't think it's that bad. It actually feels a little better this morning," he lied. "I think it'll be okay, I just didn't want to give you a start. How's the knee?"

"The knee's fine," she lied back. "Okay, whatever you think. See you soon."

Ryan sat on the edge of his unmade bed, a mass of conflicting emotions. He was drawn to this steady, beautiful woman, no doubt, but he knew nothing about her. He tried his best to quell the voice in the back of his head reminding him that Theresa had been with other men. She had mentioned it in an offhand way one time. "It don't matter, Ahmo," he chided himself. "You ain't exactly no virgin neither." He had been with a lot of women, but that was different, they were just a distraction, entertainment. This one had gotten inside, and for some reason it mattered. What if it came up? How would he react? And what if she drank? "Damn, Country," he scolded himself, "are you going to screw this up, too?" Trust didn't come easy, but somehow he knew he could trust her.

Ryan drove the two miles to her apartment very slowly, hoping for — what? That his nose would return to normal? That his heart and head would stop their pounding symphony? That he would wake up back at his place in Toronto, beside this wonderful woman — or alone — and everything else would be a bad dream?

He slid out of the car and headed to the front door of her upscale apartment. All the old feelings of insecurity crashed into him, and he almost returned to the car and left. Almost. But he strode on up to the building's front door, brushed past the shocked, inquisitive look of the doorman, and pressed "7" on the elevator pad just like he had done it a thousand times. On the long ride up he gradually shrank to that little boy in the eighth grade, and it was almost as though he had to reach up to press the doorbell at the oak encased front entrance to her apartment. What the hell, he scolded himself, this isn't the first woman you have ever gone to see. What is your problem? Before he could answer his own question, Theresa opened the door, stifled a gasp, and then with complete calm said, "Good morning, won't you please come in?"

She asked if she could take his coat and hat, he said sure. She returned from putting them up and asked if he would like some breakfast, had he eaten already? He gave her a quick glance; she had just asked him that same thing twenty minutes ago on the phone. Maybe she was a little nervous too? The thought eased him a bit, and he answered, no, I still haven't eaten, teasing. She smiled slightly, a nervous smile, spun on her house slippers and went into the kitchen.

"Do you like scrambled eggs, or would you like something a little more sophisticated, like eggs benedict?"

He would have eaten fried dog biscuits if she had offered. "Scrambled sounds divine."

She spent the next five minutes preparing their breakfast, increasingly at ease, at home. By the time he thought about offering to help, she had already finished their simple fare and put it on the table, an elegant oak table with equally elegant faux leather parson's chairs. She lit the candelabra in the center of the table, and the whole image was so warm and inviting — it was almost intoxicating.

"Theresa, I'm sorry. I'm sitting here like I'm afraid the couch will take off if I don't hold it down. I should have offered to help. I'll wash the dishes and clean up afterwards." As soon as he said that, he glanced at the stainless steel dishwasher, and mentally slapped himself. What a loser. But if it bothered her, it didn't show.

She turned and looked at him. "Thanks, that is sweet of you."

Ryan searched her eyes for a hint of sarcasm, but there was none. The two of them sat eating their breakfast, making small talk, how was the show going, when are you returning to Toronto, what about this weather, wonder who's going to win the election. And then, in that awkward moment when the food has all been eaten, before the distraction of clearing the table begins, she said "Ryan —" at exactly the same time he said "Theresa —" They both laughed nervously, self-consciously, and then she said, "You go first."

Ryan suppressed another urge to bolt and run, and slowly began. "Did the fellow that shoved you in the car have a thick German accent?"

She looked at him with her steady, unnerving gaze. "Yes, why?"

"That was my fault, but it won't happen again."

"That's great," a hint of sarcasm. "Go on, please."

Ryan took a deep breath, and plunged in. "Okay, here goes. I grew up in the country, a county called Lancaster. Have you heard of it?"

She had.

"I went to school with a fellow named Jonathon. He was, well, the class bully for lack of a better description. He was always in trouble, semi-serious trouble, like breaking the gym windows, throwing smoke bombs at the chorus rehearsal, that kind of thing. For some reason, he has always hated me." The eighth-grade grown man paused and looked out the window at the new sun. "I had cousins who also went to school there, two years behind me, and they were troublemakers too, but not in Jonathon's league. I kind of looked out for them best I could. I always suspected he egged them on as much to make my life even more miserable as anything. They were amateurs, he was a pro."

Theresa didn't say anything, didn't interrupt, just sat on her couch with her left leg draped elegantly over her right leg, left hand resting on the knee, sipping her mimosa. He had refused her offer of one for him. Let him talk.

"Home life was no picnic either. My father was a farmer, sort of, and a drunk. You never knew what was going to set him off, so we — us kids and my mother — learned to pay a lot of attention to other cues. I pay a lot of attention, I guess."

"It sounds like you have worked at this?"

"At what?"

"You know, paying attention, listening."

Ryan looked at her for a minute, decided she was sincere, and continued. "Yeah, I have. I've been part of various groups of children of alcoholic parents off and on, and it has helped some. I still feel like I'm responsible for things that intellectually I know I'm not."

The sun was shining for the second day in a row, and a beam streaming through the window hit the crystal flute she was holding, splashing a kaleidoscope of color on her white cotton blouse.

"One day when I was fifteen, I had enough. The verbal abuse had finally moved to physical, and I hit him, hard. I knocked his hat — knocked him to the ground. He hit his head on a piece of iron. I don't know how bad I hurt him. I don't really want to know."

"It sounds like the bully deserved it. Jonathon you said his name was?"

Ryan looked at her sharply. "I hit my father."

Theresa sat there for a minute, and finally said, "I don't think you are the first son to ever hit his father. How do you get along now?"

"We don't. I've never been back, never talked to him."

"That seems like a bit of an overreaction to me. What does your mother think about all this? I bet she would like to see things patched up."

"I haven't talked to her either."

Theresa did a quick calculation in her head. She didn't know exactly how old this man was, but probably in his late twenties. So he hadn't talked to either of his parents in — ten years? "You know, Ryan, I have had my share of disagreements with my father over the years, he's no saint either, but I still talk to him. And the older we both get, the less we remember what the problems were about anyway. It's a short drive out to Lancaster County. Have you thought about giving them a call and running out there? 'Course, you may want to wait 'til your face heals up a bit, eh?"

Ryan smiled slightly, giving his face an even more distorted, almost comical, look. He sobered and continued, "I can't. There's more." He was obviously having a difficult time telling her about his past. He swallowed and continued, "My family was killed in a house fire. Every one of them. I had two brothers and two sisters. I wasn't there for them." His voice dropped to a whisper, "They say my father set it deliberately."

His eyes glistened in the reflected sunlight, brimming, almost spilling. Theresa stood, walked to him and laid a hand gently on his shoulder. She said simply, "I'm so sorry." Ryan put his hand over hers, heart swelling and breaking, and then motioned for her to sit back down. He rose, walked into the kitchen, poured a glass of water and returned to his seat, composed again.

"Let me finish the part about the German. It seems that Jonathon found out I was living in Toronto, and by this time he had progressed to some pretty serious drug dealing. I talked to the twins every once in a while, they seemed to need that, and I guess one of them gave Jonathon my phone number. They were selling his dope on the street, here in Philly. Jonathon was evidently getting the majority of his stuff from this German fellow, I don't even know his name, and told him that I was coming to Philly to step into their trade, that Jonathon and I were enemies from way back. I really don't know what all lies he told the guy, but I started getting these anonymous phone calls late at night, and finally put it together that Jonathon was somehow involved. So, I was coming to Philly anyway for the horse show, and decided to track down Jonathon to — I don't know, ask him to quit — kick his ass — something. As you can see the ass kicking didn't exactly work out."

He picked up his cold coffee, took a sip, trying to calm his racing heart again. "The twins were in a car wreck. Maybe you saw the story in the paper. Killed one of them on the spot, instantly. One of the twins lived long enough to make it to the hospital, and I talked to him right before he —" Ryan looked down at the floor. "He told me he had come clean with the German, that Jonathon was using him to harass me." He was still looking at the floor. "He died while I was there."

Theresa finished her drink, and sat there, hands folded on top of her left knee, listening, silent.

"I finally decided to call the police, something I should have done a long time ago. I don't know, maybe I'll still go try to find Jonathon, make all this stop. But at least the German guy is gone and you won't have to worry about him anymore. I'm really sorry about that."

Her pulse had quickened at the mention of the German. She had not taken her eyes off of Ryan. "So are you a drug dealer?"

Ryan looked at her, at this beautiful woman and replied, "No, I'm not. But —"

Ryan had a habit of looking out the window when he was searching for words, and she decided to let him take his time. She wanted to know everything she could about this intriguing man. He shifted his position on the black leather recliner and continued.

"Have you ever for to heard — have you ever heard of the Amish?"

"Yes. But I really don't know too much about them. They drive horses and buggies and don't have electricity, I know that, and they spend most of the day praying, except when they are making furniture or farming. Why do you ask?"

He was still looking out the window. "My parents were Amish," he said simply.

The impact of this slowly sunk into the worldly woman sitting in her upscale apartment in Philadelphia. It didn't make any sense. How could this handsome, successful, apparently normal man say he was raised Amish? "You mean — you dressed with, uh, hats, and suspenders, and —"

"Yeah, that was me. All dressed up and no place to go. I'd show you some photos except we — they, didn't allow that. I can't tell you how weird it is — was, to suddenly, at age fifteen, leave everything you know and go out into a world that has been pounded into your head as evil, dangerous. And then, sure as shit, I fall into this world of drug dealing, the one thing I wanted to put behind me, way behind."

"What do you mean put drug dealing behind you? Amish don't use drugs." She was thoroughly confused.

It was too late to turn back now, and for some inexplicable reason, he wanted to tell her all about his life.

"Okay, here is a little history lesson. The Amish religion, beliefs, began in the early 17th century, with a man named Jacob Amman. It's where the name Amish comes from. The early Catholic Church was into everything, including — especially — government, and this Amman split with the official religion over the issue of infant baptism. He believed strongly that a person's soul can't be saved unless that person makes a conscious decision to join the church, and how could an infant make that decision?"

"What the hell does all this have to do with the price of plywood in Plymouth?"

"Be patient for a bit, you'll understand. The Amish have a set of guiding principles set out in the *Ordnung*, but only a handful of Bishops have the training to read, let alone interpret, these teachings. They encourage education, kind of, but only through the 8th grade, and most of the education is around the Amish way of life. So, for the most part, the various Bishops have decided that at age sixteen, Amish kids are allowed, encouraged, to go out into the world and see what it's like and decide if they want to return and join the church or not. So these poor kids are tossed into the world of drugs and booze and sex, with not a clue how to handle any of them. This is called *Rumspringa*, literally 'running around,' and it is one wild, continuous party. The crazy thing is, almost all of the kids go back and join the church. They literally get the hell scared out of them. I left before my Rumspringa, but I'm obviously one of very few that didn't go back."

Theresa needed another drink. This was a fantastic story. Could any part of it be true? Maybe she was wrong about this man.

"I went to Philadelphia when I left the farm, and worked my way up in the construction trade. Then I moved to Toronto, managed to buy a few fixer-uppers, and made a nice pile of change. And the horse training pays pretty good. The money has worked out." Ryan had seemed pretty familiar with the city, Theresa had noted. So that was it. He used to live here.

"So why did you move to Toronto in the first place?"

"I kept bumping into Jonathon here. And my old friends that were here working. Seemed like everyone knew I used to be Amish. And I had some other trouble with my cousin Phil. I lived with him for a while, and one night I came home and he had 'borrowed' all my money. I don't like banks, so all I had to my name was what I had on me plus my clothes and tools. He was a junkie and small time dealer. I don't know why I stayed with him as long as I did, I guess I just — I don't know. So I left, moved to Toronto, changed my name to Ryan. I wanted a fresh start, where no one knew me, my past. I seem to have this pattern of running, until now, since I met you." His blue-eyed glance gave her Goosebumps. "My first name is Ezra, Eshra to the German."

The two strangers from different worlds sat there for a while, saying nothing, looking at nothing. Finally, Theresa spoke. "Ryan, or whatever your name is, I need time to absorb all this. Obviously, there is — was — chemistry between us, even you sensed that —" he flushed — "but this is all a bit much. My life is uncomplicated, going well, and I am not sure about all this."

Ryan knew the risk of telling her his story, but he had to. It could go either way. "Would you like for me to leave, give you some time?"

Theresa was still looking out the window and didn't respond right away. Finally, she said, "Please."

The former Amish man rose stiffly from the chair. He saw that she was not going to get up, went to the closet to retrieve his jacket and hat. He stepped out into the hall, gently closed the front door behind him and headed slowly towards the elevator. The ride down was as long as the ride up, and he had just stepped out of the elevator onto the polished marble-floored lobby when the doorman approached him, "You have a call," he said, pointing to the dangling lobby phone. "Miss Theresa wants to talk to you."

Heart pounding again, he picked up the phone and said simply, "Hey."

"Hey yourself," she responded. "Look, this is overwhelming, but, honestly, I've never been as stricken by anyone as I have by you, and if you walk away, I may never see you again. I'm going out on a limb here, but I would like to get to know you. So — do you feel like coming back up?"

CHAPTER THIRTY-SIX

Philadelphia 1976

"I think you should go, Ez," Theresa said gently, taking his hands in hers. "You've been talking about going for a long time, I think you should. I thought about taking the twins over to see Father this afternoon anyway, so why don't you go. Take the Jag if you want."

Ryan looked at Theresa, grabbed her to him, nuzzled her soft black hair on his cheek, and looked over her shoulder at his twin boys playing on the floor in the next room. The bigger one had blond hair and blue eyes, just like his father, and the other one had his mother's olive complexion and fine features.

"Okay, I guess I will. It's beautiful out. I wanted to go on a pretty day." He shrugged into his sports jacket and grabbed the car keys, kissed her on the cheek. "Say 'hi' to your dad. I'm ready for him too, if you think we should."

Her smile faded, just a bit. "Let's don't rush it. It'll come."

The usual ninety minute drive stretched into two hours. The weather was perfectly crisp, multi-hued hardwood tree leaves swirling everywhere. Ezra passed a Philly-bound bus going the other way, Amish kids hanging out the windows, laughing and waving. He smiled and waved back, remembering his ride to town so many years ago.

The county line sign slid by, and Ezra marveled at the change to his old country, how it looked so different from the front seat of a car going fifty. He pulled into a new convenience store, bought a Coke, climbed back in, and decided to go to his old home, go the back road, see some old haunts. Ezra drove slowly past Jonathon's old house. The side was caved in, roof rusted and drooping. The yard no longer existed, taken over by weeds and creeping alfalfa from the nearby field, black raspberry, and tall weaving grass. Vines climbed through busted out windows, like bony green fingers sticking out of a toothless mouth.

His old place was two miles over, down the road, then left at the intersection that still did not have any road signs, half a mile further and then left again. The final turn was difficult, and for an instant it seemed as though the steering wheel wouldn't steer, wanted to go straight, or turn around. But it finally gave in to the driver, and Ezra slowly pulled off in a wide gravel spot next to the road to what used to be the entrance to his childhood home. He turned the key off, and the gleaming silver Jaguar stopped purring. He climbed out, looked first at the puffy white clouds drifting east, brilliant blue sky above reaching all the way to eternity.

Someone had put a new barbed wire fence along the road, and the entrance to the field was moved to the corner. The old lane was gone, plowed into neat rows of field corn, brown husks lying on the ground, a mute reminder of the four-row gasoline powered corn picker that had been here. Ezra could see the occasional gleam of a missed ear of corn, its rows of yellow gold grinning up at him.

He walked closer to the fence. The old concrete culvert was still there, under the weeds, and at one end, the remnants of six small faded wooden crosses laid disarrayed. A faded array of plastic flowers from years ago was flattened against the earth. Ezra looked up, and other than an old maple tree, probably the one outside the back door, saw nothing but field all the way to the rise of the small hill in the distance.

The young sheriff's deputy pulled in behind the new Jaguar, lights off and spoke into his radio. After several minutes, he climbed out of his idling car, putting his captain's hat on in the same motion. "Can I help you?"

Ezra turned and said, "No, thanks, I was just looking at the country."

"This isn't really a parking spot." He could see the city man was very quiet. "If you need directions or have questions, I can probably help, but otherwise you really need to move your car. It's a traffic hazard parked here."

Ezra finally turned from the field and walked over to his car, hand on the door handle. "No, but thanks, I'll head on."

He opened the door and then turned back to the deputy. "What happened here? Someone in town said there used to be an Amish family who lived here, but I don't see anything."

The deputy squinted at the man in black. "I can't say for sure, it was before my time. Rumor is the old man went berserk and set fire to the place. Killed them all, except one. The oldest kid, a boy, ran off when he was a teenager. I guess he and the old man got into it all the time." He was looking at Ezra, hard. "Do I know you?"

Ezra thought he recognized the young man, but wasn't sure. "No. I live in Philadelphia, at least part time. I've always wanted to come out here and see this country. The Amish are so fascinating."

"Fascinating? Yeah, that they are." He turned to leave and over his shoulder said, "You be careful. And you really need to be moving on."

"OK, I was about to leave, have a good day." Ezra slid back into the luxury car, turned the key, and without looking back, nosed the shiny little jaguar leaping off of the hood towards Philadelphia for the last time.

3869023

Made in the USA
Lexington, KY
02 December 2009